By DéLana R. A. Dameron

How God Ends Us: Poems
Weary Kingdom: Poems
Redwood Court
Fairfield County

Fairfield County

Fairfield County

A Novel

DÉLANA R. A. DAMERON

THE DIAL PRESS
New York

The Dial Press
An imprint of Random House
A division of Penguin Random House LLC
1745 Broadway, New York, NY 10019
randomhousebooks.com
penguinrandomhouse.com

LIBRARY OF CONGRESS CATALOGING-IN-PUBLICATION DATA
Names: Dameron, DéLana R. A. author
Title: Fairfield County : a novel / DéLana R.A. Dameron.
Description: New York, NY : The Dial Press, 2026.
Identifiers: LCCN 2025038969 (print) | LCCN 2025038970 (ebook) |
ISBN 9780593977811 hardcover acid-free paper | ISBN 9780593977828 ebook
Subjects: LCGFT: Fiction | Domestic fiction | Novels
Classification: LCC PS3604.A4398 F35 2026 (print) | LCC PS3604.A4398 (ebook)
LC record available at https://lccn.loc.gov/2025038969
LC ebook record available at https://lccn.loc.gov/2025038970

Printed in the United States of America

1st Printing

First Edition

BOOK TEAM: Production editor: Loren Noveck • Managing editor: Rebecca Berlant • Production manager: Katie Zilberman • Proofreaders: Deborah Bader, Julia Henderson, and Emily Zebrowski

Book design by Kevin Quach

The authorized representative in the EU for product safety and compliance is Penguin Random House Ireland, Morrison Chambers, 32 Nassau Street, Dublin D02 YH68, Ireland. https://eu-contact.penguin.ie

A good horse gives you wind in your face, a brave,
big heart, and a whole new world—wings.

To Stokely, my first horse, who catapulted this journey.

To Shadrack, my horsey love of my life, who
taught me to fly.

To the land. The sand. The pines. The red clay.
The open fields we run across.

PART I

1937–1976

Chapter 1

The dust had settled from the Great War long enough for folks like Moses to see a few feet into tomorrow's horizon and think there might still be a future for Fairfield County.

In the years after the war, farmers fought the boll weevil on their cotton plantations and lost; sold the used-up land for pennies on the acre. The land was useless, terrorized, plundered.

White farmers figured they'd rather have cut their losses and move on. So they did. They say that's how Fairfield County came to be populated by so many Black folks: day laborers who saved up enough to buy the land their family worked on for generations—first as slaves, then as sharecroppers. White landowners had just up and left the land for ruin, looking for a new industry.

Word was granite was growing. Managing a quarry took less manpower, fewer natural disasters to have to survive in order to pull a profit. Fewer variables in God's hand: mercy or otherwise. Figured, land management was easier than raising cattle, so buying them at least fifty years of use.

So came the availability of land, and years later with Roosevelt's New Deal, loans and capital, and right on the other side of the property line from Moses's parcel, a new parcel had come up for sale. He had watched the surveyors: trying to figure if it could be a viable location for more granite excavation. But that was the thing about this part of the Piedmont: one foot could stand on sand, one foot could stand on bedrock, and there could be a dividing line of red clay. No rhyme or reason. It was why when cotton ran its way through the soils, the land was then turned to pine for harvest. When the pines were logged and processed, then time came for pastures and so the cattle came.

For folks who never thought they'd own much of anything, the land was a timer: about seven years from a return on any investment. Moses didn't mind; he had learned to think in generations like the white folks who brought his people here centuries ago. Whatever evils lay in their hearts to round up whole humans like livestock, ship them across an ocean, and craft a whole country identity, a whole economy—whatever they had deep within themselves that gave them the ability to devise such an operation was thinking with the longest vision.

Not to say Moses had wanted to think like them, but he saw value in the idea of trying to make decisions and "investments" with an eye towards a future so far ahead of him he might never see it to fruition, but that maybe his offspring might reap. That alone filled him with purpose towards enlarging his territory. For the things that are seen are transient, but the things that are unseen are eternal, according to 2 Corinthians.

That's how he got ninety-eight acres of land—an increase from his inherited thirty-eight. Whenever anyone asked how he came upon the additional sixty acres, his response would be some version of "they practically gave 'em away." And it was true.

On the property, there was a small creek near the back pine parcel. It curved just enough that when the pines were logged and the land to pasture, he could have a water source for other livestock outside of horses he might want to keep. With almost a hundred acres, Moses could raise a drove of cattle and he'd have enough space for rotational grazing, providing a constant supply of roughage, and with time the bovines would sow nutrients back into the soil for whatever riches might spring up next. And then, he'd repeat the cycle for as long as God saw fit to keep him upright on his two feet and above the ground. And then, again God willing, one day he would have someone to take it on. He didn't know who or how, but he held his mustard-seed faith like a talisman to keep marching towards the future's horizon.

He was born just a few steps outside of a life of bondage; the inherited scar tissue showed up in Moses's rush to create a self-governed life: Marry publicly, and in a church. Have children and get to keep them. Buy a house if you want it—things his grandfather could only imagine.

Going through the motions, he came to wonder if that was supposed to be his life. Moses had found himself unevenly yoked with someone who wanted different things than he did. He knew deep down he should pursue the family way. Losing two infants in such quick succession made his first marriage as short as a winter's day. He had wanted to do right by her, but he also wanted to be his own man. Make his own decisions. Not rush into wedded bondage—how he was seeing the weight of his wife and her desires.

What other way was there to pursue a life? Moses wanted freedom and land and horses in pastures. The life he fought for. He wanted to reap the bounty of his struggle, despite being born a Black man in 1888 in Fairfield County, South Carolina, on the land he would die on. He was the son of slaves who had transitioned to sharecropping after Lincoln signed them papers declaring *all men free.*

For eleven years as freed people, his parents worked the land, worked horses, sold horses, trained horses—just as they had done when they were owned by the Boltons—but now they were armed with their own enterprise and dreams. Ones that they could see and taste. Eventually, Moses's parents had earned enough from this work to make a land purchase of one acre not long after Moses was born. *Inheritance making,* Ezekiel had said each time he handed over the cash for the first parcels. Then later, five more. Then more until they came to own twenty-two acres in total.

His parents were the lucky ones. After manumission, his Aunt Hagar made her way back to Fairfield County having walked the whole way from Hopkins. Like salmon swimming back to the place they were born, many blood Boltons of their time saw the town of Ridgeway as their homeland, and no other dirt to lay their heads until their last breaths would suffice. She never did find any of the twelve children she birthed. But she was able to live out the rest of her life with family again. When she finally laid down to her eternal rest, her ten acres reverted to Moses, who she saw as a son. So then he had enough land for the horses he'd keep, and enough land to farm, and enough land to live and breathe the clean, free air.

In the new world made by emancipation, white horsemen found themselves having to now pay for the services readily available to them. Having to step into the gap made when the once enslaved went about manifesting their own destiny. For some of those men who decided to stay in the business of Thoroughbred racing, they knew their chances of remaining in the winner's circle relied heavily on the skilled Black horsemen and their descendants who helped build the industry. They would cross the increasing color-line boundaries if it meant a wreath of roses and a fine payout.

Word was that Moses was *an exceptional horseman.* He had only just set out his shingle when his father retired, and folks came like a steam engine—tick by tick—looking for his expertise. A man had come by once, inquiring about his services, took one look at his herd, and exclaimed, "I tell you, there's nothing like a horse trained by a nigger!" The man slipped his hands into his pockets. He knew what he said. Meant it exactly like he had said it. Twirled the piece of hay he was chewing. Moses nodded. He was free to live his life, sure, but he knew there was only so much one could do under the thumb of white men who feel their whole lives been turned upside down, having found themselves in the embarrassing position of needing a *nigger's* help. But Moses knew that won't no one for miles of here that had his seat. The word went around by mouth. Moses could put his hands on the withers of a bronc'ing horse—that couldn't no one get to *not* be a kite in the sky—and have the horse bending his neck around him in a hug, almost purring.

At first Moses had traveled to their plantations, or their parcels, back into the bellies of the beast, so to say, to do his work. He'd wake up and travel day after day. Sometimes for two seasons, staying at each post as long as he could. Every descendant of former slave masters being varying degrees of sufferable until it just made sense for him to start his own operation on his terms on his land: folks—whoever wanted to do business with him—would bring their horses and he'd make of the horses what they wanted in the off-season. *On his time. On their dime.* (That was how he described the new setup to Lillie.) During the racing season, well, he was back on the backstretch of the racecourse like a young man again, bunking with his ward until he couldn't handle the hard ground for long stretches anymore.

As he aged, and his body started to fail, Moses took on apprentices, his son Lloyd being one. Lloyd, his only child with Lillie, the one who lived after so many years swearing off trying to have children. Moses believed Lloyd would be the one to bring the work of the Black Bolton horsemen forward. Moses counted on it. If you had asked Lillie, she'd say he counted too much on it. *All your eggs in the tail of your shirt.* She loved that turn of phrase, since that's how Moses collected the eggs, and not in a basket. Moses had put so much weight on Lloyd's back he hadn't considered how easily Lloyd could break.

Chapter 2

When asked what number Pal O Mine should run under Moses had said, "Number 7 or number 3. Them's divine numbers, alright. God made this whole world in seven days. And He's a trinity: Father, Son, Holy Ghost. Cain't go wrong with three neither."

It wasn't often that a Negro at the racetrack was asked his opinion, but Moses was respected by the horse's owner, so when it came time to prepare for the 1938 Carolina Jessamine Invitational, Mrs. Pynchon-Grant went right up to Moses and told him to pick the number.

The number 7 slot would have put the stallion too far right in the field and closer to the stands of crowds, and so would have caused further distraction that would have leaked through Pal's blinders and earplugs. That far out in the field and the thunder of the spectators' cheers would drown out the footfalls of Pal's competitors, and so the number 3 would put the colt closer to the center of action and increase the odds of victory—should he be able to run.

He had come to the track with slim odds: 50–1. In fact, Pal was on the bench the whole week leading up to the big race, only used to breeze the contenders as a pacing bunny, until favored-to-win Blazing Time was inspected, it was determined that his right-hind hock was warm to the touch, and they decided to scratch the gray colt from the race.

The backstretch, where the stables and the people whose hands made sure the horses were ready for the big day—the night watchmen, the hot-walkers, the stall cleaners, the grooms, many of them Black—was quiet but moving how a tributary moves: rolling, rolling.

When the news came that a horse had scratched, a great stir rose, and several of the grooms who were sitting in the stalls with their horse wards scurried to start their brisk brushing to get the pine shavings off and used their jute sacks to spit shine the coats slick. Hoping their horse would be the one picked. It could be anyone's chance.

Moses had asked which horse? His question rose above the stalls like steam. Someone yelled out, "Blazing Time," and he whispered in Pal's ear, "That's 'cause they bought that horse off looks alone. His little dapple-gray coat shole is pretty and all but it hid the fact that his back leg 'bout cripple as a farmer's scythe, ain't it?"

Moses chuckled and Pal jerked his head up seemingly in response right at that moment, even though to the untrained eye, you'd think it was because Moses was running the jute sack right at the base of the neck, in the crease where the neck met the shoulders and it felt good to the horse, but Moses knew when a movement was a movement versus a response. Could feel it. Pal agreed.

It could be anybody's chance, but Moses's gut started to twist with anticipation. Only a superstitious man when it came to race day, he couldn't make any grand gestures, or else Pal might sense his excitement and use all of his energy getting to the starting gate.

If they were to be chosen at this late hour, Pal would be walking the Valley of Roses—what the fancy called the path from the backstretch to the front—by himself since Moses knew the imaginary line marking where he could move freely and where he couldn't at the racecourse. Where the horse passed from the care of one to the other. For all intents and purposes, Pal would be walking onto the field alone. Yes. Pal would have the jockey. Of course. But the jockey sees Pal almost like a piece of equipment. Like the saddle. Or the reins. The jockey, to Pal, was another thing to carry from the start to the finish. He'd have to do it alone until he crossed the line again to the backstretch where Moses would be the one to see to it that Pal returns to himself. Checks in. Checks the body. Walk him until his nostrils unflare. Scratch him behind the ears and say *good boy* over and over so the horse might tire of hearing it, but he never will, cronching his peppermint in sweet victory—even defeat. Moses always rewarded the try. It was Moses's race as much as it was Jockey What's-His-Name's, and Mrs. Pynchon-Grant's.

Moses breathed deeply and prayed number 3 would be drawn up. It didn't matter how many times he made it to the backstretch over the years. Each time was like the first time. He was fifty years old and had practically been born in a stable not unlike this.

The weekend of his birth was a race weekend, and Moses's father, Ezekiel, concerned that his mother, Maryam, would face complications if she went into labor alone and her time was near, insisted she camp out with him at the track. Won't no amount of protest on her part could change his mind. So she laid up in the stall with Ezekiel and his horse ward on top of an extra layer of wood shavings.

Even from the womb Moses felt it then, the importance of the day. The story was he waited to be born until after the horse left the stables, and since Ezekiel couldn't go to the track to watch and he had a very pregnant wife, he returned to the stall to find Maryam's water had broken and she had started to push just as he walked back to check on her.

His horse won't a winner that day, but Ezekiel was.

The labor was quick. It had to be. Ezekiel was due to receive his horse after the race, but someone stepped up for the cooldown and cold wash to give him more time. After they checked for vitals, counted all the fingers and toes, waited for the wail, Ezekiel and another groom, who helped by wringing the hot towels and cleaning his paring knife for the umbilical cord, brought the baby boy back to Maryam. He was wrapped in a jute sack, and someone else scrounged up some clean straw bedding and had put him in a basket. When she saw it was a boy in a basket, she chuckled and said, "Well, I might as well name him Moses."

Having literally been born into this whole thing, horses, Moses couldn't imagine what other life he was supposed to have. Sure, the government called him up to fight, and like the rest of the world, he stopped his life to serve, but he knew every day in the trenches, in the mess hall, in the rocking ocean liner crossing the Atlantic, what he was coming back to: a life, a life of horses. That's what kept his head on straight in the trenches, even when his socks got bogged down with mud and soldiers flanked on either side of him caught shrapnel or pneumonia. The thought of a horse's warm body beneath him, breathing when he breathed, galloping through a field, or his grand neck wrapped around Moses's back while being groomed—that's what kept him whole and brought him home.

Like a game of telephone, Pal O Mine's name rang out on the backstretch until it reached Moses's ears. It was Pal's time to race. Moses could put his real game face on and settle into his prerace routine—even if a bit rushed—to get Pal in the zone, and then send him off into the Valley of Roses to pick up his jockey, then on to the starting gate.

Pal lined up in the number 6 position—on account of his late addition, he took the empty spot rather than having to shuffle the rest of the horses already lined up, waiting. Moses watched from the fence.

"Give him his face," Moses said to the jockey—a cautionary warning to not hold the horse back with the reins before the race even started—even though won't no way the jockey could hear him where he stood. Even if he could hear, the jockey would not be looking for his opinion. Usually, they at least come gather their mounts for call time, but Jockey What's-His-Name got someone else to gather Pal from the Valley of Roses and sent him back to Moses. Never once did he have even a glance of greeting for Moses, but it won't Moses's business to mind. Pal was his business. That Mrs. Pynchon-Grant was happy with him and so still paid his wages was his business. Whether a handsy jockey, who hangs on a horse's mouth rather than ride him, paid him any mind was the least of his worries. Thankfully Pal was forgiving, and didn't hold a grudge for poor riding like that chestnut mare Solaris—after every race with Jockey What's-His-Name, Moses would hop on Solaris and sing made-up songs until her jiggy-jog turned into a quiet walk and she lowered her head instead of lifting it like an ostrich-stringy neck whenever anyone reached for the halter.

"Give him his face," Moses said again. This time, Jimmy, who also had a horse in the race, hummed in agreement, then commented on his own jockey's performance.

"Get out the middle, you get stuck there. Make a move," Jimmy said.

"You don't want him too tired, they barely halfway in," another groom said.

"His face! He needs it—you jamming him up holding him back!" That was all Moses could focus on. That was all Pal needed to separate from the pack. The ability to balance himself with each stride—for the jockey to get out the way.

During practices, when Moses breezed Pal on the track, every time he let the reins get a little drape—*let go, give Pal his face*—Pal O Mine dug deeper into the turf and blazed past the pacesetter, even though they were supposed to stay just to the setter's hip. Never pass. Of course, Moses knew the whole purpose of the exercise, but he also knew what it meant to allow the horse to know his own powers, that he *could* do it, go faster, be the fastest horse out on the field. Most often what kept Pal out of the money won't the training or the fitness or the readiness, but conductor error. How you can set a steam engine on a track and let it run, but if the conductor don't apply the brakes then *let them go* at the right time around a curve, well, that's how we get derailments.

Pal rounded the last turn of the course and it was the closest on the whole racetrack Pal would be to Moses. Jockey What's-His-Name had let up some, but not enough. Pal had moved up a few places. Near the front-middle of the pack. Moses could hear and see from the footfall, and how clean or not they landed the jumps, that the horses in the front were getting tired.

"They must only ever run the course or less," Moses said out loud. "Don't know how to tuck away some energy for the last bit."

He shook his head, but saw Pal's cadence remained steady, and as the horse got closer Moses noticed he had pulled more reins from the jockey's hands, freeing up his face. But still not enough.

Now Moses was jumping and yelling. "FACE! He needs his face!" That was for the jockey.

"PAL O MINE! Take 'em to church!" That was for the horse.

Moses slapped the fence and hollered and stomped his feet, figuring if a horse can feel a fly land on its back, surely Pal would know the weight of him, the full weight of him, pounding the earth through the turf, the way his heart had sped up as if he were in the race with Pal. He'd *feel* it.

Finally he had his face. Moses sent his intentions to the finish line and watched Pal O Mine's neck lengthen—his stride triple in length as he passed fifth, passed fourth, stayed steady on with the third for too many paces. The announcer and crowd started to go wild.

"Odd-chancer Pal O Mine snuck out of the stables and is giving the podium racers their paces! He's gunning for it! Neck and neck with number 3. Now look, his jockey found the seventh gear and he's caught the hip of number 2—this was a horse on the sidelines, I mean literally on the bench, only fifteen minutes ago and now he's a *contender*!"

"Been a contender!" Moses called back.

"He's vying for the winner's circle for the 1938 Carolina Jessamine Invitational. He's running. He's digging. He's second place. He's second place. A minute ago, he wasn't a contender and now he's a contender—*oh my God*—"

"My God—" Moses echoed. Pal O Mine was doing it. He couldn't imagine how Mrs. Pynchon-Grant was handling watching this. He pulled himself over the top of the fence so he'd have an unobstructed view. Pal O Mine's nose caught the tail of the front-runner.

"My God!"

Pal O Mine was at the haunches. Only five breaths to the end of the course. Five reaches. Pal O Mine was head to the other jockey's chest. And that jockey was flapping and flapping about the top of his horse lookin' like he was doing the chicken dance—elbows jumping this way an' that, but the horse was spent. He was cruising on the last gear as best he could, trying not to lose any steam. Couldn't go no faster no matter what. Jockey What's-His-Name finally realized Pal O Mine could take him home. He grabbed mane and held on.

"Finally" was all Moses could say as Pal took over the lead for the last three lengths of the course.

Then Moses lost it. He absolutely lost it. His colleagues on the backstretch had already been creeping up to the fence—not unlike Pal making his way to the finish line into first place—with a feed bucket of ice-cold water. Who cared that it was a chilly April 2, and an ice-water bath would surely lead to a sickness, but this was *tradition.* His horse had won. Pal had come off the bench. And was victorious.

"We won! We won!" Moses shouted before they dumped the ice water over his shoulders.

"We won," he whispered into Pal O Mine's ears when he retrieved the horse from the Valley of Roses.

"We won," he said again, when Mrs. Pynchon-Grant pulled him just to the edge of the frame of the photo op for the *County Chronicle.* Moses had been there to collect the horse; had crossed the invisible racial line so that Pal O Mine could get his breath postrace and rest. Mrs. Pynchon-Grant pulled him into the moment and with that gesture acknowledged his Negro self as part of her team. What a gesture. They had won. He had repeated it to the journalist—*we* won—who went on to name all of the players he thought made the win possible. Except Moses. It didn't matter. Moses was the victor with Pal O Mine; no one could take that from him.

Look, he'd say, showing off the article with its photo: everyone else in that photo was looking at the cameraman as the lightbulb flashed to capture the moment.

Moses was looking at his horse.

Chapter 3

In the before-years, before the Depression, then the dust, before everything shut down for the second war, after everyone who could climbed out of it all with what they had salvaged intact, in those golden years, Moses was a name that was called in all of the racing stables to come and make another Pal O Mine; to make another something out of nothing. To make a champion for them.

He lived at the racing stables. Slept more on a pallet of hay next to his athletes than he did his own cotton-stuffed mattress Lillie made every morning and turned down in hopes, in anticipation, that more than one night a week he might warm her up.

When they first understood they were pregnant with Lloyd, Lillie had joked maybe she was the Virgin Mary; how else could she account for carrying a baby considering how little she saw Moses? He had heard the tinge of pain behind the laughs and promised the sacrifices won't be eternal. Promised her a quiet life on the farm enjoying whatever simple pleasure her heart desired. Her eyes cast wide and she said, “A herd of mustangs?” Holding her belly, indicating she did not at all mean the wild horse variety, and Moses had frowned his face at the word “mustangs” before he too understood she had meant more children. She wanted a life filled with children, and it was this, alone, that amplified their age difference when on any given day he had seen them exactly as they were: two lovebirds set on spending the rest of their lives together in the nest they built up in Fairfield County. That would be enough for him: A man having marked almost half a century of life already. And his young bride, barely past the beginning of hers. But it was the small moments like her statement of desire for more children that placed the grandest of canyons between them.

Of course, Moses could have been a father before Lillie, in his first marriage. But the pure fact that he wasn’t was good enough for him. He had not been even in a position of wanting to marry again, swore he would never, actually, until Lillie had almost appeared before him how he imagined Gabriel forming before Mary to tell her about the task ahead for her life.

There was no other way to say that he could not find himself living a life without Lillie once she had planted herself, doggedly, within it.

The first time he met her he thought she was Abe’s wife, another groom at the stables. She had come around all that summer cradling a baby in one hand and a basket in the other. He’d watch Lillie hand Abe his baby and his sandwich and they’d giggle and laugh like young lovers at the beginning of their family. It went like this through the training season until he saw another woman, one child on her hip and another wading in her shadow, wandering the barn aisles, and stopped him to ask if he knew where Abraham—how she called him—might be?

"He's walkin' his horse down to the paddocks. They're about to race, Miss."

"Mrs.," she corrected. She saw his brow furrow. Moses corrected himself, then tipped his hat in salutation and offered an apology. He looked up and Lillie was approaching the two of them. Lillie grabbed the boy's hand and offered her hip for the baby. Relieved of the two, Mrs. Abe Forman returned to Moses and asked again the direction that her husband might be, and when it took a beat for Moses to register the request, she chuckled.

"Lillie is my kid sister. Our parents had a hard enough time in Georgia making it through—feeding themselves when the ground was so dry it cracked like kindling under your feet—so they sent her to us."

The look of relief must have been visible to her. She smiled at Moses now.

"She likes to visit the horses and offered to take Johnny for walks—we live only about a twenty-minute walk away and Abe cut a path from the end of our parcel straight here so she can do it without getting into any roadways, or trouble. You know."

Moses hummed in agreement. Nodded his head. Again, relief. The next time he saw Lillie, he'd introduce himself proper. Not long after that, Lillie came bearing lunch and baby kisses and peppermints for Streaker, Abe's ward, then swung by Moses's stalls and handed him a sandwich. The first time she offered, he refused, citing he knew everything was tough for everyone. But he admitted he couldn't deny how nice it would have been to eat something a woman had cooked. After the divorce, there wasn't much Moses found himself missing from their union except maybe the drudgery and burden of figuring out what to cook for himself and when each day being sorted out.

So when Lillie, in her persistence, held out two pieces of fried chicken wrapped in a cloth napkin, he could not refuse it. He couldn't remember the last time he had fried chicken. Didn't care if it was cold by the time it touched his lips, he understood in those Depression years what an offering had been bestowed upon him: Meat and flour. Salt. Buttermilk. Together. For lunch. Oh, he would savor each bite. Gristle, even. Lillie offered it, smiled, then turned and took the small child down each stall and visited with the grooms and their wards. When she circled back to Moses, he smiled thinking she had come back to visit again, and dusted off his hands on his pants, swiping hay, probably wet bran mash, an errant oat as she walked up. He chuckled towards Lillie as if their conversation had already begun.

"Sometimes, I look in their buckets and get jealous! They do eat better'n me most days."

They laughed. The baby fussed. It had been a long day. Lillie had been there longer than usual. Lingering.

Moses cleared his throat. "Didn't eat better'n me today, though. Thank you again for that most delicious lunch, Miss Lillie." He tipped his hat.

Lillie looked like she had been caught in a surprise hearing her name.

"How did you—"

"Oh! Your sister came down for one of the races and you know this whole time I been thinking you was Abe wife and so when I saw another woman with him, I was confused and also won't none of my business but she say her kid sister Lillie come with the baby and so here you are."

He wiped his brow with his handkerchief. Then tipped his page-boy hat as in a new greeting. He didn't know why he did it, except perhaps nerves. But why? She was young. He was old rough-out leather. And yet and still.

"And you are? Mr.?"

"Moses. Bolton. Pleasure's mine."

IIIIIIIIIIIIIIIIII

The guys at the barn started making kissing faces and winked their eyes at Moses whenever they saw Lillie and her nephew come down the center aisle. Moses paid no mind. He knew what it was already to love, think you're building a life, and lose it because you an' her are on different railroad tracks speeding down the countryside.

With his first wife, it was losing the baby he won't even sure he wanted in the first place. Then trying again. The midwife said the grief had taken up residence in the womb where the baby had been, and they needed to evict the burdensome grief first, heal the heart and womb—together—in order for their family to be a viable place for a baby to want to enter the world. Moses had never thought about the agency of the child, embryo, what should he call it? And its desire to occupy this earth. Did it choose? To come here? On this timeline?

Moses couldn't figure how to find the energy to promise to protect whoever emerged in Fairfield County, especially on days like the morning he woke to the news of Bear Greely strung up on a strong branch of the elm tree on the outskirts of town for—who even knows the reason anymore? All Moses knew was the week before, brother Bear was at church talking about how a truck of white boys came onto his property offering to buy it because of how close it was to the piece of land folks say was going to be a granite quarry, or maybe there was oil or diamonds—every time the story was told it had changed—and Bear, in his landowning right, asked kindly for the men to leave. And they laughed and said it was going to be their land one way or the other.

So it was a season of hangings, not unlike how the news was projecting a season of struggle on the way. Moses had gone to the shipyards when the call came for him to suit up, and had participated, as demanded, in the World War for democracy. He had only seen a front line near the end of it and he understood a different front line was waiting for him when he returned: it seemed every other day a Black man was found dead, and every other day the white boys about town with their hay straws dangling from their lips like smoking pipes patrolled the streets with their chests puffed out prouder and prouder. Years of this.

Between folks from Fairfield County staying near their station after that November day that said the war was over and there'd never be another one, and those puffed-chested proud boys strolling down the streets with two-by-fours like billy clubs, and then his wife Elaine's grief sitting in the living room with them night after night after he come in from a full day of training and grooming at the track, it was all Moses could do to look her in the eyes in a way that projected love and care. It was all he could do—won't no other air in his chest to form whatever words she might have needed to cast out the grief from her womb like the doctor say.

Hell, he hadn't an inch of time to consider his own grief on the matter of losing something he never had—never held—was promised but slipped between his fingers like the land grants his grandma said they was supposed to get when the shackles dropped. They had said a parcel and a beast of burden of choice. They themselves won't no one's beasts no more, how his grandma had said it, remembering the promise, undelivered. That grief Moses held, what he saw in

Elaine, similar. How could anyone find room to make of themselves a new life right where the old one held for her so much sorrow?

Eventually Moses gave up the ghost of the idea that he would be ready to think about what it meant to be in the family way in a time-line that might make sense for her or him—even though he knew what it all meant to her, what it could mean to him. They parted ways, as amicably as possible. He wished her luck and love and a man who could give her what her heart needed. She wished him luck and whatever it was he was after. It was enough. It had to be. In a way, free of the weight of not ever being able to meet his woman's expectations, he could turn his life back to horses, his growing career, what to make of himself besides a ship porter tied to a dock in service, and he still managed to leave the war somehow mangled.

The boys had called it ship-black lung, because the symptoms were similar to those snaking through the workers in the coal mines: shortness of breath, chest tightness, coughing black into a handkerchief. When the symptoms showed up, right when Moses returned to the barn, he thought it a hay allergy, newly developed. It sometimes happened to the best of them. Too much exposure, and the body starts to think it a thing to be expelled. But more and more of the ship bunkmates hunkered together in that windowless room next to the coal-fed engine, they all one by one got the cough. Doctors said he'd have to work hard to clear the tar from his lungs, to have, like the horses, the deep heart girth to gallop along the turf.

It was no coincidence that with Elaine, Moses felt the tightening of the sinew in his lungs, like they were held, constricted in a cage tighter than his ribs. But years later, with Lillie, he had felt like a new man and often the world around him slipped away, and cleaning stalls at the track he'd find himself humming nonsense like a little lovestruck boy:

I'm just a man with some horses,
  An' a lil land to roam—
I'm just a man, list'n for his woman
  To call him home.

He had never known something would soften the cracked leather of his heart. Whenever Lillie walked down the center aisle of the barn, carrying their own child on her hip, his basket of food in her hand, Moses knew that next to seeing a horse he had trained and groomed in the winning circle, there won't no better sight to be had on this green earth. One of those things where you just don't know such beauty until you see it. And he prayed to God that he never wanted to know another day for as many days he has without Lillie to look him in the eyes the way she do. He wouldn't be able to live without her.

Chapter 4

That song, a silly ditty that had turned into the soundtrack of the second part of Moses's life, had slowly faded away—maybe it was that he no longer toiled away at a barn that he didn't own, for white people who didn't recognize what all he did to produce the winningest horses until he quit and had set up his own operation and they had to come foot in hand to see if he'd work with their nags. So he had no reason to daydream and sing away the doldrums while completing a day's work of chores. He had bet on himself. It was the only way to see that there was something—knowledge, land, horses, a whole life—to pass on to his Lloyd, if the boy wanted it.

And it seemed that the boy did. Ever since he was born with hay in his hair, just like his father, Lloyd stood at his feet, watching. Lillie loved that about her son: his watchfulness. Children his age would look, eyes glazing over the surface level of whatever it was they were fixed on, but Lloyd drank it in. How, when he learned to form words, it was "hosey" that first came, and then when he learned to string those words into phrases and questions, they seemed to never cease. He had been possessed. "Feed hosey," "ride hosey," "Daddy hosey"—they laughed whenever Lloyd said those words at the track. He wasn't wrong—that was the thing about children: they are the eternal truth tellers.

At home, there was a picture of Moses on a hosey. His Daddy's hosey. Lloyd saw it every day, and when he was at the track, young Lloyd had seen another horse, one that looked like the one in the picture, and proclaimed it Daddy's hosey. Again, he wasn't wrong. That day, after the Carolina Jessamine Invitational of 1938, when the white press left, and the fanfare of the owner and jockey had died down, and the jockey had pulled Pal O Mine to the line marking where Moses couldn't cross to hand over the horse, a camera appeared from somewhere. Lillie had arranged it in anticipation that the outcome of Pal O Mine's maiden race would be that of a champion.

Later Moses asked her how she knew Pal would even run since he wasn't officially entered?

"You're the best. Why wouldn't he run?" she said.

He'd offer some response, ask again, and Lillie would sigh.

"I made my own bets. I wagered right."

She had asked a friend of a friend who worked at the *Call & Response,* a Negro circular in Columbia, if he'd be interested in covering a Negro trainer of the winning horse—because someone should acknowledge the man in the machine. The friend didn't know, but he'd put in a word, then Lillie had offered that she would pay to have the moment documented. She pleaded and then scraped a few dollars between her laundry service and slipped into their farm savings. She couldn't explain it to Moses, she just had a feeling that race would change their life, and she couldn't expect the white press to capture the magnitude of it all.

So as soon as Pal crossed back over the invisible force field to the backstretch, he snorted—a release. All of the grooms gathered to celebrate Moses's win chuckled, because they knew: horses understand when they're in the hands of their caretaker and not. Loved and used. Pal was with his person and his head dropped to Moses's eye level. Years in the barn with her sister and now Moses taught Lillie that Pal's adrenaline had calmed. Lloyd knew it too. Called out, "Hosey!" and of course "Daddy's hosey!" and in the comfort of the backstretch no one corrected him. Instead, Moses reached for his son and plopped Lloyd in the saddle. Lloyd squealed with his snaggletooth grin and Moses pulled Lillie to his hip, and the photographer captured the sweet moment.

Moses held his son on Pal's back all the way to the stables. Lillie hadn't signed up for that much adventure but what a far cry from their early days trying to convince Moses to have a child, or else what all was this for?—she'd ask, pointing to them and the horses. And Moses would shrug: Me. You. You for me.

"How you light me up. And horses for me: I don't know another way to be in this world. Having a kid don't automatically mean they gone want what you gave 'em. My grandaddy said his daddy tried to give him whatever he had when they ain't had nothing to own, so he gave him the fields, working the earth, had said knowing dirt under your fingernails an' how to make food from it an' you won't know hunger a day in your life, an' my grandaddy said he wanted to know how far a landscape will take you from a horse's back."

Lillie didn't know what changed but she wasn't going to stop it, even if it terrified her in that moment: her two-year-old son on the back of a two-year-old stallion. But the smile on her husband's face. The echo of her son's calls of excitement quieted the unease in her heart, and she knew they all were where they needed to be, and that nature finds a way to push the timeline of your life forward. Moses had made a replica of himself, a mirror. A place to store and find some joy.

||||||||||||||||||

It was the inherited love, the inquisitiveness, the desire pulling him like a sapling to sunlight, that kept Lloyd at the barn year after year. Sure, school would be starting back soon, and the freak snowstorm of 1948 delayed that return a few days into the new year, for which he was thankful. Everything was already so delicate after the war. Everyone walked around with the shortest of fuses, like any wrong step would set off the next atomic bomb. Everyone lifted their hands in resignation when first it was the full moon, then the four full days of abnormal hard freeze giving the snow that was to come a cold place to land and stick, making difficult winter chores harder, roads impassable, and so the town had decided to hunker down and wait for the big thaw.

Moses had just explained to Lloyd how on the first of January, all horses turn towards a new year, no matter when along the twelve months air first filled their lungs, how we mark it: no matter if March or July, on January 1 each horse gains a new notch on its age. It also marks—if all goes well and the mares carrying bide by good nature—the beginning of foaling season.

||||||||||||||||||

Reddmare had started acting funny as soon as the moon rose full above the trees. Laying down, standing up. Laying down. In his twelve years of life, each of them surrounded by horses, Lloyd knew this to be a sign of distress. Colic. A possible life-threatening stomachache. When foaling season comes, you stand watch like the volunteers who camp in the fire towers ready to call for help at the first plume of smoke in the sky. When Reddmare laid down the fifth time, he haltered her and tied her to the chain hanging from the barn rafters to keep the mare from laying down another time, and he ran to get his father.

After they learned she was pregnant, which wasn't so long ago, they were told she wouldn't be due for three months. They were nowhere near their safe date. That was clear. There was no way a vet was coming down an icy, muddy dirt road in the middle of the night, Lillie reported, having been the one to call. They'd have to get the mare through the night and assess in the morning.

"Vet says you may have to make a choice," Lillie sighed. Moses shook his head. Won't nothing fair about animal husbandry, his daddy always said, who got it from Grandaddy and so on. Nothing's fair because you can't change the course of nature.

She was an aged mare. She wasn't supposed to be on the foal watch list. Moses had planned to keep her open—she had given him so many things, including good horses over the years. He hadn't planned to ask anything else of her—just live out the rest of her days a beautiful ornament in his barn. She was his best horse. Matriarch, producer of some of his best lines. Winners, all. But out in the world, she was old news so it ain't make sense to breed her again. They say everyone's tastes had changed and folks were crossing this and that. Away from her pedigree. Trying to land on what would be *the* American Quarter Horse. That was something crazy to think about: not even a decade in and his mare and her bloodlines were already old news.

At least that's what Dale had been saying these last few years whenever he came back from a sale. Moses knew better than to load any of his colts onto his own trailer and drive anywhere with the audacity to represent his own interests at a sale, so he had asked Dale to do it. Dale was one of the few white men he trusted to do his bidding, and they had worked out that he would do it for a cut of the sale. Each year the price of Moses's colts would go down, but each year Dale would come out to the farm to see what would be up for sale.

Two years ago, Dale claimed no one wanted to pay asking price for what would cover what Moses wanted and what he wanted, supposedly. Dale brought the filly back to the farm and made Moses a low offer, but it was cash in hand. And if Moses rejected it, he'd be looking at another mouth to feed in an already lean year what with the whole of everything struggling to recover from the epic loss of workforce to the war.

Moses accepted the offer, then was later told a man had come to Dale's farm looking for the filly that was at the sale, and made him an offer he couldn't refuse. Dale came with a handful of cash—Moses's "cut"—and said: "I know it won't near what you're looking for, but I figured all our years in business, I wanted there to be no bad blood."

Except now there *was* bad blood because Moses suspected he was being cheated and had asked some of the sale-barn farmhands, who said the filly never made it to the sale at all.

Every time Moses had gone back out into the world, it showed him what the world thought of him, and each chip, especially all these decades of it, not only hardened him but made it more evident that he had to divest as best he could while also knowing how much of his livelihood, and possibly how much of Lloyd's, was intertwined. How do you leave the thing you built? He understood his grandfather better now than when he had asked, as a young boy, why he chose to stay in Fairfield County after manumission: *How do you leave the thing you built?*

Moses cared too much for the horses, and what would become of them. He appreciated that there were—despite whatever their other misgivings about him were—folks who appreciated good honest horseflesh that he produced. It was just that he had to keep carving new pathways around the resistance, and that was to keep on in the direction you were already headed—how water makes its way through rock, eventually. So would he. Or the next generation, or the next.

Anyway, he did pause on breeding his Reddmare for the Tri-Stock Sale that happened over in Augusta, Georgia. He had a few foals he was expecting that were called for through private treaty—folks coming back to the well for their own cool sip of water. When he was feeding Reddmare her rations like his other open horses but her hips started erupting through her fall, then winter coat even though her belly was reaching for the ground, Moses called the vet to confirm. It was only then that he had heard from Lloyd that one morning when he went out for chores he noticed that Reddmare was in the paddock with Ol' Mister and since they were standing grazing together, calmly—"like how you and Mama sit around the fire after dinner"—Lloyd had seen no cause for concern; he went and gathered Reddmare and Ol' Mister nickered after her and she nickered back.

"Why didn't you tell me? How did she get in there?"

It had been months since Lloyd had considered that question. He supposed since it didn't seem anyone was hurt won't no use ringing the alarm.

"You didn't think that since a mare had gone in with a stallion he wouldn't have bred her?"

"They didn't seem—" Lloyd started. Moses shook his head. Too late. Now they were on foal watch when it was entirely too early to be on foal watch because there won't a real drop date since no one knew when she was bred. Reddmare had decided what she had wanted to do with her body this season. Nature continued to find a way despite whatever Moses tried to orchestrate.

When they got to the barn, the mare was on the floor—at least her body was. Her head was still strapped into the halter about three feet off the ground that had been fixed to the chain from the rafters.

"I tried to keep her from laying back down while I ran to get you," Lloyd cried into the dark, dank barn. Moses lit a lamp and placed it far out of their reach but close enough to attempt to get more light besides the sliver of moonlight through the wood beams casting shadows over so much of the mare's body. It was hard to tell if she was still alive.

"Don't reckon that worked," Moses responded, then pulled open the stall door. Hearing Moses's voice, Reddmare jostled enough to let them know she was still alive, if barely, but did not have the strength to push herself to her feet.

Moses made his way slowly into the stall, squinting to see what was going on. Her breathing wasn't heavy like a mare in labor. It was low and slow like she was taking in her last catches of air earth-side. He didn't know why he did it, but he crossed his chest and whispered a small prayer: "Strength for my son," he said under his breath. Sure they had experienced losses: Raccoons pulling chicks through the wire just enough to behead them. A pup overcome by rabies after she had been attacked by a pack of coyotes passing through when the land a few parcels over had been clear-cut for some reason or another. Probably timber. A piglet smothered by its nursing mother, oblivious to the small clump of flesh attached to her. Each loss seemed natural, seemed minuscule compared to a pregnant mare possibly facing the end of her life.

By the time he made it to her side, there was no longer a choice. If she was in so much pain as to buckle to the floor, surely it was that her legs gave out beneath her and gravity likely broke her neck, severing her spine. What Moses thought were attempts to stand were muscle contractions.

"Her belly moving, Daddy," Lloyd whispered.

So it was. This was the choice. He had to act quickly to save something of this mess while respecting the magnitude of what his son was about to witness. He untied the halter, and Reddmare's head flopped onto the ground like a wet rag.

"Son, I need you to go and ask your mama to sharpen the largest knife we got. She probably already got a pot of water set to boil. But I need you to make haste and grab it. Grab a towel. Anything we can wipe the foal with, 'cause Redd won't be able to clean any of this up."

He cooed and felt around the belly to try to locate the position of the foal's head. Even if she was able to push it out it would have been difficult. Lloyd returned and dropped the requested items at his father's feet.

"Look here." Moses gestured, then grabbed Lloyd's hand. Together they moved along the mare's warm, quivering body. "She's trying to abort but doesn't have enough strength. Anyway, the foal is breech—trying to come out butt first. Just like humans, you want it head first. But you want it head and front legs, like they diving into this godforsaken world."

"How would you fix it?"

"In normal cases, you'd have to reach in there and turn the foal rightway and pray your mama mare trust you enough to do it that she don't try to knock you into next week." Moses found a chuckle, under the circumstances. "Me and Reddmare been down this road a few times. Her babies loved keeping me on my toes. We been in all the situations you could find yourself to be in, except of course this one. I'm afraid, son, this will be our last trip."

Moses felt Lloyd turn to him in the darkness. At first Moses nodded but realized he probably couldn't see him.

"She's not going to make it, son. So I'm trying to save the foal now, but everything is against us."

He patted Reddmare, then scratched. "I'm sorry, girl."

The work was hard and bloody. Moses's aged body, not unlike the mare's, struggling under the task. When he stopped for the second time to catch his breath, Lloyd asked what he could do to be helpful. Moses grabbed his right hand to know where to place the bloody knife, then grabbed Lloyd's left hand and pulled him closer to the mare's body.

"She passed out at the first cut. I think she's still with us. Barely. Not enough to be supplying oxygen to the foal at this point. We have a little time, I think, before we lose them both, but I'm an old man with no more steam. I need you, son. Cut here. Deep, but not too deep. Keep an angle. Don't cut through them both."

When Moses felt the boy had cut enough room, he told Lloyd to stop and reached inside the opening for the foal. He used an old jute cloth that he had once used to shine racehorses after their baths to clear the air passages. The foal arrived to the world limp, lifeless. After he pulled back the placenta, and wiped the first globs of womb stuffs from its eyes, nose, mouth, Moses had knelt down further in the bloody muck and pressed his lips to the newborn muzzle and blew with all the air he could gather in his lungs and blew and blew. He didn't stop. Lloyd got up to gather Lillie and they watched Moses attempt to breathe life into an impossible situation.

Lillie saw he would not stop on his own. Now there was the business of moving to the next task and burying the bodies. To continue to watch for the rest of the foal crop for the next six months.

"Mo—" she cooed in his ear, then touched his shoulder when he leaned up on his knees to catch his breath. "Mo—we need to stop so we can figure this out together. Figure out how we moving the body. Bodies. I'll get the lye for now."

In a crisis, Lillie thought steps ahead with reason, while Moses moved molasses-slow and with his heart. Especially when it came to horses. She loved Reddmare like a daughter when it seemed that would be the closest she'd get, and she was mourning too, but it wasn't going to do anyone any good for them both to get caught up in this. She had to gather Moses and had to teach Lloyd. Forward motion against obstacles. Move like water.

Eventually, Moses relented. Later, he'd tell Lillie the truth: that he would have breathed for that foal as long as it would have taken for it to stand up on its own two feet, but the circumstances of his age and those years at the shipyard caught up and he couldn't ask his boy to do anything else for him that night or surely he'd walk away from it all. He had to stop.

Walter down the way had come to help figure out what was to happen next. Whatever it was, it had to be done swiftly. In the hours since, a new day had come, and with it, flies blanketing the barn, and the stench of blood, placenta, innards, and other bodily fluids soaked into the sawdust slapped you in the face. No one who didn't see it with their own eyes ever believed Moses when he recalled he had to move the body quickly because when he had woken up, all of the horses faced the barn, standing vigil. Not one of them touched their breakfast. And then, when the pieces of Reddmare and her unnamed colt were tractor-dragged across the land, back past the family plot, and the cypresses, out by the maple that spread far east to west instead of north to the sky, all of the horses faced that portion of the property, every evening for three days as the sun was setting.

On the fourth day after they buried them, Moses checked Lloyd's temperature on the matter. Sure, the boy had gone on to complete his daily chores, including night check. Sure, the boy had helped his father strip the stall and lay new bedding. No one was sure who it was for yet, but they did it anyway. He went through the motions, but Moses noticed the questions stopped. A light in his eyes, dampened.

"You alright?" was all Moses managed to mutter while they were dishing out the oat and corn for evening feed.

"Yes sir."

"You quiet. You want to talk about it? That was a big day for all us."

"No sir," Lloyd started. "I mean, I know it was a big day, but I don't got no words for it."

Moses hummed in acknowledgment and waited a few beats.

"I know I talk about life going on, nature's way and all that, pushing you to the next thing. Farm life don't never stop and whatnot. But it's alright to have feelings. I don't know that I'll ever recover from that night myself."

Moses shook his head, recalling the first deep slice into the mare's belly, the first struggled breath into the foal. How the gases released from the belly. How a moan escaped from the small clump. How he apologized then, tears forming in his eyes.

"We lose so much of what we love in this life, son. I had hoped you had a little more time before you felt that sting like I know it."

Reddmare had been the horse he saddled time and time again to ride out into the open fields, into the woods, out to check fence lines, into town. When folks found their way to owning their own automobiles, he would holler out as they passed him on the road, kicking up dust.

"One red horsepower is all I need to get me where I'm goin'!"

When Lloyd had added the *r* to what was the only word he knew, and said the word "horses," Moses pulled out Reddmare to teach the boy what it meant to be cared for under saddle. That was the difference in his way of things. He didn't have broodmares in the way white horsemen had them: a tool for turning more profit by birthing more babies. In the racing barns, the broodmares were unhandled except at breeding and if, like with Reddmare, there were complications, thrown back out to pasture after being bred again. They almost never had a name except maybe So-n-so's dam. But according to Moses, won't no better—absolutely no better—horse to teach a child how to ride, how to take care of it while also being taken care of, than a mama horse that's still gentled to human touch.

She taught Lloyd how to ride bareback when she was too big carrying a foal to be saddled but he was small enough not to cause no trouble. Moses had to get a handle on his own jealousy the day he and Lloyd both went out to the pastures and she walked to the boy. She loved him. It was probably why, while he was standing vigil all night, she had tried to be strong and got up each time he asked until he walked away, and she tried to leave, quietly, without her little boy

Lloyd watching. Moses knew this as well as he knew his boy would be forever changed by that night. He won't know how or when the grief will take over his life, but Moses knew in his heart that his boy would meet a day that presented Lloyd with a big choice. A big impossible choice. When that day came, Moses knew the answer would only make sense to Lloyd. And he would have to let that choice stand. No matter whose pain, whose costs.

Chapter 5

"You almost twenty-five, son. You think just 'cause you inching near a quarter century on this dirt you got life enough in you to think up something new? Every generation try to outshine the past ones only to find that the past everlasting. Try to put a tuxedo on a hog. It still a hog," Moses said.

He was standing at the rope fence that demarcated the track from the spectator field. Won't no bleachers or what the white folks called a "grandstand" like at the field that held the Carolina Jessamine Invitational—where the folks who paid top dollar to witness which horse stretched his neck across the finish line set high up in the Carolina-blue sky. Won't no tents with canapés and crudités . . . for the service folk to wrap in cloth napkins and carry home after the last spectator disappeared. No pomp and circumstance—no pledging allegiance or presenting colors. The Track, if he could call it that—but he supposed he should 'cause that's what Lloyd called it—was a tilled path across the property, kicking up the bright white Carolina sand. It was a fast-when-wet, slow-when-dry sand, because the horses sank a good four inches with each galloping step in the dry sand.

"This the ground that separate athletes from wild babies," Lloyd said, standing next to his father, surveying what he could see of the field—the portable starting gate was ready to receive the four horses signed up by their owners to test what kind of horseflesh they were to continue to invest in.

Lloyd dug the toe of his boot into the ground. "This the place *your* bosses come to pace out their new blood before sending them to your Evergreen Gardens turf or whatever." He lifted his hands and made a gesture to mock where his father had worked and groomed and trained for decades, which was where Moses's father worked and his before then until the names were lost across the water.

Moses chuffed at the gesture. "Y'all young menfolk think you inventing and reinventing and doing things better an' whatnot. I get it. You get your little track and make you a little money that don't pass through white hands and think you cracked a code us 'old-timers' ain't never thought to crack."

"Well," Lloyd started. "Ain't no white folks 'round here pretending you're not there . . . pretending that it ain't *y'all* own sweat and time and knowledge run the whole enterprise. No. They stick y'all behind a fence and come out with they cigars and bourbons and bets like they had a hand in any of it."

"They pay for it," Moses offered.

"So do we," Lloyd said. "We pay for this." He twirled his fingers in a circle above his head.

"Yeh, an' hope the officials turn a blind eye and find something to keep them busy while y'all all corralled out here. It would be so easy to round y'all up an' lock you up 'cause it ain't sanctioned."

Lloyd shook his head. He supposed it was futile trying to teach an old dog. How they say. Won't never learn new ideas. The horses being led out to the field came into their field of vision and saved him. Right on time.

"They rounding 'em up now," Lloyd offered the obvious. He pointed to the ground. Then turned to his father. "Looka here. You get to stand at the starting gate, which, with this out-an'-back course, is basically the finish line. How many of your races have you been able to witness the finish for yourself?"

On that, his son had a point.

"I remember sitting on your shoulders so I could see the field over the fence," Lloyd said.

The announcer could be heard between the crackles of the loudspeaker making its way above the commotion. This was a fast race. Done before you really settled in. "We won't spend our time telling you about the horses, y'all about to see who gets dusted an' who will do the dusting. So just sit right back an' get your greenbacks out, folks. Who's gone make you some money today?"

No pomp. No circumstance. Moses found himself missing the very thing this place was supposed to skip over: Tradition. The parade of it all. He always enjoyed how the announcer had to fill a lot of empty space between the first horse to line up at the gate and the last horse to cross the finish line. Stories of who the horses were, who trained them, what kind of race history, their odds for winning—all of that. It was how he got to know the horses that ran the circuit with him, before he met their handlers or grooms on the backstretch in the stables. But here, Lloyd always stressed that folks really want to see the horseflesh run. The reason to gather and gawk at all.

"Pop, we the sons and grandsons and nephews of y'all folk who we know to be the *real* stewards of the horses. What we look like saying all of what don't matter? When we know the truth? We know whose sweat really mark the horses' backs. We wanted to create a space for y'all too. Out here. To stand tall with us and the horses. You can stand tall right here with me."

The announcer said something about seeing the horses getting anxious and it being time to get the show on the road. Moses looked around for a race official then laughed when he remembered where he was. The only man standing near the gate when it was called for the track to be cleared "of any animal not wearing a race number *and also* four legs." He grinned at that, but frowned his face that the person to fire the starting pistol was also going to be the one to call false start or anything. No separation of church and state. No checks with no balances.

"This just a free-for-all," Moses mumbled. Lloyd asked what did he say? And Moses shook his head. He won't gone start with his son today.

The horseflesh, though, for what it was worth if you had asked Moses, was exceptional. There was just something about the quarter horses that caught his eye a smidge deeper than those Thoroughbreds. Even after all those years at the long-distance racetrack. It was the hind end—the engine. Someone figured out that a horse can only pull through the turf with his front end for so long in his life or else it starts to impact conformation, overall performance, and health—was why so many of them tapped out of their careers after a season or two of racing. Moses knew this fact, but that was just the nature of the beast. It was how he had a string of good-lookin'—but not yet usable—horses in his barns year after year; and frankly, where folk really came to know him as a true horseman and trainer.

As a groom and galloper, only one or two folk know what work he really did, or the importance of doing it well: the jockey, the trainer. Neither of whom can ever find themselves in a place to speak the groom's or galloper's name when it comes time to sing praises and talk to the press when they standing in the winner's circle. That's why everybody looked at Mrs. Pynchon-Grant like she had six eyes when she pulled Moses into the frame of the photo op. She knew. That was her thanks. A rare breed. Otherwise, the owner never knows neither, 'cause *if*—a big if—he rides at all, he (or she, though less often) is almost guaranteed to be too big to make the weight requirement on account of they living a big, rich life. And besides, that won't even what they were in it for. Either way, unless those owners mount the horses, how he could turn a wiry Thoroughbred into an exceptional hunt horse or even a family pleasure horse they won't know for themselves.

"I make 'em just a good listening and thinking horse," Moses would describe the horse, having transitioned it into its new job—whatever he trained it to do as a next career. "When they come off the track, they just a ball of muscles, reacting. They reacting to the starting gun. They reacting to the energy of the course. The other horses. The jockey whippin' its ass with a crop whip. Yankin' its head left. Justa reacting. If you take that horse home and think you gone ride it like a normal horse, well, that's when folks get hurt. The horse hear a crinkle of a leaf in fall and just get to reactin'. You can't reason with a horse like that. So I make it my business to teach 'em to think in they next life. They got the muscle. They got the heart. The good ones got the courage. I'll take those on, then I just remind them they got a brain an' can use it."

The look on the owners' faces when they got their racehorse-turned-something-else back let him know he was in business, and the first few head he took off the track like that, Moses had refused payment and simply asked the white folk speak his name whenever any of their colleagues asked who they should send their horses to if they were looking to invest in a second career. Hell, speak his name when they tired of racing it even if that won't what they were lookin' to do.

But those quarter horses at the Quarter Downs track had what Lloyd said so often, "the brain an' the caboose." Moses cut his eyes in Lloyd's direction the first time he heard that particular turn of phrase and asked, "Ain't you mean the engine? The caboose just come along for the ride."

Of course he had known what Lloyd meant, and that was why, when given the choice himself for what kind of horses he wanted to keep, and later breed, it was the quarter horse, because they climbed out the womb with the heart, the brain, the courage, the caboose. The work then was convincing them you were smart enough to be in their presence. Moses loved that challenge.

It was mostly quarter horses that were raced at the Track, that and what they called appendix quarter horses—quarter horses mixed with Thoroughbreds—those are the ones who moved the breed above sixty inches on average. Had longer backs and their cabooses angled a bit towards the ground rather than rounded like the curve of a question mark—the true physical distinction of a quarter horse. Moses noticed two of the four horses at the Track were appendix, and so if he were a betting man (which he wasn't) he wouldn't dare put his money on them to cross the finish line first on such a short course. They were bound for the longer course, more time to stretch out, and find their groove. This was a dry run for the big games for the appendixes.

The crowd had settled a bit when the horses were taking their mark, but the hum of chatter started to rise in the lull before the starting gun.

"Folks, we had a few last-minute registrations, and a pull. We got enough draws to run a second race instead of load this field. Sorry, y'all. Bear with us," the announcer called over the murmuration.

Lloyd walked over to the part of the rope fence within earshot of the two men who had appeared on the field to open starting gate number one.

More than usual, the horse in the first gate was attempting to rear up—pull his front feet into the air. Because of his size and the design of the gate, the horse just kept banging his hooves on the galvanized steel, causing panic among the other horses. Moses had noted this to the gentleman to his right, who asked if he might know what was up since he did look like a horseman.

Moses tipped his hat. "Yes sir. I am. Lookin' like that there horse might be juiced up an' they didn't get him out the start gate fast enough to hide it. Now everyone gone suffer. Horse an' rider—all. They gone have to reload or else wait in them stocks. That ain't no good for no one. Yeap."

Moses pointed to Lloyd, who had grabbed a stethoscope from someone who brought it to the field. He waited for the horse to exit the gate and the jockey to dismount, and the horse's handler tried his level best to get the horse to stand still so Lloyd could check the heart rate. The horse was dripping sweat.

"Ain't no need to check the heart rate, Doc, we see it," Moses said out loud.

"Folks, we have our field doctor out here, Mr. Lloyd Bolton, to make sure everyone is aboveboard," the announcer said.

Moses pointed to the horse. "He dancing 'round at the end of that lead line like he a kite. Done sweated himself to foaming an' ain't even stepped on the real turf yet."

Lloyd shook his head and pointed towards the stable. That was that.

"Yes, folks, number 47 has been pulled. We'll call number 52 if they're ready to join up, and give these jockeys and their mounts a chance to reset if they feel the need. We're still gearing up for the fastest race on dirt, folks! Stay tuned!"

At least they had someone to make sure the horses are running fair. *Least they got that,* Moses thought.

Lloyd had come back, wiping his hands on his pants. He had started to explain.

"It was clear as day, son, that horse won't clean." Moses shook his head. "Clear as Easter morn."

After a few minutes of commotion around the track, the announcer tapped on the loudspeaker.

"Alright, folks. This is it. We got sparkly-clean horses in the lineup, with thanks to Doc Bolton keeping us on the straight and narrow. We're ready to run now. Can I get an all clear from the field?"

Lloyd held up his hand and pointed down the track. Ready to go.

"Doc says let's get a move on. So here we go. Hope you got your purse settled and your champion dreams on the right horse."

Moses squinted and then nodded in the direction of the starting gate.

"It's the red boy for me," he said. "That's the one gone get it. If I were a betting man."

"It's always the red ones for you, Pop," Lloyd said.

Moses shrugged. He knew the danger of betting on a pretty-colored horse. "Well, history tell the truth like I do. Red most likely to come up roses. Be in the winner's circle. You go on chasin' color 'cause you like to look at 'em, standing there looking pretty. If you like your wallet, you'll mind me."

"You did Thoroughbreds, Pops. This quarters," Lloyd countered.

"You go back a few generations in quarters an' you'll find red Thoroughbreds, son. See, I'm talkin' y'all need to know this stuff to push any of this forward. Me, I had to know five generations back of any horse in my care. Anyone would walk by and ask who made him, and they won't asking about the owners. I needed to be able to answer it. Then, I made it my business to know that about as many horses as I could. Daddy made sure of that, too. In his day, spilling over into mine, we were the record keepers, the walking breed registries. We held the score. The primary sources for the journalists at the races. Answered who was who an' whatnot. We brought the stallions to stand with the mares and it would be the grooms—*us*—tellin' the owners who begat who, what kind of horse-cross they was making. Calculating the odds of breeding a champion. You know. So when they crowning the winners with them floral wreaths *we knew* what blood produced it."

Lloyd rolled his eyes at the umpteenth time he heard that story and nodded.

The gun blasted. The crowd shushed just long enough to see who launched out the starting gate first. Then the roars unfolded like waves. Lloyd was shouting for a horse—not a red one—he had in the race as part owner. He had convinced a few of his friends to go in on his seal-brown piece of dynamite he called Pilot. Pilot had a white star in the middle of his forehead like an Ash Wednesday cross and no other white on any part of his body. He was stunning alright. Great to look at. A pretty good caboose. Still years left to his career. Lloyd didn't tell his father who he was to him; this was Pilot's first race on the track.

One-fourth of the way in, Moses remarked, "*My* horse lookin' to do negative split on the second half, must be."

Lloyd chuckled, "Or else he just slow."

Moses shook his head. They were halfway done; Pilot was in the middle of the pack. "*My horse* nostrils ain't flaring yet. He coasting. He got 'bout three more gears. There," he pointed and watched his red horse move up two places with three strides.

"Yeap," Moses said. Lloyd was biting his bottom lip—a habit of his when he got nervous. Pilot was one of the first out the gate and now trailing the others.

"That black one ain't got no wind left to shoo a fly," Moses said. He turned back to the front of the pack, to his red horse. "There you go, boy," his voice louder.

"There you go, boy," he repeated louder again.

The announcer called out as the horses zipped by Moses and Lloyd, kicking dirt into their faces: a badge of honor. Neither flinched.

"Come on. Come. Come," Lloyd said under his breath. Pilot picked up a place back to third as they approached the finish. It was mostly fine. Good, even. At the Track, one of the big things Lloyd fought for was that every place that crossed the finish line if it started the race paid out, so his partners will get something back no matter what. And with Pilot, he had something to work *to attain* rather than attempt to maintain if they had won. A much easier journey for the two of them.

"And here it is, folks, your winner!" the announcer called out.

"In his red suit." Moses grinned at Lloyd, and cuffed his shoulder. "Genes will come through every time. I'd bet on that. Yes sir!"

Chapter 6

In those later years of Moses's life, his eyesight had started to fail, and on the ground on his own two feet he hung on to Lillie like she was a walking stick. He'd wake up, and ask her to help him get ready to tend horses, and he'd slowly make his way around back to the stables he was so thankful he had tacked onto the back of the house—how would he have gotten to them so easily otherwise? No way he could make it to the old barns how he used to, almost skipping across the pasture, but in the presence of God's angels (what he called horses) he felt young again. His ailments wafted away. He stood upright, found his core, and could do what he needed to do.

That kept him young, and being a grandfather. When Lloyd announced that he and Delores were expecting, the fading light inside him flared up. What he hadn't realized he yearned for—a lineage, a long one—coming true, and he would witness it manifest. All this time he thought it too late in the season of his life. Lloyd was at the top of the game of the space he crafted for himself and made space for a family. It was possible. He wanted it all. There was no choice for him. He'd have Delores, the love of his life, Quarter Downs, and his string of winning horses and—he wasn't shy with his request—a boy to imprint it all upon. Of course he'd love whatever God gave him. Of course. But a boy would just put him in the best winner's circle. Everyone pre-celebrated Lloyd's good fortune (according to Lillie, God's favor) each month of the pregnancy. Lloyd had the horse picked out. Moses too. They'd fight over whose horse would be the child's horse. The settlement was one at each farm. Lightning Jet at home. And O'boy—third generation out of Reddmare—at . . . what would Moses be called?

"Don't make it difficult. I'm Grandaddy," he said.

O'boy would be the child's mount at the Bolton Plantation.

On the day the baby arrived, doctors didn't seem worried when Delores came to the hospital with waterlogged ankles and shortness of breath. She said her head hurt too, and they nodded, proceeded like a normal labor. To the untrained eye, maybe it was. Everyone was there to welcome the next generation: Lillie, Moses, Lloyd nervously sweating, wringing his hands. Lillie pulled Moses out "so they can have some air." Later, she'll say she knew the signs of trouble and it needed to be between husband and wife.

When Lloyd walked out into the waiting room, Moses gathered himself as quickly as he could, quicker with Lillie lending an arm. They held their breaths.

"A boy," he said. They smiled.

"Congrats, son." Lloyd stood not looking at them, or anywhere. Lillie cleared her throat, but she knew.

"And how's Mama doing?"

"She's—"

Everyone in the room, listening or pretending to, understood.

"Oh, my baby," Lillie offered, rushing towards him with arms open for an embrace. Losing his lean-to, Moses crumpled back into the chair, thinking of the sorrel mare, the decisions we inherit, and started to understand Lloyd was already checked out, leaving—gone. On that day, the big impossible choice finally came for Lloyd in the face of his grief. What Moses braced himself for every day since he tried to breathe for that foal he cut out of Reddmare all those years ago.

Won't no way to prepare Moses for Lloyd's departure without his newborn. Won't no way.

||||||||||||||||||

When they were confronted with the necessity of being the caretakers for their grandson, Moses was much too old to take on a young boy like a son, but Lillie insisted—where else was Dwayne to go? Lloyd had only said he had to leave. There was no sign of when he'd return. Besides, Lillie nudged, Dwayne is the next generation. Moses still had something to give, so the boy could be the one to *truly* carry it all forward.

"How do you just walk away from all this?" Moses asked. Lillie was present, but she knew he wasn't looking for an answer. "How do you just—keep on and just live your life?" He couldn't understand. All he knew: he was put on this earth to be in communion with horses. There was nothing else to know.

In Dwayne, Moses believed he had been given one last chance, like a large breath before your spirit sends itself off to see the Lord.

When Dwayne was old enough, Moses scooped him up and plopped him right on the back of his red horse, O'boy. Wasn't any gear—no bridle, no saddle. No prep at all: Moses had run the back of his hands along the length of the horse's back in quick sweeps like brushing crumbs off a sitting chair. Then swung the boy up—his legs falling to O'boy's sides. They swayed like curtains in front of an open window. Dwayne wiggled, trying to find some stability, his hands grasping for something to hold on to. Moses said balance comes from *here,* and pointed in the middle of his body, lifting his shoulders, puffing his chest.

Dwayne said, "The heart?"

Moses said well, that too, yes. The heart, too.

Dwayne grabbed a piece of O'boy's mane—the only thing graspable up there—and Grandaddy Mo made the smooching noise like blowing a long-distance kiss to a lover, and Dwayne felt his heart skip a beat as O'boy launched forward into a steady lope across the yard. After a few flops left and then right and left again, Dwayne tried gripping O'boy with his legs, and he grabbed more mane further up O'boy's neck, and tried crouching low.

"Unh-unh, Dewy. Not like that just yet. That's how you tell him to launch out into a gallop like you a jockey at the races, you can't hold on to him like that."

"But Imma fall, Grandaddy," Dwayne had whimpered.

"Sit up like you the King of Fairfield County. Like you trying to keep that heavy 'spensive crown from falling off your head. Like you know how valuable you are."

Dwayne straightened his spine and remembered his heart. Grandaddy Mo was moving his hands in slow, deliberate gestures like he was a choir director and the horse—carrying his future—loped circles around him.

Moses nodded. That was good breeding alright. O'boy was the son of Mister, the last live colt out of Reddmare. Those bloodlines went all the way back to some of the horses traded by the Spanish and Indigenous horsemen—what started the quarter horse breed, who were faster than fast at the sprint, and sturdy. You couldn't break them if you tried. And Moses tried. That was part of the training, and why he was so good at it. Take a horse like Boss, Reddmare's sire, and you could fire a pistol off him with black powder flinging by both ears and marvel that all four legs would remain on the ground. At her best, what made Reddmare so valuable to Moses's breeding program was that she was so unfazed by anything and scared of nothing that if she decided she didn't want to do something, you just simply couldn't make her. You had to *negotiate* with Reddmare. She had to pick you as her partner, or else it won't no use trying to ride out into the field or beyond with her. Sure, he'd lost a lot of horses, but he hadn't grieved one so deeply as his Reddmare.

But it was that unbreakability that Moses sought—horse after horse—along with the ability to sense good people, that was what he wanted to breed, and he succeeded in O'boy. O'boy outshined everyone with the smarts. It was like winning the lottery after all these years trying: a horse that was eager to get up and go to work every day of his life, who was quiet enough for Lillie if she ever had the urge to hop aboard and ride out into the horizon and have a horse that would bring her back home safely (she chose the mules and wagon, but still Moses wanted her to have the option). It was such a shame that this horse had come so late in his life. The things they could have done together! But maybe that was the right way—he had now the best ride he'd ever produced, and his grandson could partner up for the long haul. First, though, Moses had to see if Dwayne had inherited the seat. That's why he tossed the boy up there with no tack. Let him feel the horse's movements. Let the horse feel Dwayne's intentions. He'll know within the first few moments if they'll get along, and so far, they made a team.

"Talk to him if you have to. Sing to him. He knows you're scared so he's getting worried thinking he gotta run from something 'cause he's trying to protect himself but also not knowing the fear he senses emanating from you, the thing you scared of *is him.* You gotta be brave enough for the both of y'all."

"Hey, 'Boy," Dwayne whispered, the word "boy" falling out of his mouth like a long exhale. It was all he could think to say or sing. The horse quieted to a walk just like that. How easy it was to slow the big animal down had caught him by surprise.

"Grandaddy, look! He stoppin'!" he squealed. Grandaddy Mo nodded his head and pointed a finger to the right and clucked. Dwayne breathed deeply as the horse changed directions.

"I'll teach you everything I know, just like I taught your daddy, and like my daddy taught me," Grandaddy Mo said, following the boy and his horse. "How you use it is up to you, but this your inheritance."

O'boy had strolled around the lawn for the rest of the evening with Dwayne along for the ride until Grandma Lillie called them both inside for supper. The day so perfect, Dwayne never forgot the feel of his first ride, nor the meal after. The feeling of what it must be to fly. Country ham. Flat beans. Grandma Lillie's hot-water cornbread with a glass of buttermilk. The taste of everlasting summer.

It was all he could think about: the next ride on O'boy. Became all he could talk about: O'boy this. O'boy that. Grandma Lillie whispered to Moses one morning while they were lingering over breakfast and Dwayne was already out at the stables brushing his horse, "That horse just might give him the hope he needs. What for all he's been through in his young life already. That boy needs something that'll be steady. Dependable."

"That's O'boy, alright," Moses said, saying the *O* harder to differentiate between the horse and the word "boy" they used also to refer to Dwayne. "He's proven every day that he's the horse I made him to be."

Moses smiled, and he and Lillie watched the boy and his horse lope across the field past the pair of cypress trees and into the woods.

Chapter 7

After church but before supper every Sunday, Lillie and Moses would go into town by mule and buggy. Holly, the mule that was attached to the cart the Boltons had used, would watch them come down the drive in their automobile and wait at the gate. It was as much a treat for her as it had been for them. To loose themselves of the newfangled technology and rig up a good sturdy mule and wagon and rock back and forth along the dirt roads and sometimes gravel roads and sometimes paved roads into town. Sometimes to pick up what vittles Lillie would need to round out her Sunday plate, but most often to drop in: sit a spell with Rose, gossip a minute with Earl at the meat counter about how the price of a chop had jumped ten cents on account of the corn being dried out this summer with the drought—the domino of it all. Holly would wait patiently at this stop and that, and nicker at Lillie when they exited the General Store, smelling the sweets in her pockets. A mint for Holly and two mints for Dwayne. Ms. Mozell, their neighbor who felt like family across the street, was happy to give them this afternoon time anytime, almost suggested it even: One day Lillie had come to see if she had three cups of flour for her soda pound cake to tide them over until they made it back into town. Mozell had remarked on her appearance, but in a loving way—how someone who cares about you might point out a hair out of place because they know how important keeping up appearances is, and it was clear to Mozell that appearances weren't being kept. Lillie gingerly tucked the errant lock of hair behind her ear and remarked how much more busy life was these days: "I had forgotten how energetic boys are. Lloyd . . . he was quiet, reserved. He watched. Internalized. Dwayne wears his emotions and energy like a rain poncho—a different kind of protection barrier. I thank God he's taken such a liking to horses. I guess how could he not? So, he's outside occupied with Moses most of the morning, day, night, but—"

Mozell interrupted her. "Why don't you send him over here sometime? You know I got the two boys for now; they can run around and entertain themselves so I'm not really watching nothing and the two of y'all go do something for yourselves again."

Dwayne remembered all those Sundays watching from Ms. Mozell's window as Holly bopped down the road with his grandparents in the wagon, licking the peppermint residue from around her lips. He'd see them pull in front of the house and then unpack whatever they bought from town and take it inside. Dwayne always, always tried to rush back across the street to meet them, and Ms. Mozell, feeling his antsy feet shake her floorboards, would holler from wherever she was, saying *let them settle. I promise they ain't forgot about you.*

Often, he'd crane his neck as best he could to see far, far down the road in order to beat the sound of Holly's clunky hooves and the wooden wheel-squeal calling out as to the reason he wanted to go outside. Because if he was out, well, he'd run down and hitch a ride on the back of the wagon kicking his feet in joy during the small ride back. It was the ritual of it all over the years that didn't immediately signal anything was off is what Mozell always said so many times those first few days, weeks, months—almost a year until the investigation was complete. And then later, she repeated it only at the anniversary, as though those were her only remarks: "It was just a normal Sunday God chose to change the courses of our lives. A normal Sunday with no signs things was going to be changed forever."

It was the repetition of this idea—that there might be signs just before any life-changing event—that led Dwayne to always be on the search for them. He became wary whenever the sky turned red at night. A storm was brewing: Was this his ending? Absolutely anything could be a sign. The cardinal that swooped onto the porch every morning. (That was true, Mozell said one day: our loved ones often come back as red birds. It could be Moses; it could be Lillie.) The fox slinking across the yard each evening at dusk. He never made the connections to what anything was signaling, because it seemed his world—however changed it was—went on and on but that didn't stop his worrying.

The smoke wafting into Ms. Mozell's kitchen when she had not yet found a need to start her fires for the season was the first strange thing on an otherwise ordinary Sunday. She called out to the boys to come inside in case it was a brush fire, and anyways they didn't need all that smoke exposure. As with lightning storms, she instructed them to sit and be quiet. When she rushed out to investigate, she saw the first plume of smoke coming from across the street and not near either of the two chimneys. She rushed back and reminded the boys to *sit still, don't move,* and called about town looking for the Boltons.

They had just left the Masseys' not even a half hour ago.

They didn't stop by the Fords'.

Pastor told them he wasn't going to be home after church service, so they didn't stop in. If they did, he wasn't there earlier.

Finally, Mozell caught up to them at the Walkers', having a quick tea before their ice block melted in the wagon and groceries spoiled.

Mozell spoke quick short breaths to stress the urgency. Hung up the phone and paced the living room trying to figure what to do next. She called John Henry the Black firefighter and told him all hands. "We know what hay do once it gets a taste of them flames."

Dwayne heard the *clip-clop-clop* of Holly's hooves at a lope, a hard thing for a single mule hooked up to a wagon carrying two folks. He heard Moses smooching at Holly, asking more, faster. The crack of the whip that he had never used. Not once. Except now. The speed lifted the wagon wheels then slammed them down with such force with each step. From Ms. Mozell's house, Dwayne watched red and orange light up the windows like the brightest sunset—fire making its way through their house like someone walking through and turning on the lights one by one. When he heard O'boy neighing, he sprang off the couch. Ms. Mozell blocked the door.

And then, it seemed like in an instant, Dwayne settled into the goneness of his life: Both of his grandparents, perished in the flames. Along with his horses. His father, vanished. His mother, though they barely met earthside, taken, too. Somehow Holly was still standing hooked up to the wagon when the fire snuffed out to embers. When the fire trucks and coroner and well-meaning neighbors left, everyone had forgotten her in the rush to try and save the human lives. Dwayne had tried to say something but was shushed or ignored. Finally, when Ms. Mozell retired for the night, even though the sky still had amber light—just enough to see—he crept out to see about Holly. The ground was damp and hot from the flame licks. He heard her labored breathing and rushed back to gather water to offer. There had been stories before of horses, donkeys, mules so frightened by whatever commotion that they ran off—wagon and all—until their heart burst from no longer listening to their body. They heard only their fright, and didn't have sense enough left to slow down—not for food, not for water, not if they had been caught up by the wagon rigging. They just, as they say, would run until the wheels came plumb off. Then there were mules like Holly. Who waited to be relieved, off duty. Sitting in Ms. Mozell's window, Dwayne thought she was probably looking for Grandaddy Moses to come and offer his wither scratches and a handful of oats. That's how faithful every animal over which Moses had dominion was. They waited. Despite their natural proclivity to flee the unknown, they waited for their steward to show them the way out.

But Grandaddy Moses was gone, so now it was up to Dwayne.

Ms. Mozell heard Dwayne readying to leave the house again after he got the water and got up to stop him. Prepared for this move, he held up his arm and pointed, tears forming for the first time. "Holly is just standing there. Been a whole day with no water, no food. Nothing. She watched everything burn up just like me, but no one thought to move her. Grandaddy wouldn't want that." He wiped his face with the back of his hand and started to walk out, and this time Ms. Mozell cleared the way.

From across the street, it was impossible to take in the full breadth of all that had occurred. There was the smell of all the burned flesh:

horse carcasses littered the ground, and whatever flesh remained was picked clean by the usual scavengers. Even while marching over, Dwayne had to shoo away a gang of vultures. The fire must have taken the manes and tails; there was no way to distinguish any one horse from another. Stepping around the smoldering ruins, he jumped in surprise at a hot spot: How was Holly standing so still among this, and for so long?

Usually straight up and forward, Holly's ears draped along the side of her face. She lifted her head for Dwayne's attention and started to nicker for him.

"I know, girl. I know," Dwayne said. He saw evidence that the flames—maybe small fire offshoots—had attempted to catch near her and burned her hooves, but thankfully did not climb her legs or worse. There were blisters forming, and when he reached to touch, she stomped her legs.

"I know, girl. I'm sorry, Holly," Dwayne couldn't think of much more to say. So he got to work unhooking her from the wagon. In the back of the wagon there was a piece of rope he tied around her neck—something to hold on to as he unclipped, unlatched, untied what seemed like the hundred straps of leather rigging. Then finally, he reached towards her ears and she flinched again. He retreated, then moved slowly, humming so she might be soothed by the lowered frequencies and his own breath and heartbeat forced to slow down as well. He couldn't think of a song, so he just kept the octaves low and slow: Holly turned in to him then. Legs and feet still locked into place, and craned her neck about him. A hug.

"I know," Dwayne repeated. He scratched her neck in the embrace. He was crying again. They stood in the ruins for a while, mourning, before he picked up the rope about her neck and led her across the street—home.

At first the only thing that mattered to Dwayne was keeping Holly alive. Ms. Mozell's place wasn't set up for large four-legged livestock, who'd need strands of wire along a fence line and large amounts of grass to graze and roam. But it was the face he gave her, and their joint understanding of all he lost, that made Mozell acquiesce. Besides, she knew the boy would need somewhere to focus his grief, maybe later his anger, and a project and a pet could keep him busy, distracted. The first night they drilled an eyehook into a tree and looped a quick-release tie knot between the metal eye and the rope about Holly's neck. She was a good girl who Moses let graze around the farm most days, anyway. Worst she could do if she fancied getting loose would probably be to venture across the street, especially, say, to the hayfields. Otherwise, she could stand on soft ground not heated by a large fire and breathe a bit clearer air and not be within eyeshot of the skeleton graveyard of her former herd.

||||||||||||||||||||

In the days after the fire everyone whispered, "Where's that boy's daddy?" or "Lloyd should be here" or "If Lloyd don't take care of his boy, who's gonna do it?" But no one raised their hands or offered their homes.

One day at the farm stand, two women had started in on their *it's a shame*s, *can you believe it*s, and *what's gone happen when Mozell tire of him? It's not like she gone get a check like them other boys she take in.* Mozell, standing behind them, cleared her throat and stepped forward to hand her cash over for the bag of collards whose leaves were as broad as serving trays, a bag of rutabagas, and a jar of honey. The women's jaws dropped, of course, when she stepped between them, saying only: "Them Boltons blessed me and my family as long as we both existed in this county on our same land as bonded men and free. I'm happy to attempt to repay through loving that boy as my own and not ask any questions. I didn't see no one else offer their beds to the unfortunate . . . I just don't want to miss my opportunity to entertain an angel unawares. On that great getting-up day, I know my blessing is gone come due." She twirled around and marched back home.

Dwayne remembered Ms. Mozell and other neighbors had gone through the house ashes to see what might have survived the fire. His grandmother's cedar chest had evidence of flames licking it, but it was mostly intact—water damage being its contents' biggest issue. Among other ephemera he would learn about later, as if the Boltons knew their time was near, was a letter inside the chest addressed to Lloyd, containing instructions for burial: Wash the bodies and style any errant hairs. Ivory dress for Lillie. Moses had selected a navy-blue suit with Carolina-blue top and royal-blue tie—he wanted to look the color of the sky he was going towards. They had packed a suit for Dwayne, too, but having been prepared when he was eight and not thirteen, it was too small now.

Other instructions included: a small gathering in their living room for the wake and funeral. This posed the biggest challenge, and so Pastor offered a weekday afternoon in the sanctuary instead, where he presided over the few who could step away from their labors to pay their final respects. A few volunteers sat in the choir pews and marched the attendees through standard funerary hymns—coming to the river; one day they'll fly away. Pastor recited oft-quoted scriptures about living a good, long, Christianly life, and how servants of the Lord not unlike the Boltons would be spirited away to sit at the foot of our Heavenly Father as their reward for earthly suffering, and so on. Even though there was no house for the funeral or for the official repast, everyone knew by then Lloyd had not come home—or at least, into town—and no Boltons had sent for Dwayne. Weesie and Teeta, cousins in Columbia, came to comfort with their girl Rhina, same age as Dwayne. Wringing their hands. If circumstances were different. Feeling like burdens themselves, they had been crowded up into Weesie's brother's house with four of his kids. Ms. Mozell, having in her possession at her home what seemed like the lone survivor of the family, was the default choice of residence to receive the casseroles, cakes, punches, fried chicken, and salads for the repast and a few sympathetic setting-up days after.

The Boltons' final request was to be buried on the land. There were instructions about a small clearing in the woods. If you were standing on the back porch, facing west, there was a grove of oaks in a semicircle whose opening faced east overlooking a nearby horse pasture. There was a cypress marking the southern point of the entrance, and another cypress marking the northern point of the entrance. In the years of its established designation, there had never been proper headstones. What the descendants of the gone had done for generations was place a flat rock at the feet to anchor their physical bodies to the earth and allow the spirits ease in their travel heavenward, so they believed.

No matter the season, it was easy to know where their loved ones rested because of the evergreen cypresses like a gateway entrance during winter when all other leaves had fallen, or in the spring the cove would be covered with periwinkle, offering a bright splash of purple in the sea of green. Blessings. Moses had been the last and only caretaker of this unmarked cemetery and had witnessed or overseen the placement of so many in his eighty-eight years. There was a small diagram of what he knew, but no names, and then there was one rectangle that was written in his perfect Spencerian script *Lillie + Moses,* indicating their choice of burial plot. The undertaker lent them his tractor (the wires of Moses's tractor were melted) and backhoe to dig eight feet into the ground, where they lowered Moses first, and then Lillie, and covered with the remaining dirt.

No one could have predicted it would be the burial that would undo Dwayne. Everyone remarked how well he was holding up, considering. Like Ms. Mozell predicted, he had turned so much of his energy to Holly—fashioned her an enclosure as best he could out of scraps and things from his grandfather's farm that hadn't perished—and that kept him busy in the days between the fire and the funeral, which were more drawn out than anyone would have liked because the coroner at first refused to release the bodies to anyone but next of kin. Enough folks called the coroner to reason—everyone in Fairfield County was likely kin if you thought about it hard enough, and would he want his parents' bodies sitting in a morgue in limbo for that long?

Dwayne had held through those days of folks stopping by and setting up with Mozell, who entertained those who came to mourn in community. He sat through going into town with the designated funerary dress and asking if the cleaners could make the outfits look like new? Ms. Mozell had culled from the ashes a pair of slacks and a shirt and asked a seamstress to fashion something for Dwayne before she carried it to the cleaners. He held through being fitted in his grandfather's clothes cloaked in soot. He was dry-eyed through the funeral and the Lord's Prayer at the Bolton burial ground. And then, when the undertaker's crew threw the last shovel of dirt onto the coffins, he collapsed in a fit of grief so big it made the hair on folks' arms stand up. *It was loud enough to raise those poor souls from the dead.* Ms. Mozell lifted his driftwood body into her arms and squeezed.

"I know, honey, let it out," she said. He cried louder, and she squeezed harder. Folks stood around them—tall oaks in a semicircle. Some whispered prayers of comfort, others just stood by in witness of a boy born new that day.

PART II

1976–2014

Chapter 8

When Holly died of old age, grief, and probably loneliness, everyone thought Dwayne would put it all behind him: any reminder of his past life. And he did. He never populated Ms. Mozell's place with horses; he didn't see the point—*Where am I going to find a horse worthy enough to replace O'boy?*

It took a while, between high school responsibilities and his life, but eventually he took down the paddock he built for Holly. You'd have to squint to see the desire lines she paced from her hay to water trough to gate—almost the exact rectangle perimeter of the whole thing. Ms. Mozell said he could bring a horse if that would help him but he shook his head. He was moving on. He had his studies, and he followed Gwendolyn from place to place. He had shut the door on thinking he might too have a farm one day, raise and ride horses.

"Is the door locked?" Gwendolyn asked one day when he had said something to her about shutting it all out.

"I don't know, but it's a door I don't know if I can open. Or what occasion I might open it for," Dwayne said.

And then, over time, their love grew deeper. She asked again if the door was locked—if he could build a life on the land, with horses and all. He said for her, he might find his way back to it. For her.

As high school sweethearts, Dwayne and Gwendolyn would dream together building their forever home on their parcel of the Bolton Plantation. Young and in love, Dwayne had imagined a world where he would be beyond his grief. Maybe he'd have some pigs, a peck of goats to assist with land maintenance, of course chickens. Donkeys. Even a horse or two or three—yes, even the horses. He had dreamed, in the dreamscape before war—before Iraq, before Kuwait—that maybe there would be a day he could usher children onto the land his grandaddy had set out for him, even when it became clear his father couldn't or didn't want to or wasn't able. Dwayne had mapped out a way forward, to march across the street from Ms. Mozell's to his family's homeplace and set the foundation, to erect the walls, to set the pitch of the roof, the A-frame pig-farrowing stalls, the coop. He would clear the Virginia creeper vines that took over their firewood shed, would set irrigation lines back out to the cattle fields that were just beyond the corn and soy. Would spray for weeds and fertilize the hayfield. Would refill and restock the pond with only the fish worth scaling and frying on Friday nights: Perch. Crappie. Bass. Catfish. He'd erect three walls to bring his budding small-engine-repair business home and run electricity to the workshop. He'd set every wood post along the perimeter for a fence, but low enough so the several families of deer he watched leap through the fields all these years would still come, like a blessing at the beginning and end of each day no matter the season. Just because Gwendolyn had asked him to dream it. Isn't that love?

Dwayne would clear the pastures again. The riding arenas. The ground his grandfather worked down to the Carolina-gold sand from running the horses in circles, the same circles he ran O'boy and all the rest of the herd for exercise training. And how could he know it then, in the days long before all the hurt that would come, when he and Gwendolyn strolled in wanderlust over the parcel, making promises, dreaming up what future children might come to make of themselves . . . how could he have known that he would work so hard for grief and love to coexist within him so that he could bring along his grandaddy's horseman's trade, could steward the same land, could offer a future?

When he first met Gwendolyn, she always seemed the girl too far out of his reach, so he never pursued her. She'd used to say that he walked around with such a profound sadness about him it made her want to know him even more. So, she pursued him. First as friends, then she let him take her out to the dairy bar, then the drive-in, then she started announcing herself as his girlfriend in the hallway between classes. She ran track. He joined track just so they would spend more time together after school, on weekends. He'd suffer through the shot put and discus drills for the thrill of wrapping his arm around her in the darkened back seats of the activity bus on their way home to Fairfield County after a track meet. Before then, nothing gave him more pride than to watch with the rest of the folks gathered at the track for the final thrilling event of the night: Gwendolyn taking the baton around the last bend of the 4 x 100 meter race and crossing the finish line first.

Coach said her legs could write her a ticket to any college she wanted to go to, and she would smile and grab Dwayne's hand (he was never too far away) and say she only dreamed of staying in Fairfield County and running a farm with him, maybe raising a few kids; she loved gardening and dreamed of a learning farm where the next generation of kids would understand the importance of land stewardship, and didn't Coach notice how the impulse to send us up and away for college was what drained the county of its local talents? Who comes back to small-town country living when they've had a taste of life beyond dirt roads?

How was Dwayne to know that last line was prophecy? He had spent so much energy in those early years after they graduated trying to make a life. That's what happens to dreams—you get so caught up trying to chase them you don't realize you're so far off the path there was almost no way back. He had tried to work up the nerve to figure out where his father was in the world, from what post he had been sending his letters. Often all Dwayne had was a city and state and the APO stamp, denoting he was still on an army base at least. The letters—if you could call them that—had come from Fort Jackson (Columbia, South Carolina), Fort Bliss (El Paso, Texas), Fort Carson (Colorado Springs, Colorado), Camp Dodge (Johnston, Iowa), and Fort Knox (near Louisville, Kentucky), from what he remembered. Every two years a different state. Every year a stale letter with no real return address. Dwayne wanted to ask Lloyd how to take over the land as he approached adulthood, and he also wanted to tell his father that he had a girl who he wanted to wrap his arms around forever.

He recalled the day Grandaddy Moses had said—holding his arms out wide, pointing from one imagined corner of the property to the other—that one day all the land before Dwayne would belong to him, when he was ready. He wanted to tell Lloyd that he was ready to take on the land, and could he have it?

In the meantime silences, Dwayne stayed on with Ms. Mozell. Every time the proverbial clock ticked towards his having become an adult, and she'd catch him staring longingly across the street from her porch steps just like she had seen that day of the fire, and she'd remind him that this was his home, too.

"Ain't no need to rush out into that crazy world like you on a deadline. Family don't have timelines, you know."

But Dwayne would need. He got a job after school and weekends working with Mr. Vance to finish his apprenticeship mastering metal and small engines. First, Mr. Vance watched his work so closely, Dwayne could feel the small hairs on the back of his neck sway each time Mr. Vance breathed. Then, he'd loosen his grip and let Dwayne make farm calls for the bigger machines or cover the shop on days he needed to go into the city. Of course, Dwayne liked those days most because he could practice what it meant to have his own business, and on principle, Mr. Vance let him keep the lion's share of the day's earnings, because Dwayne had done the lion's share of the day's work.

And almost like clockwork as soon as Dwayne started to earn a bit of money on his own, the universe would find use for it. That first year after high school, a hurricane crawled up the East Coast after having made landfall in Florida. To be so far instate like they were in Fairfield County, where folks from the coast evacuated *to*, schools would shut down and become temporary shelters. Farmers would clear out spaces in barns or open up pastures for livestock needing a place to weather the storm. Sure, they might have a little wind damage here and there, a little more water pooled about the streets and farms than usual, but never anything like the sheer battering the coast got year after year, sometimes multiple times a season. Hurricane Billy crawled a snail's pace from Florida to North Carolina, stalled out—turning and turning like on a wash cycle—just around the Congaree, as predicted.

What wasn't predicted was the size of the storm, its arms stretched for miles around the eye, and its direct hit to Richland and Fairfield Counties. Weathermen said it was like no other storm in recorded history. Everyone hunkered down. Folks in town said it was like the time Joe Frazier took Muhammad Ali for fifteen rounds. Mincemeat. When they got up the next morning, birds were singing as if the winds weren't a pack of yipping coyotes the night before. Dwayne got up to survey the damage. He looked across the street: His pear tree, standing. His oak tree that was just outside the back door where Grandaddy Mo hung a swing—nobody knows how it didn't get swallowed in flames with the house that day—was still standing, too, though he saw a few limbs on the ground twisted up like haystacks. Then he turned to Ms. Mozell's property. A pine tree had given up the ghost and was on its side as if waiting to be put to bed. The Bradford pear out by the chicken coop, which had provided shade and roost, had snapped about two feet off the ground and upon further inspection, it seemed like lightning must have hit it. Either way it would probably be some days before eggs showed up after the girls got such a fright. A gutter slouched towards the ground near the bathroom window, and he counted fifteen shingles loosed themselves from the roof—which he had suspected because in the living room, there had formed bubbles on the ceiling overnight. So much work to be done now. That would set his savings back for some time.

That fall, Dwayne understood what Ms. Mozell always muttered nearest to the beginning of the month when she counted out her army-widow pension. The cost of repair and replacing all of the food in the icebox because electricity didn't come back on for five days (that is, the electric company serviced city, suburbs, country folks in that order, so they were last in line). She had said, "When it rains, it pours," and Dwayne felt the weight of it himself, and more, when he went to check up on Gwendolyn and her people, after the roof situation was taken care of as best they could before the professionals came, and they had cleaned out the fridge.

Not knowing the conditions of the road for driving or biking, he chose to walk to Gwendolyn's. It would take him about an hour, but he was fine with it—he could survey the rest of the area along the way and stretch his legs. When he got to the end of her drive, he saw Gwendolyn's father pushing fallen leaves onto the grass. On all accounts, except for the few pieces of debris on the ground, it seemed as though they made it through unscathed. Dwayne had said as much in a greeting to Mr. Howard, who nodded, then beat Dwayne to the punch: "Gwendolyn's not going to be able to see you, son. Thank you for stopping in." Then, he turned to go inside, as if he was only outside waiting for Dwayne to pass by.

When Dwayne returned home, he tried calling but the line was busy. When he tried a third time, Mrs. Howard picked up, sounded exasperated when she heard Dwayne's voice, and all but repeated like a parrot what Mr. Howard had said, but she said his name, and then before she hung up Dwayne heard Gwendolyn's voice, like a whimper, call out to him, begging to speak to him.

Ms. Mozell, eavesdropping, asked if there was anything she could do, and Dwayne was helpless to think of a solution to a problem he did not know how to diagnose. No symptoms. No indicator lights like on his tractors pointing to the area in need of attention. Just the other day, they were together, making up, dreaming up a life, drawing farm plans, saving literal pennies that passed through their young fingers, and then the storm, and now where were they? Dwayne shrugged to Ms. Mozell and reported that Gwendolyn's parents were icing him out.

"Probably stressed from this storm. I know I am," Ms. Mozell had said.

He reported there wasn't any real visible damage from where he stood. That Mr. Howard was just pushing leaves across the lawn with a broom.

"Maybe the storm happened for them on the inside, then," Ms. Mozell reflected out loud.

Without the everydayness of school, Dwayne had to think about how he was going to get to Gwendolyn to figure out what else had blown in with the winds.

He had concocted a plan to rap at her window like some young lovestruck boy, and in a way, he was exactly that. She had gotten him to return to himself. Imagine a living beyond his deep grief. With her, they had planned whole lives together—it would take some time as most plans do, and even now with the setback of helping Ms. Mozell with the roof and coop and he even skipped a day's labor with Mr. Vance to dig a new ditch to send the pooling water down and away from the house's foundation; even with that, he wanted to be on track to figure out how to take ownership of the Bolton land and erect a small one-room house. The water—a later addition when Grandaddy Mo was alive—was still accessible in the pump house. He knew there was a septic tank that was added about the same time. The neighbors and cousins had chipped in to bring Grandaddy Mo and Grandma Lillie into the twentieth century. Said 'cause they were raising a modern boy, they needed to have modern-boy amenities, but Dwayne didn't know that people didn't go outside to relieve themselves or that there was an alternative to that or that it was a misery until he had a choice. But if he had to go back to having an outhouse and outdoor showers heated by leaving a hose stretched across a lawn in the sun in order to build the life he wanted with Gwendolyn, he could. If he had to swallow the pain of what might have become of his life before the fire, he would. Just to have *anything* that was his.

Dwayne found his way to her window late one night and laughed to himself. He was Romeo. He hadn't prepared what he was going to say—what was there? He threw a small twig, and then another, and then another, and finally it worked and she had come to see about the noise and he lit his flashlight beneath his chin, not supposing the shadows cast would distort him so indistinguishably that Gwendolyn squinted, turned away from the window, and just then he had two twigs that he threw in quick succession hoping she would turn back. Instead, silence. Until the back door opened.

"Dwayne, you're going to get me in more trouble, coming back so soon," Gwendolyn said, before he could even say hello. Who was this? Before the storm, they sat under the oak tree swing and pointed to where each piece of their homestead would go. Before the storm, they decided on horses, yes, and decided to follow the faint traces of the old pasture fence lines. She had said she only wanted horses if she could have a palomino and name it Butter.

"Everyone names their palomino horses Butter," Dwayne chuckled in response. He thought about Grandaddy's prized racehorse, who he never met, but for so long Dwayne thought it was the color of a palomino with a name like Pal O Mine, until he saw the newspaper clippings from the race. He was as red as O'boy. Similar builds and faces. Gwendolyn had punched him in the arm under the oak swing when he joked back, then turned to look him in the eyes.

"You would do that for me? Horses?"

Dwayne had looked out on the empty parcel and grafted the barn onto his view. The training ring made of young pine harvested from the land. The colts, bucking, would bounce off of them due to the slight bend. Once, one horse had knocked a panel loose in an otherwise solid siding and that had become the hook Dwayne used as a child to slip his boot or sometimes bare feet to mount any horse Grandaddy Mo had. And then, as quickly as the visions came back to him, they were swallowed by the fire. Yes. He would walk back through the fire for her.

"If that's what makes you happy. I want to do it" is what Dwayne's young heart said in those before-storm days. She looked at him then, as if to say something. She started, then just laid her head on his shoulder.

Outside her house, after the storm, Dwayne recalled those words and he still meant them. He didn't know what to do with the cold front that had rolled in with those strong winds and wedged its way between them.

"So you know I tried to come and call to make sure y'all were alright after the storm? Did your parents tell you?" His voice raised and Gwendolyn lifted her finger to her lips in an attempt to get him to speak quieter. "What's going on?"

Gwendolyn inhaled and her shoulders lifted up to her earlobes. She exhaled longer, again. Dwayne shifted his feet, simultaneously inching forward.

"I'm—"

She cleared the frog in her throat. She brought her hand to her face and Dwayne assumed she was wiping tears from her eyes. His own breath quickening in anticipation.

"I *was*—"

She exhaled like she was hyping herself up for the final run at the state track meet.

"The stress of the storm. I thought it was my monthly, you know how I had—have—heavy flows? Well, you don't know, but I tell you all the time. I usually only bleed heavy with bad cramps on the first day. When I saw you last it had started when I got home, but the cramps got worse. The most pain I had felt in my life. When Mama saw me reach for the second Kotex too soon, she asked me if everything was OK, and the winds were howling and my heartbeat was rising—you know I hate storms, and I was in the bathroom trying to catch the blood with the second pad and a sharp pain went from my toes to my neck. Full-bodied, 'Wayne. I thought I had been electrocuted. I froze from the pain. Mama burst through the door because she said the sounds coming from my mouth were so wild. When I saw her, I burst into tears from relief, that I had help. She said I passed out."

He stepped closer. She moved back, lifted her hand—*don't.*

"You OK now?"

From where he stood, he could see Gwendolyn's silhouette look up to the sky.

"Winnie—" Dwayne whimpered.

"It's gone," she said.

Finally, Dwayne understood it all. He rushed to her then. Damn her protests. He squeezed her and she buried her face in his chest.

Eventually, Gwendolyn hiked the mountain of her own grief. That summer after graduation, she didn't come back to him. Instead, she enrolled at the cosmetology school in Columbia and found an apartment to share with two other girls, also aspiring beauticians. She went on to get her beauty license and rented a stall at Miss Dot's salon on North Main Street. Miss Dot liked having her around because Gwendolyn brought youth and youthful clients—

the next generation of salon-goers to ensure she'd be alright until retirement-ready. With youth came a new energy. Girls giggling in the wash-and-dry room. The real youngins whining and crying about burning edges, too-hot dryers, tender scalps. But it was a welcomed annoyance. Dwayne appreciated knowing there was a place he could drop in to see her—like their school days—that wasn't mediated by her parents who, ever since the miscarriage, held some distance from him that he had never experienced. In all their knowing each other, it was like the presence of the storm and blood brought with it the realization that their daughter was planning a life with Dwayne. While they weren't intentionally trying to conceive so soon the two of them had names and nicknames picked out for both sexes—just in case—which was mostly led by Gwendolyn's desire. Dwayne was agnostic about the children piece of the deal and often asked her, *Won't the two of us enough? Don't two people make a family?*

He realized his earliest visions of family were his grandparents: content in their own two ways. But of course, they had children. That's how he got here. Only, their relationship, as he experienced it, was as man and woman, husband and helpmeet, *perfectly yoked* (as Grandma Lillie would say), and when he thought about it, that was really the life he was after. A simple one, with some acreage, some livestock, his woman, and the Carolina sky.

Mostly, he mourned the loss because Gwendolyn did. When she uttered the words, he understood he was loosed of the burden of dreaming up a life in the ashes of the farm after the fire took it away. Even still, he mourned this loss and what it all had meant. He had whispered, "We can still have horses," thinking it a suitable consolation, not knowing what else to offer in that moment to the two of them, having lost a thing they barely had. It was more like a gesture. An idea. A seed attempting to germinate into a sapling of an offspring, and then announcing itself only as it was leaving. Didn't know at all what they had before it was gone. He dared not say he was relieved, that he had been saved from something maybe. But getting Gwendolyn back meant new conversations, concessions, intentionality.

He eased his way back into her life by calling the shop and asking her if she had eaten lunch? And could he bring it to her? The young girls made googly lovey noises whenever he walked in—the only man not a husband or father to a client to pick up or pay for services rendered, but a semi-attached handsome man that darkened the doorway, and yes, he was tall, but did not have to lower his head to cross thresholds. He did it anyways, as he walked across the tile floor to hand Gwendolyn her two-piece meal—dark meat only—with a roll and extra crispy fries from Millie's. Some older woman would ask about *her* lunch and did he bring it this time, and he'd smile and say *no ma'am, I got you next* in his collegial banter, then turn to Gwendolyn with a more serious face that pleaded *please,* pleaded *take me back,* pleaded *I'm sorry* though he never really understood what he was sorry for—loving her?

With no future family prospects, he had put the farm dreams aside. That's how he lost track of it—life was happening. Real life. Life he could hold on to, work at, build. Ms. Mozell was getting older, despite her mouth still running a mile a minute on the phone, in town, on the porch whenever she managed to make it there to sit. All those years taking in children filled her life with such purpose—"I never got around to having any of my own," she said one day after Sunday dinner, and the two of them sat out an early-evening storm rocking on the curved feet of the rocking chairs.

"Every time I turned around the house was full of children who needed me for some reason or another, and I just knew it to be why God saw fit for me to be on this earth—if at least one boy or girl don't go hungry or freeze out in the elements on account of me, I guess I get my angel wings." When her hands were better, she'd have had a basket filled with a bushel of snap peas between her knees. Lately, she shuffled her waterlogged ankles to the rocker and held on to the armrests as she pushed back and forth—to get her blood flowing again.

"Now I know He was set to give me a real son anyways," she'd say with a wink.

In the silences between them, Dwayne was certainly glad Ms. Mozell took him for the afternoon on the day his grandparents went into town—like any other day—and then didn't say anything else in those days after the joint funeral. She just went to the linen wardrobe and pulled out an old quilt, a sheet to protect the couch, a pillow—the same each and every night until he got a room of his own in the house. She also set the table with one extra place. Every night. When the first letter from Lloyd came in the mail, the postman hand-delivered it directly to her so as not to be intercepted by Dwayne or one of the other boys boarded up with her. Ms. Mozell read the letter—it was so short she sort of glanced at it—flashed the wad of cash and told Dwayne she was going to put it up for him, and stuffed it in the front of her apron, and then handed him the card. A Christmas card with a drawing of a donkey standing next to a manger with a North Star.

> Sorry I can't be there with you at this time. I really want to. But I can't. Maybe one day you'll understand. I'm sure it will still be a Merry Christmas, because even though I can't be there, I love you. All ways.

Dwayne kept the first card, though he wasn't sure why. It felt special. Temporary. Then the other letters came, and it felt routine. Whenever he returned to the card, in the lost afternoons thinking about his grandfather, mostly, it led him on a wild-goose chase to be caught up in all of his ephemera that he had—what they had managed to salvage from the ashes, and the sympathy cards and notices, and then the cards from his father. As he got older, and continued to read and reread that short note, there was never any address to him, no "Son" and no sign-off that might suggest his relationship: "Daddy," "Dad," "Your father." None of that. It could have been a letter from anyone to anyone.

Chapter 9

Save for his years in service when he fixed the sheet corners into crisp envelopes of whatever bed in whatever state or country he found himself in, Dwayne woke up every morning in the two-room farmhouse on Ms. Mozell's property.

That the actual house was so close to the road was more of the county's doing—*they* had decided that a state road needed to branch off Highway 21, and it was so. They plotted a straight line down the road between the two houses, and favored and then crossed over Mozell's property line, bringing the road mere feet from her front porch while the Boltons had significant easement.

That the new branch off Highway 21 never did become another main highway like predicted didn't make it a big deal; mostly, for the Boltons, having a state-managed and paved road helped their bums riding with the mule and wagon, and when they got cars, it kept the dirt and dust low. When the roads washed out with winter storms after expanding and contracting and freezing for months, the county fixed it—so maybe there were some benefits. It was alright so long as traffic remained low.

Mozell herself inherited the house from her parents, who got it from her grandparents, who were the first hands to turn it from a meager sharecropper shack, complete with newspapered insulation and outhouse and singular hearth, to pine-board interiors, a wood cooking stove, a heated stove in what became the bedroom, and eventually adding a fireplace and interior walls.

In the 1920s the property and house formally entered into the record as having been owned by Blacks, even though the land had been deeded basically immediately when word came that the slaves were free, because the white Boltons had understood that many of their former property considered this piece of land their homeplace, so might still work it if given some type of ownership. So they implemented a lease to own, payable by crops or cash, and allowed building up, personal farming—so long as it didn't interfere with the big crops and other enterprises for which the white Boltons needed the physical labor. Mozell's people, the Camerons, sold okra and watermelon and peanuts—boiled and roasted. That's how they made their money to buy the land faster than whatever calculations their former-master-now-customer set the deal for. They had some autonomy, yes, but only so much. When the deed transferred, and the property—a hundred acres, a mere fraction of the whole—was owned outright, it was collards that paid their way generation after generation.

When God didn't see fit for Mozell to have children of her own—mostly due to being the last-born girl, and so inheriting the duty of caring for her parents in their later years—at first, she joked: What use did she have birthing children when she had two at home?

Her parents were the generation to bring the water well from hand pump to electrical, and so the house had only one outlet per room, and it took all of Mozell's energy in the sunset period of her parents' lives to convince them that the electrical currents were in fact safer than kerosene lamps, and so never ventured too far from the homestead or else risk an errant fire.

Her mother went first. It was a surprise, because in the Cameron family, women often outlived the men. Mozell could see the years gathering in the folds of her mother's face. The grief of waking up each day to relearn who she was, who she had become. Relearning the strange woman in the house caring for her was her daughter. And for Mozell, hell was the daily litany of calling out the names of her mother's children, and then naming who was among the living and who passed on.

Eventually no one counted out the deaths as they came. Or the deaths already come. In those days, to her mother, everyone was alive, always. The damage to her psyche—losing children she had forgotten then had to remember she had—had been done. The dementia progressed. She stopped eating. She no longer cared to sit on the porch and look out at the horses grazing across the street, the sun warming her feet. It was all Mozell could do to get her to slurp okra stew, and then any meat or vegetable or bone broth—she had tried them all—and finally, nothing. Soon after, she was dead.

And then, as if in a cosmic shift, her father Carl came back to his senses the day of her mother's funeral. Young Lloyd, who had taken to helping after school and on weekends, had pushed Carl's wheelchair casket-side at the last viewing.

Everyone saw it—the click. Carl pushed himself out of the wheelchair, turned to the fellow mourners gathered at Palmer's Funeral Home, and said, “My lovely bride,” and then he turned to the body, and whispered, “My lovely, lovely bride,” and bent down to kiss her hand and then her lips.

A guttural growl rose up from the ground, then a holler, “My bride,” and he collapsed on her brick-stiff body in the coffin. When Lloyd reached to grab him and set him as best he could to his feet, it was as if in that moment Carl’s knees recalled they had not held the full weight of his body in years and he crumpled onto the floor—and everyone thought grief had taken him then, too.

But he lived. Mozell had a week of her daddy back and called him that in those early grieving days: she cooed it almost: *Daddy,* are you ready for supper? *Daddy,* tell me a story about how you got that land from those folks. *Daddy,* what was Mama like when you first met? All of those stories that felt like a chore listening to before, when it never seemed she would face a day without them, she relished them now. And almost as quickly as he came back, he left.

Expecting banter at breakfast, she almost sang his name: *Daddy,* want to sit on the porch today? Mr. Moses got the horses grazing in the front pasture. Your blue boy out there looking for you. But his response was a vapid stare across the dining room at the fire in the fireplace, the rest of him frozen in place. Her song turned to desperation. *Daddy?*

And just like that she was an orphan. Just like that. Mozell looked up at the empty land, empty house. She dared not say it: empty life; except she took the opportunity to reframe it: a first opportunity to shape it all for herself.

In her caregiving years the foliage on the land crept closer to the house than she would have liked, but what was she to do? The woodshed was taken over by wasps. Muscadine vines ran up the trees, across the clothesline like a trellis. The rust-colored barn leaned with the weight of decay, of rot, of Virginia creeper pulling at its sides, bending the beams towards the earth.

When she got portions of her life back, she devised a plan: she knew men who knew how to work the earth in Fairfield County and so rented out whatever pieces of her parcel they sought to clear for their purposes, and that's one of the ways she was never lonely. The other way was being a safe home for some of the county's lost boys that came to know about her because one day the nephew of one of her landlessees asked if she needed any yard clearing. She relented and the boy came out every day of the growing season with his uncle, and she found small jobs for him for small sums of money. Sometimes lunch. Sometimes breakfast and lunch. It took the frequency of these visits and the proximity for Mozell to learn that he was trying to stay out of his parents' house because it was no longer safe for him. His uncle barely had room or means himself. The boy was behind in school, mostly because he never had a quiet place to work on his studies. A sad situation, his uncle reported to Mozell when she finally inquired.

"I don't see why he can't bunk here," she offered one day at the end of their shift. He was a help, after all. And polite to her. Always offering "ma'am," despite her insistence on being called "sis." He compromised with "Ms. Mozell" the day he moved in, and that started the string of boys who found haven in her house, generations of them being built back up before going out into the world.

It wasn't until Dwayne, though, that Mozell felt she had a boy that felt something like a child of her own. Shopping for him, she'd try motherhood on for size at the register: *For my boy, Dwayne.* Or with him: "Ain't he just the most handsome? My Dwayne." It didn't matter that Dwayne always kept the community moniker for her—Ms. Mozell—mostly to keep in line with the boys passing through. And maybe it was the fact that Dwayne was not passing through. When it was abundantly clear that Lloyd wasn't coming back, she was the stopgap from him becoming a ward of the state, in the hands of some social worker who could place him literally anywhere in South Carolina. Mozell knew that that boy's life going up in flames in front of his eyes ain't no fault of his, and she had the room and the will—and the love—for him to stay right here in Fairfield County. As close to any home he would ever know.

When Lloyd said he wasn't coming, couldn't come, she sat Dwayne down and proclaimed: *This is your home as long as you want it. What's mine, your'n.*

Year over year, her refrain. *It's mine, so it's your'n. Can you deal with the landlessee? It's practically your'n. If you want that barn house to be around another hundred years when it's your'n, Dwayne, you gotta take care of it almost like you help with our house.*

One morning, sipping coffee on the porch, she told Dwayne the story of his parents, how Lloyd helped around the farm, helped her find the lessees, which kept change in her pocket, kept enough money in the bank for tax bills and so on and so forth.

"And it's just what you do when family is in trouble, I guess," she said, first referring to Lloyd's help, but also how she helped Lloyd. "If you mean it—that folks is like family—you do it with no expectations. No timeline."

She hadn't imagined her help would be forever, but she won't counting, either.

Dwayne had believed Ms. Mozell all those years when she said what was hers was his. It was impossible not to. He had taken on the care of the property and house as one who would be proud to inherit. And she *was* family. He felt it every day he woke up in her house since that first morning after the fire.

When he enlisted in the army, set on being the man she believed him already to be, he had named Ms. Mozell as his emergency contact, labeling her relationship to him as "Aunt," though he thought for a long while to just write "Mother."

Chapter 10

Two years later, when he was convalescing in the medic in Kuwait after a covert operation, nurses asked who they could call on his behalf. Without hesitation Dwayne called out Ms. Mozell's number, and though he wasn't injured in the way Sonny, his friend and comrade, was—or the other men had been—the on-call nurse said he had done enough for his country, he should let her do something for him, and held the phone to his ear.

Ms. Mozell picked up the phone and he immediately said *don't cry, don't cry. I'm OK.* Tears rolled down his cheeks and the nurse wiped them while Ms. Mozell prayed for him, for Sonny, for that poor boy Brian, who they lost. She prayed that God send Dwayne home to her.

When she got off the phone with Dwayne, Ms. Mozell called Gwendolyn. They were back on again in their relationship, and the poor girl had been walking around Fairfield County like a zombie—it had been weeks since Dwayne went dark communication-wise—won't no telling if he was among the living or the dead.

Within the hour, Gwendolyn was at Ms. Mozell's door with a bucket of fried chicken and appropriate fixings.

"Baby, he ain't dead," Mozell chuckled and finished opening the door, and as soon as she set the chicken down, Gwendolyn burst into tears and buried her sobs in Mozell's neck. "He's going to be fine. Dehydrated from the desert. A little dust up. But fine. He'd be home sooner but he say he want to wait for Sonny to be cleared for the long haul home."

Mozell rubbed Gwendolyn's back, like she had for all those flip-flop years that she was with Dwayne. Over the little fights. The big fights. She had counseled Gwendolyn in those off years, even. "Baby, I know I'm not a relationship expert, but I know love, and love ain't perfect, but it will keep showing you where it's coming from, where you should direct it."

On the phone with Mrs. Howard once, they both remarked how Gwendolyn having moved to Columbia would do it—finally sever the tie. And yet.

"They got a magnetic force field neither can escape," Mozell had said. "They meant to make something out of this life. That's for sure." And when, just before he shipped off to Kuwait, Dwayne had come to Ms. Mozell's to announce his intent to do it right this time, to marry Gwendolyn, to figure out how to get that land finally and start again when he got back, Mozell reached across the dining table and placed her hands over his and proclaimed: "Y'all keep trying to make something of the ruins that hurt you so. Maybe it's not yours yet. That's why God letting it slip through your fingers. Why don't you just bring her here? This is your home. Build a place anywhere you want. Or build me something and take this—you know I wanted all my life to have my porch set back further from the road.

Put me in the woods outta sight—just let me see my grands y'all making. I'll be good."

Dwayne chuckled. He was ready to try again. He had wanted Mozell to have grands.

"This must be the best deal. Forever, I wondered if I missed out on being a grandma because I didn't have no kids. Blood kids. You know what I mean. But I'll wait for yours. Ready for yours. You raise them here."

That promise and new dream kept Dwayne floating through basic. Through the grueling marches in full gear ten miles before daylight. When he saw Gwendolyn before he left, he revised his earlier promise, unrealized. *Here. Home. Let's make one. Fill it with children.* He hadn't figured how much he yearned for that part of his life to be complete until it seemed it would forever be an open wound. But this time, Gwendolyn had hesitated. It was her flesh wound. She had bled that windy night. She mourned every day. She was not sure if she could go through that pain, that loss again, but they could talk when he got back stateside. She'll consider.

"I love him, Ma," Gwendolyn had said to Mozell, reaching for a piece of chicken. Gwendolyn had taken to calling Mozell that no matter her status with Dwayne. The old woman allowed it and had doled out mother-energy without the baggage, though once Mozell did speak sternly the last time they were on the outs: "My boy deserve a steady love, all he been through. You need to decide if you gone be the one to give it." And here she was at the dining table worrying over Dwayne and when he'd come back to her.

He did come back. Not quite whole though. Even though Mozell had insisted that the nurse, over the phone, count out all his fingers and toes, eyes, ears, nostrils, hairs on his chin. He was all there, the nurse promised. Mozell asked her to count again, to be sure. She reported to Gwendolyn. But when Dwayne got back and seemed to walk through his days with a cloud over him, it was clear whatever plans he might have had with his longtime love would have to be returned to whatever stores inside them they place the lovey-dovey feelings they unshelved every few seasons.

Caring for his surviving comrade Sonny was now his occupation; Dwayne had room in his heart for nothing else. Sonny had woke up from surgery, and when they asked who they could call for him, his eyes had filled with tears when he said they were all gone. Everyone who loved him had died, and that's why he had enlisted anyways. He was alone. Before Dwayne. Even though he grew up in Fairfield County, and probably if they dug deep enough they might be family, Sonny was a listless boy without home roots, so he went in search of a place that would give him some. He told the nurse through his tears he only had his army brothers, and even they had lost one. Brian. The doctors said he was a most-lucky man. That there was, in fact, an exit wound, which is to say the bullet that hit him passed clean through his shoulder before releasing its shrapnel. If it had been different, he might have lost his arm altogether. If it had been a few inches lower, he certainly would have died. The worst of his ordeal would be physical therapy. For Sonny, the "worst of it" was his army career ending the day he lost brother Brian. No seeing the globe. No real pension. He had what he made and saved and that was it. No good use of his shoulder for the foreseeable future, if ever. How some exercises gone bring that arm back, like new? No one worrying if he had ten fingers or ten toes. Where was he to go after this?

So Dwayne brought him back to Fairfield County, and to

Mozell—so used to taking in lost boys. She unrolled her spare linens onto the couch where he laid for months while he continued to recover.

This meant that Dwayne and Gwendolyn's plans were put on hold again. And again. The space widening between them.

After he got his shoulder back enough, Sonny scouted and bought property in Fairfield County just down the road some from Dwayne and Mozell's place with what he had saved.

"Since leaving Fairfield County, I've lived so many places—going from base to base to base, I never knew what was home. I don't feel I can go back there now—that was so many lives ago, and I never felt a connection to anywhere else. Here though feels special. I love the landscape especially."

Sonny went on to describe what Dwayne had come to know: on one parcel you can get it all: Pillowy moss and prickly cactus. Towering pines and strong oaks. Lush grass making way to bright white sand. Perfect climate for year-round planting and the right livestock.

"Wasn't shit like this, for us, what we fight for and protect? I don't know that I ever dreamed this in another life, but it's what my soul needs now. Living off the land—to want for nothing; have everything within my property line—the little creek bringing fresh water through," Sonny said.

The well-drilling folks say any bit west or east and Sonny woulda been drilling through deep layers of bedrock.

"How much more perfect can you get than a well drill slicing straight through the earth to the cleanest water there is? It's perfection. Like this place was waiting on me to return and finally see it," Sonny said.

Knowing you really need to go through all four seasons in order to know where permanent fixtures go, Sonny and Dwayne worked through the year watching how rain traveled and maybe pooled around the property. How the sun moved through the sky in winter and summer. It was the summer line of the sun to worry about before building a house: too many west-facing windows and he'd spend almost all of his electric bill keeping the internal temperature below eighty-five degrees.

That's what Dwayne loved about Mozell's house: they cut the shade oak down when the road came through, but only the bathroom window faced west. During the height of summer with the sun lingering in the sky until nine P.M., it tracked over the roof of the house, save for the few hours peeking into the bathroom window before dropping below the pines. He had been noting this information, including what side of the property would hold all the horses he'd long promised Gwendolyn—he'd need established grass that wouldn't immediately turn to sand with horses on it, but enough sand that the pastures would drain quickly after a heavy storm. As bad as no grass and hungry horses is, horses standing in mud is worse—the moisture eats away at the hooves.

"No hooves, no horse," Grandaddy Mo would say. "You take care of the feet, and the chain reaction is how you keep 'em healthy."

So much had been swimming in his head and his heart about the land. Sonny leaned on Dwayne's knowledge for his own homestead. Now separated from the whole ordeal, and healed a little, when Sonny was ready, Dwayne asked how, in the desert, Sonny knew so much about horses when he didn't grow up with any?

"I mean, sure, I had a few when I was little and with my family. But I didn't pay them any mind," Sonny said. "Then, on one of the bases I lived on the longest, they had a stable for some of the families who had horses, and I drove by them every night to throw my head on my pillow. I was like a moth to a flame—I couldn't think of anything but! One day, I lost a dare, and so me and one of my platoon members had to sneak over, jump the fence. To finish the dare, I grabbed a stick mimicking what those jockeys use to get the horse to go at horse races, and a handful of mane, and somehow we stayed on as we ran through the pastures under moonlight. That was our escape."

"A crop," Dwayne corrected. "That's the thing jockeys use to get their horses to go." Sonny nodded. Dwayne added, "You had a good seat then."

"You know the words of what it all means. Like how you explained it to the brothers out in the desert, clear as day. How do *you* know so much about this stuff?" Sonny asked.

Dwayne hadn't figured what it might mean to be living, as a civilian, with his war brother. Wasn't the code that what happened over there, stayed there?

Here, in America, he had the promises to make of himself a life after service. Over there was no time to explain how either of them came to know whatever they had known about horses—only, they had a job to do, and lives and freedoms depended on it. In so many ways Dwayne succeeded. In others, his failures haunted him back to America. Dwayne knew he had to do this for Sonny now. He was the one, the leader, back in Kuwait. He was the captain of the ship who was supposed to sweep the deck for any persons, any bodies, before leaving. If he had gone back, maybe Brian would have lived. He was the stronger rider. But he had left Brian behind. He had not counted his brothers and noticed the missing. If he had gone back, maybe Sonny wouldn't have been shot. He should have been at the back of the pack to make sure no one was left. So when Sonny proclaimed he was going to go back and get Brian, Dwayne should have been the one to ride back into the desert, into the line of fire. He should have been the one taking the bullet to the back. How many times can singular events change the course of your life? It was the fire again.

He didn't want to get lost in the mire and muck of guilt like his father, so he leaned into his friend instead.

Here, at home, the wide-open days and landscapes waiting for a purpose, Dwayne's project became Sonny and Sonny's project was emerging: horses.

"Did you name your guy out there? I did. I called him Grasshopper," Sonny said. "Before my daddy died in a work accident, you know he had some horses but like I said I won't interested. I wanted anything but what he had. But he did have one horse, Cricket, and I laughed when I saw the horse you put me on and said he look like Cricket come back to me, so I named my guy Grasshopper."

Dwayne thought about his answer. He had named his horse, too. Pal. He had thought first about the faithfulness of O'boy—the first horse that taught him he could ride the wind, but it was Pal O Mine that Grandaddy had always bragged about—if that horse was with you, Moses would say, you could *be* the wind. That's what he figured he needed out there. To be the wind.

"I named him after my grandaddy's racehorse Pal O Mine," Dwayne answered. They had been through so much. And now, truly brothers. Who else could he tell but Sonny?

Sonny looked at Dwayne as if he was just introduced to him for the first time, and in many ways, he was.

"Your grandaddy had racehorses?"

Dwayne looked down at his fingernails and started picking his cuticles.

"Yeh. I mean, kind of. He was a groom and an exercise rider. You know, a groom? They take real care of the horses, get them ready to race. All that. And you know those folks spend more time with the horses than anyone—save the two minutes on the track if it's a steeplechase; save the few seconds postrace if they're in the winner's circle. He came from a long line of men who raised, trained, rode—all of it—horses. Even when we was in chains."

Sonny grew wide-eyed. "So horses run in your blood, huh?"

They were setting posts for Sonny's horse pastures, the first two. Digging and grunting; digging and grunting. It had been years since he thought about it all, but so much of the build of Sonny's place—to the best of his recollection—was a pretty close replica of his grandfather's farm, landscape allowing, and save the barn that Moses had built that was attached to the house.

"People told me my father Lloyd went his own way—onto the bush track. Unsanctioned racing in the back of someone's farm. With quarter horses. Full-out speed, so a shorter distance. Grandaddy ain't love that his love and life of horses was governed by white folks, but I guess when you think of it he was nostalgic for ceremony, pomp and circumstance, regulation. The horses at the center. Even if it meant he disappeared within it. He always said he knew which horses were his: *the winning ones.*"

They both chuckled.

"He never understood what he say my daddy was up to with his own flavor of racing the few stories Grandaddy told me about it, but he did say he appreciated the horseflesh. That's how he started bringing quarter horses home. Student becomes the influencer.

Grandaddy saw you could rough them up a bit more. Sturdier. For his use, training other horses, working the land, Grandaddy actually preferred them to the racing Thoroughbreds."

Sonny stopped stabbing the post-digger into the earth and wiped his brow. Dwayne took the break to wipe his as well. It was late spring, but the humidity made sweat stick to their skin like honey.

"You never talk about your daddy."

Dwayne went back to work. Kept moving, using the momentum to push him through the telling. Sonny was right. He never did talk about his daddy.

"I guess I ain't got much to say. He left after the fire," he said. He knew the hole he was digging was good and deep enough, but he couldn't stop, couldn't look up. Not now. "Well, he left when I was born and my mother died. Everyone guessed he needed time. He popped in here and there, but I don't got no big memories I can recall. Then years passed. Then my grandparents died going into the house and barn fire trying to save their damn horses, and we all thought maybe that would be the thing to bring my father back, maybe he would show up then. But he never did. There were pictures of us on holidays, things like that when I was really young. When my grandma coaxed him to come around. I seen when newspapers reported on the races and whatnot, and he'd be quoted, or sometimes pictured. But I cannot tell you what his voice sounded like, what he smells like. I imagine he might look like a younger version of my grandaddy now, but I don't know."

He stopped. Looked at Sonny.

"I watched them burn, Snoop. My family. Burn. My horses. Burn. All but one mule. Gone. Ms. Mozell picked me up off the floor and gave me a life, but practically it was hard, emotionally, it was harder to think I was supposed to carry any of that forward."

Sonny saw Dwayne wipe his face again, but this time, lower than his brows. He walked over to Dwayne and cupped his shoulder. It was clearer to him now.

"Thank you for helping me build my dream, man. Even for all the pain it must be causing you," he said. "Look at all you still have, swirling inside, to be manifest."

Chapter 11

These days, Sonny loved to pass a good Sunday afternoon on the ground at his place throwing loops of rope around his dummy steer head attached to a hay bale that had caught too much moisture to feed out, so was perfectly good to be the body of his practice steer. He had enough horseflesh and tack and using ropes—those too worn to catch a real live steer with but fine enough for folks to come and play cowboys with.

Sonny invited the Crew to venture out of the Spot on the weekends, and onto the grounds of his place to "change things up." The gaggle of veterans that found each other in Fairfield County and then later clung together put up a garage-type dwelling on Sonny's land and called it the Spot. They gathered just about weekly, throwing back longnecks. Talking about the past times. Remembering this operation, that. Skipping the hard memories. Singing mess-hall songs and such. Whenever Sonny offered they should venture outside of the Spot, he mostly wanted to not be tied up inside all day, and while they were there, it could give him a chance to do some big projects at the farm with some muscle. They'd fall in regimented line and follow whatever instructions Sonny barked at them, and before he knew it, he'd have a new paddock built—post holes dug, T-posts set, wire hung. A thing that would take him days took hours.

When Dwayne first started bringing his little girl Nikki to the Spot—saying something with rolled eyes about Gwendolyn intentionally messing with his free weekends—initially Sonny was annoyed: How was he expected to entertain a child? Since coming back from Kuwait, Sonny watched Dwayne fall back into the icy-hot games with Gwendolyn again and again.

"You givin' me whiplash, Dew," Sonny said. "A few months ago you said you're through, and now you're telling me y'all having a baby?"

Nikki emerged almost fully formed into their lives, and Dwayne couldn't at first comprehend how thankful he was for her. How despite whatever was between him and Gwendolyn, he had Nikki, forever. He'd do right by her, he promised Gwendolyn, when she asked what to do? What to do? Dwayne said *keep it,* and though it surprised him that he said it, he meant it. Whatever that would mean for them, he wanted Gwendolyn to keep it. And it meant making space for a little girl in his life. In his life with Sonny. In the life he crafted back in Fairfield County after the war. And now Sonny—initially inconvenienced—found himself making space, too.

What he had loved about his time with the Crew was that no one was expecting anything special of him. They all knew that if he was out working, he had his out-working outfit: Carhartt overalls that were once a navy blue but were worn so (he joked that he might be the one to put them to the test) that the color was closer to a steel gray. He'd 100% have strands of hay in his beard he let hang about four inches from his chin that was increasingly being peppered with white. And, as with a man that spends so much time on the back of a horse, out in the field with a horse, and so on, had a constant slight musk of horse and sweat and grain.

It was hard to explain what it really smelled like, but when she was around seven or eight each time Nikki came close enough to give him two fist bumps, followed by a quick opening of the hands and snap to finish it off in a choreographed greeting, she'd sniff the air and proclaim: "Uncle Sonny, you smell like peanut butter!" One time it was "moldy bread" and that was after he had to open and then throw out a whole bag of wheat grains that had overwintered in the back of his storage shed and had gotten ruined by exposure to too much moisture. Nikki loved figuring out what scent he donned, and despite his initial hesitation, he began to appreciate her time on the farm. Someone he could share his gifts with. Someone who knew what it was to partner with the animals. She walked straight up to him and watched for a bit before she picked up the rope herself and tossed it over the dummy steer's wide-stretching horns.

Sonny was surprised how Nikki took to roping. It wasn't pretty, but it was something to work with. Something Sonny could work with. *Always reward a try.*

"Keep your elbow still. That's it. Now wave your arm left to right like a windshield wiper," Sonny instructed.

He was crouching behind her, holding her elbow in place. "Now rotate your wrist, that's how you throw the best loop, the circle the loop travels over your head comes from your wrist, not your elbow." He'd mark the rhythm she should follow, *left, right; left, right; left, right* while Nikki swung her arm in the air without a rope.

"Now you got the rhythm in your body, here's the good stuff, the almost-real stuff."

Often, while talking or thinking or just being outside, he'd start looking for something to keep his hands busy. It was the only way ideas or words downloaded clearly into his mind. Most often he'd grab a rope and pull out a loop, then twirl it next to his body. Every third loop he'd pull, Sonny would swing it just over his head and throw it out, his open palm facing in the direction of the object he was looking to rope: a water spigot, the patience pole (with or without a horse tied to it), a fence post, Pup—his farm dog who became his farm dog after he just showed up one day looking hungry and Sonny fed him and named him Pup. Stationary or otherwise, if it could fit within the loop he pulled, it was probably roped by Sonny a time or five. He let Nikki stand on the back of his side-by-side and swing out and they both giggled when she tossed the rope loop and caught Dwayne. The loop had gone through the air like a Frisbee, over his head and then hooked his left shoulder. She knew not to yank her slack too hard but did tug on it and knocked her father off-balance, moving him a step closer.

"That's a half-head you caught there, on a mean ol' bull. He's too big for team roping though. I'm surprised he's not a rib eye yet," Sonny chuckled.

"Looks more like chuck roast to me!" Nikki countered—all those hours and days in the shadow of her father and her play uncles gave her razor-sharp quick wit and a grittiness Dwayne was growing to be thankful for.

"That girl ain't never gone wear a dress in her life, you know that, Dew? Look at her—"

And Nikki would be off somewhere messing around with this or that. If at home with Dwayne, she'd be driving a tractor—how kids in the suburbs twirled around on their Big Wheels, ten-speeds, or Power Wheels.

If at Uncle Sonny's, because she had graduated from brushing and petting his horses supervised, most often she was scratching Easy's wither and whispering tween things in his ear as often as she could, mostly on the weekends when not with her mother, rarely after school. Easy, living up to his name, had apparently grown into wanting nothing more out of life than being spoiled by a horse-crazy girl, and if Sonny and her father ventured out of sight she would coax Easy over to the gate of his pasture, which she knew would hold her because it was where she stood and climbed the rungs to get high enough to scratch his ears before she started just walking out to him in the pasture. Ever since the day they met, they bonded. Easy followed Nikki everywhere with or without peppermints in her pocket, and so she'd coax him to the gate and from the ground, tap his shoulders to move the front half closer, and tap his butt to move that end closer. Just enough for her to squeeze between Easy and the gate, and she'd grab a piece of his mane with her right hand, and the gate with her left, and spider-climbed the two until she was high enough to fling her torso across Easy's back, then a leg. And Easy would stand still as stone. A bulldozer couldn't move him. He was in on their little secret. Finally, Nikki was sitting upright and tapped his sides with her calves, asking for forward movement, and he would offer a gentle walk-off. The first time they had done this, it was like a tiptoe—as if he knew he carried precious cargo.

Wandering around the pasture like this of course put Nikki within eyesight of the adults. She was squealing, but not in the way that raised the hairs on Dwayne's arms; they were squeals that allowed his shoulders to fall away from his ears. Relax. Her smile so bright it seemed the sun reflected off of it.

It was only a matter of time, Sonny told Dwayne one day, not unlike the day they saw Nikki sauntering on the back of Easy like they had already formed into a centaur. Only a matter of time before what they knew was inside her—horses—would make its presence known.

"Cain't stop nature from finding its way," Sonny had said the first time they caught a glimpse of Nikki trotting across the lawn. "Like trying to stop a river from flowing where you don't want it. You can *try*. But nature still find a way where God intended for it to go."

What else was there for Dwayne to do but to lift his hands in resignation to this statement? He shook his head, more in reluctant acceptance than anything else. Sonny was right—every time man tries to stop nature, it come back to bite him.

There wasn't much else of Nikki's life when she wasn't desperately trying to make her way to her Uncle Sonny's place with her father.

One day after school, she had convinced the bus driver—Mrs. Esther—that her daddy was going to meet her at Uncle Sonny's house and she could just drop her off there. It was a big wager, Nikki knew. What if her daddy won't at Sonny's when the bus came squealing down the road? Would Mrs. Esther let her off? Would Sonny be home at all and not off trail riding?

Mrs. Esther knew Dwayne, having grown up with his father, and enjoyed spending part of her days making sure the kids made it safely to and from school. She was retired from the post office, but when an urgent call came for bus drivers, particularly the routes out in the country, down the paved and still-existing dirt roads of the mostly Black part of Fairfield County, she thought she owed it to her younger self to heed the call. Besides, she already knew where everyone lived, and everyone already knew her from the decades of bringing bills, holiday cards, eviction notices, tax bills, and so on.

As a young girl, she had been forbidden to ride a bus—even when they closed the Black school and she was forced to attend the integrated school across the county. How did she do it then? Walk that whole way? Her short legs. Those heavy books. Those white men in pickup trucks, honking. Swerving in any mud puddle hoping to fling it her way. Those kids sticking their bubblegum-pink heads out the school bus taunting and throwing wads of school paper. It was Lloyd that offered to meet her part of the way and walked with her into the school hall.

Her grandbabies can drive themselves now, thank God, but she promised every parent she met along the route that she would treat every child in her care as her very own. Reminded them to let her know if they needed anything, *anything at all.* Sometimes that meant driving off-route to Blythewood or Columbia because Tyrone's grandma was in the hospital, so he had to stay with his daddy who was a construction worker, which meant won't no way he could come all the way up by Winnsboro to take him to school or pick him up, so Mrs. Esther stopped the bus in front of the construction company main office and nodded at the receptionist and Tyrone skipped off the bus, his book bag flapping behind him like a shield while he greeted Ms. Oscarine. They'd both wave in thanks to Mrs. Esther.

That was small-town love. *We take care of we,* she said to Nikki the day she asked to go to Uncle Sonny's house like she had stepped into her own personal taxi. Mrs. Esther wondered why neither of her parents had arranged it with her at morning pickup, but it didn't matter, *we take care of we,* and she waved the girl in and headed south along Highway 21.

"Mrs. Esther! Uncle Sonny! It's Uncle Sonny!" Nikki knew that horse's butt anywhere, even from any distance. Besides, only

Uncle Sonny was crazy enough these days to ride his horse along the highway like it was a regular car. She had heard stories of how once almost everyone in Fairfield County had horses that they rode everywhere, but most days it was just Uncle Sonny tip-tapping along the shoulder of the highway or side road with his horse with the puff of blond hair at the top of the tail. Dimples right where the rounded part turned into a leg. "That's the part look like a chicken leg," Sonny joked when he started teaching her parts of the horse, and that part was called "haunches," or "in plain cowboy speak, the butt." Yep, that was Easy, alright. Uncle Sonny was riding Easy, holding the reins loose with his right hand resting on the saddle. Nikki called directly after him, hanging out the window as the bus squealed to a stop. Before Mrs. Esther could pull the lever to open the door, Nikki was at the bottom step, her hands on each door panel, attempting to push them open. Nikki knew she had to catch Uncle Sonny first, have him look her in the eye, before Mrs. Esther asked him was it true.

"Hey, Uncle Sonny," Nikki said, jumping off the bottom step. She started loudly: "Remember I was 'sposed to come to your house after school 'cause Daddy had an appointment?"

Easy had tried to step forward to meet Nikki's reach for his muzzle. Sonny lifted his hands on the reins and clucked, pulling him back. The kids on the bus were chanting "horsey!" with increasing fervor, and while this was the quieter part of Highway 21, it *was* still a highway and sometimes truckers loved to careen around the corners of it knowing damned well that it took upwards of seventy-five feet to come to a complete stop. That's how that little boy a few years back died in front of all them kids that time. Sonny pulled Easy three steps back from the road so he could keep everyone out of harm's way. He looked at Nikki then, at first not sure what appointment or arrangement she meant, but when she winked, he understood and tipped his hat at Nikki and echoed the same words to Mrs. Esther.

"Yes ma'am. She right. Nikki 'sposed to come by my place, but it's clear I plumb forgot," he chuckled, leaning forward to pat Easy on the neck. Mrs. Esther asked, well what was she to do? He won't at home exactly, was he?

"No ma'am. I'm just about a five-minute mosey 'round that way," he said, pointing to the opening of a path leading into the thick woods.

That was *cowboy talk* and Nikki, running her hand through Easy's mane, smirked. Ladies melted like butter whenever he did it. She had heard Sonny use it like at the parades whenever women came to admire his horses. His twang would linger the way the strong scent of diesel fuel refuses to go anywhere even hours after you pour it. Mrs. Esther fluffed her curls like a flirty schoolgirl, then a car honked. She was holding up traffic.

"I'll be alright, Mrs. Esther. I can ride Easy, too!" Nikki offered, lifting her head and nodding. Sonny removed his foot from the stirrup so Nikki could have some help. She wedged her foot into the triangled leather. He reached down and counted, "One, two, three, *up*!" and pulled Nikki into the sky almost, except she landed where she intended: riding Easy. She wrapped her arms around Sonny's torso.

"You gone get me in trouble, lil lady," Sonny whispered to Nikki. He tipped his hat for the second time to Mrs. Esther and let the bus and its backed-up traffic roll by before he said to Nikki, "You do the honors."

"Alright boy, giddy up!" she said, clucking at Easy and clicking her heels three times at his sides like Dorothy at the end of the yellow brick road.

⁞⁞⁞⁞⁞⁞⁞⁞

After the first year when he and Dwayne set it up, Sonny would choose a quadrant of his parcel to work on, improve, build upon, or change—as his needs of the land changed. In the middle of the yearslong transformation, it was hard to see where it was all going. Won't no real schema to it so far as he could see. There was a firepit and a few chairs but mostly railroad ties placed in a hexagon around it for seating. Just to the right of that was what Sonny called a round pen where he worked his young colts. If you actually looked at the round pen, you'd notice it won't round at all, more oval, with some straight sides and all but it got the job done. Both the firepit and round pen were right dab smack in the middle of the farm. The heart of it. Then there's the pastures that surround it all. Three of them make a U shape around the farm hearth and the fourth has two horses and a double-wide inside it. Ask Sonny why he living in a horse pasture like he an animal himself and Sonny would first chuckle and say, "Maybe I am. An animal, I mean."

Nikki begged Dwayne to let her head over to "the barn" after school. She got to spend more time with the horses, and with Uncle Sonny. It was only net positive for them both, Dwayne wagered. One day at dinner, at home, Nikki remarked on her observations of her uncle, how his place was set up. Marveled, really.

"His closest mounts walk up to the first two steps of the deck he built off his trailer and nicker for a treat," she said. Then, after a thought, she'd offer, "That's called real horsemanship. Uncle Sonny says them fancy barns lookin' like castles is for *people*. Horses wanna be outside. Horses wanna be with they horsey friends. With their herd. Horses want good grass and good hay. You want your horses close, pull up close."

When asked directly, Sonny offered to Nikki that's how he can keep a better eye on the herd's welfare. Just get up and look out the window. Step off the porch.

"If horses can hear my heartbeat from several feet away, then they'll know how I'm feeling soon's I wake up. Hell, maybe before. They'll know how I'm feeling when I'm rustling in my kitchen fixin' coffee. When I settle into the evening in front of my television. That's conditioning just as much as pushin' 'em around and around my pen. It shows up when I toss a leg over to ride—they can know where my head and heart is at."

Dwayne straightened his back when he heard the word "heart," recalling his Grandaddy Moses once talking about heart and horses. Sonny paused. Dwayne changed topics. Nikki danced off into the waning light after another horse.

Chapter 12

"You riding in the rodeo?" Dwayne asked. They were easing into the end of another day around the firepit; as usual the sun set an hour ago but it wasn't yet dinnertime, so he let Nikki continue to piddle around with the horses before he gathered her.

"Are *you*?" Sonny countered Dwayne's question with his own. Besides being annoying in general, he was prodding more lately. Ever since Nikki's natural-born instinct/affinity for horses started emerging, it seemed all Sonny did these days was ask him about what *he* was going to do with horses. Dwayne sucked his teeth at the questions.

"Come on, man. That's foul. You know where I am with that," he said, raising his beer in the direction of a horse pasture. "Whatever is brewing in her, I aim to support it as best I can, and I support you and y'all at the rodeo by being one of the loudest voices in the stands."

"I know, man. I just—" Sonny jumped in, trying to stop whatever freight train was coming his way. "I just. Man, Nikki has *it*. She has it: what you told me your grandaddy had? She got it."

Of course she did. He was trying not to see it, but over time it emerged a stronger part of who she was. Days he'd come to peel her off the farm he hoped she'd be off horse already. If he got there and she was riding, Nikki would call him over to watch.

"Daddy, Uncle Sonny says I have a balanced seat! That means—"

"You know how to keep the horse between you and the ground!" Dwayne chuckled.

"No, Daddy! It means I don't wiggle all over the horses' backs like a spaghetti noodle! I sit up straight, use my body, and—" She pointed in the middle of her chest. "I keep my shoulders so that I don't even need the reins! Look!"

Nikki held her arms out like an airplane and smooched. Wasn't any denying how easily Nikki and the horse loped off and rounded the pen. Never rising out of her seat. Never reaching for mane like she was unsure of her partner. No. They were in unison. One song. The three-beat footfall of the lope lured Dwayne into humming *row, row, row your boat*. That's how Grandaddy Moses helped him find a steady loping rhythm. He'd holler it and tell him to *sing it* out loud. Grandaddy Moses would start the verse *merrily merrily merrily / life is full of dreams*. Then he'd start to the *rowing* part. And here was Nikki, finding that rhythm on her own. All her own.

"You working with her?" Dwayne asked Sonny.

"I thought about getting her ready for the rodeo. But no, I'm not doing much. Showing her how to throw a loop. Tell her to sit back here and there. 'Cept for the fact I have to tell her I need Easy when I need to pony a colt or something, she out here on her own. Doing her own thing. Maybe she ask me stuff like *how* to keep a horse, like the life of it, but the rest . . . that's her own doing. I can't take credit for it."

Me neither, Dwayne thought. Sonny cleared his throat. "But for real, man. This rodeo. You know unless they trucking talent in, I'm the only Black cowboy out there. It's getting old. Especially when there's folks out here in Ridgeway that can *ride*—you know what I mean. I convinced Rogelio to enter with his stud. They gone heel for someone. But you know. It's not the same as saying there's more than just me out there."

Dwayne watched Nikki. She'd call out *hooo* to stop the horse, then turn the horse, then smooch and lope off again. Didn't her arms get tired? The times Grandaddy made him ride like this, he won't brave enough to lope. It required too much heart work. Balance. Trust in the horse. Except for maybe the first time, ignorance is bliss and all that, Dwayne needed the reins.

"You can't control everything, 'Wayne," Grandaddy Mo had said back then. "Riding horses well is about letting go. Let it go." Dwayne would drop the reins for a step or two then sweep them right on back up. But Nikki . . . he squinted in her direction . . . does the horse have reins at all?

"Nikki been wondering out loud lately, when I catch wind of her over here."

Dwayne had heard "wandering" at first. "Where she wandering off to now?"

Sonny tried again, slower. "Wondering about what's nature, you know, in us, and what's . . . taught. I tell her I ain't really teaching her much, so she goes, 'So it's natural?' and I have to agree. I can't lie to her, Dew. She knows when I'm lying. Once I told her Easy was lame so I could have some horse for me to practice my bulldoggin' runs and I swear she trotted that motherfucker out across the pasture and said, 'Looks fine to me,' and what was I gone say then? Anyway. She asked out loud if her ancestors rode horses just yesterday."

Dwayne turned to look him in the eye.

"I said maybe. I said *maybe,* man. But listen, you need to talk to her. She wants to do the rodeo, and if you let her and the *County Chronicle* gets involved because there's a bona fide Black woman—"

"—girl," Dwayne corrected.

"Right. Either way. It'll be a story that a Black woman broke the rodeo race barrier, then they'll dig up any old photo of Black people on horses they might have in their archives, and you'll have to explain y'all come from a family that been created with horses from the dust when God was making this whole world them seven days and how you been riding longer than her little memory."

"I get it, Sonny," Dwayne stopped him. He was always going into his ideas at the most inconvenient time. Had Nikki heard his line of reasoning? Enough to make her own inferences?

"She asked me what even she might could do at the rodeo if she did go. She wants to go *and compete.*" Sonny started again. "I told her obviously she needed to check with you, but Dew, she could do breakaway or barrels. You know, the lady events and all. But just the other day we was playing around in the pasture and she caught a steer just so, and then I scooted my horse up to get into place so I could heel it 'cause I always stay ready and I yell out, 'Dally an' turn left! Hook left!' and she did, then when I got my loop around the dancing back legs, she turned and faced just like them professionals, Dew."

Dwayne sat with the idea of his girl becoming a rodeo rider and wondered who he might have been if his life had turned out differently. He'd watch the spring turf races on television and tried to imagine himself, like his grandfather, parading the giant Thoroughbreds around the green, spit shining them, galloping in the early-morning fog, during the hours before night turned over to day.

Or would he have been on the dusty clay tracks at his father's feet? And then standing on his own? How would he have handled the dwindling numbers of that industry—fighting sanctioning and all? Each time he smells the sweat-grain dander on Nikki, he feels something like homesick for a life he only really got the beginning of.

Dwayne knew his daughter. She wanted to run with the boys since she could stand on her own two feet.

"She'd be bored with breakaway—just hookin' and letting go like she a young gun fishing for minnows on the shoreline," Dwayne said. Sonny raised his eyebrows that they were actually having a conversation about it.

"You right. So, I say if—and I mean obviously it's up to you—but I think even now she'd give some of them cowboys callin' themselves professionals a run for they money if she team ropes. I'd heel for her, of course. And you know where I stand on that, but for her, *for you,* I'd do it. They'd be so surprised there was a woman—I mean girl—doing team roping, much less a Black one. Out there in the arena, under the big lights, doing real cowboy-like shit."

Chapter 13

Everyone knew fall had arrived to Fairfield County when bright red-and-white rodeo signs started popping up all over town like weeds—mostly places folks knew the people who frequented said place would care about such an event: The Feed & Seed store. The General Store. Waffle House. Used to be, they would advertise in the *County Chronicle* but it was turning into a classifieds-only circular for real estate: whose property was up for grabs on account of tax delinquency, estate disputes, or—more likely—folks trying to escape the growing urbanization sneaking up to their property line, and so placed an ad in the hopes that maybe some developer would offer them the payday of their life to leave it.

'Cause of that stuff filling up the columns of the *County Chronicle,* won't room for much else when you take into account how Charlotte, the city to the north in the other Carolina, and Columbia, the city to the south in the real Carolina, were trying their level best to annex the whole ninety-five-mile corridor of counties like Fairfield between the two cities. Its inhabitants becoming collateral damage of this late-century new-millennium manifest-destiny-type pursuit.

Those who cared, though, knew that as soon as the sun started setting a little earlier—signaling a change of seasons (not always the weather)—was the time to turn their attention to the rodeo that set up in the empty field lot just off the Interstate 77 exit. Some said a developer owned the land but no one knew who exactly. Everyone called the patch of land "the Rodeo Field," 'cause it always, always had one row of stadium seats year-round left over from the weekend event, and whenever anyone referenced the land's fate, folks always started with "They say—"

"—it's going to be eighty-eight townhomes when they're done using it up by making money off us for the rodeo."

"—it was supposed to be a playground or park, but then someone came and bought it up, so they say it'll be storage units."

"—the Rodeo Field gone be a car wash even though we got two of them in a three-mile radius already."

The one that went around the most, though, and was the longest rumor, was the one about how a developer was going to take over the Rodeo Field to expand the interstate, and that any parcel of land from Blythewood to Ridgeway to Winnsboro was subject to eminent domain because interstate projects included the state, and its government, and everyone knew that once the government got involved in land conversations won't nothing you could do to stop it.

So whenever anyone moved in—it didn't matter if they were in Blythewood, Ridgeway, or Winnsboro—folks would be barely moved out of their boxes or had time enough to turn on their utilities or inspected their septic tanks before a neighbor would trot on over in welcome and warning.

"You know they say they're going to exit the interstate right here," and they'd kick the dirt on which y'all stood. "Then, they say won't be no large-acreage properties. They coming for our way of life, I tell you."

Wasn't much more than "a developer" that could unite small-town white folks with just about anyone no matter their color nor creed who was on their side against so-called "progress." Against "change." It's one of the moments they remember they have neighbors at all, truly. Let a yellow town notice sign pop up near a wooded lot and here come Neighbor What's-His-Face knocking on your door talking about "they say an Amazon warehouse," and so on. Any other time they'd growl at you because they believe your dog found his way onto their lawn, never mind you know they themselves sneak through your own property's weak fence line because everybody knows the cost of lumber and steel skyrocketed and don't we all have things that need to be fixed? But when those standing dead pine trees fell, well, a way opened up for them to hunt the deer that took up residence in *your* woods. All these desire lines keep popping up from their property to yours. One day you caught them because they thought you had retreated for the night and became their same, usual cantankerous neighbor-self because they were confronted about the trespass. How dare they be challenged for being in the wrong. White folks are *never* in the wrong.

It was these folks, mostly, who put on the rodeo in Blythewood, who sponsored seats so their little business signs could be hung in the arena. Tractor Sales, the electric company, the local grocer, the bed-n-breakfast, the restaurant in the town country club even though it won't open to the public—someone decided they needed to make a statement of support so forked over the fee to have a banner hanging. The real bigwigs worked to have their logo on the lawn signs next to rodeo and whatever October date it was that year.

Every year, Sonny made it a point to call the office to enter the rodeo. He didn't keep steers at his place anymore because the dailiness of fence repair became too much for his operation, but the body keeps the dance of bulldoggin'—jumping off the back of his moving horse and onto the back of the steer. He was kept in a straight line by the hazer on the other side and Easy, who, like the hazer, understood his job was also to keep running next to the steer even though the rider was now off its back, trying his level best to grab the steer's horns and flip it off its feet.

Sonny knew he could probably take home a check in team roping or tie-down roping. But it cost too much. Instead, he always wagered if he was going to be the only Black cowboy on the field, Sonny wanted it to be for the event that white folks actually credit a Black man for its creation as a rodeo event at all. If he had an activist bone in his body, that was one way. Roll up to the rodeo to take home the cash in bulldoggin'.

Folks would walk up to him milling around the contestants' side of the rodeo field and ask him, "You ridin' tonight?" Probably out of fear of competition. Riders knew he had the right kinda roping arm—he'd catch as many steers as ropes he threw. Which came as a surprise to him, on account of his war wounds and all. But his arm had grown stronger as the days and years rolled on. Many a thousand of hours of pasture roping—the day work at local folks' cattle operations he sometimes gets catching they little jerks who broke fence and ended up somewhere they won't supposed to be. He knew how to hunt the steer down, put his horse in the right position behind it, and his horse knew once he locked on won't no letting up until that thing was caught. Sonny'd throw a good loop, snatch the rope 'round the horns, then he'd dally it right quick 'round his saddle, and the next real skill in team roping was turning and pulling the steer so its legs would kick up in a rhythm ripe for catching—the heelers loved him for this fact.

Sonny figured won't no use paying to do what he get paid to do out in the pastures, where he loved to shine—not confined by a 150 by 200 foot arena. The wide-open spaces is where he preferred to rope; there was more unpredictability. Requiring more finesse. Intuition. *Feel.* Which way was the steer gone go? You had to know how to read 'em. In those rodeo arenas, they only really had one way to go—straight forward—coming out of the chute, and that won't no fun for Sonny. No real challenge. No matter how much people begged, or what percentage of the win he was promised, he only ever did one event: bulldoggin'.

For Nikki, all those years growing up in Fairfield County, she had believed the signs weren't as big or as loud for the rodeo until this year. How something is nearly invisible to you because it doesn't quite or yet or at all apply to you and then as soon as you work a thing or idea into your brain, it appears everywhere. In conversation, on the radio, flyers posted in Lizard's Thicket, bulletin boards at school, in Piggly Wiggly. It was getting realer every day she thought about the event: riding in front of hundreds of people on a Friday night.

Sonny had told her what it's like—the adrenaline coursing through your body until your fingers tingle.

"You gotta shake it out," Sonny said. "You'll feel the tightness in your chest, and if you let it linger an' listen with your seat, you'll feel the horse's back tighten. So you breathe deep, wiggle your toes, and then shake the nerves out of your hands."

The more she thought about it, the more she didn't understand how she got here. More and more Sonny kept gassing her up every time she found her way onto a horse's back and encouraging her to show the world what she was made of.

"But also. Have fun! I don't know how to tell you, it just feels different. It won't feel like riding at home. The energy. The competition. Easy loves a crowd—you'll feel his chest puff out with pride as soon as y'all enter the arena. And then you just ride as you do at the barn. Push 'em, push 'em, then open up and swing the rope."

"I've never tried to rope a calf. How do you hook it without the horns?" Nikki asked.

Sonny nodded. "In a way, it is harder. They're faster. Smaller. You right, no horns."

He had a young colt at the end of a lead rope and while they talked about the rodeo, he waved the rope around, sometimes tapping the colt. Surprised, the colt would flinch, and Nikki stopped talking to watch. She wanted to know why it was so important to compete, why not just enjoy the horses at home. Sonny scratched the colt's neck then went back to swinging the lead rope.

"You just ride different when something is on the line. More intensity. Learn where you can focus energy to be better, because it's not downloaded into your muscle memory. You come back home—even if it's with a check or not—and start thinking about what to work on to be a stronger rider. Competition teaches you better than I can."

Nikki just hadn't thought about competing on a platform like this before. Even in school, she was fine being in the middle of the pack. The quiet one. Hopefully invisible enough to make it through the day to tend to her life outside of the classroom. Horses became a thing that lured her to the end of the day, and mostly an independent endeavor. She'd still be independent in the arena, sure, but with the largest audience she could imagine.

"Wish I could team rope with you," she said. "I mean, I have to go out there all alone." Nikki made a fake frown and drew out "alone" into a small whine.

Sonny chuckled. "Welp, I don't team rope on the off chance Imma get paid to do what I already get paid to do. So *we* not going to do that. Unless you want to. But anyway, you mostly out here all alone."

Sonny mimicked the way Nikki had said it, opening his arms out to indicate the whole of his farm.

"Just imagine you're here. But you're there."

"With a big audience," Nikki said.

"Cheering for you."

Nowhere in any forecast in the days leading up to the rodeo was there a chance of rain, even though for the last six years, without fail, no matter what the weatherman said, a surprise shower would pop up somewhere about fifteen minutes before the national anthem.

And like clockwork, the rain came. The announcer welcomed folks to grab their last-minute snack, asked the vendors to pause their sales, the mechanical bull to stop bucking, and then, like part of the script, said some version of "God, bless us with a good rain if that's our lot tonight. One that gives these cowboys and cowgirls good footing for the greatest show on dirt."

The crowd cheered as folks hurried along looking for any makeshift reprieves from the surprise shower. They came independently to watch their daughter for the first time in the arena, but Dwayne and Gwendolyn had found each other in the kettle-corn line.

"Caramel?" Dwayne asked.

Gwendolyn nodded yes. Dwayne had asked for that and a large cinnamon and paid the gentleman before Gwendolyn had time to reach for her wallet.

"Oh—why thank you, sir," she said, in a bit of actual surprise, and Dwayne tipped his hat. A few days ago, when Nikki confirmed she was going to try the rodeo for the first time, she also asked that Dwayne get a *real* hat.

"Not the one landscapers wear that look like wicker baskets upside down, Daddy. Go to Pistol Creek and get a real one, please." And so he did, and he appreciated how it made him walk taller. He straightened his back. For his girl, he put the starched crease in the front of his blue jeans, and dusted the dirt off his boots. He even tucked his shirt.

"Nice hat, Cowboy 'Wayne," Gwendolyn had said between bites of popcorn. They both started walking to the stands, quickly, because the mist had started, even though they were walking to an uncovered arena, being in place felt something like seeking shelter.

Dwayne wondered if Gwendolyn thought he was dressed for her, how she smiled her old smile when she saw him in line, and it had melted him into a teenage version of himself, the one who still had dreams despite everything, and dreams with her, even. He cleared his throat, looking at the sky. The rain checked him. They were there to support Nikki. He would have sat anywhere there was an open spot. The seats they were choosing happened to be together. And now the rain made him act more gentlemanly towards Gwendolyn than maybe he would have otherwise.

"It's not supposed to be this dark in the day yet. That's real rain clouds. Go ahead and sit. I think I have an umbrella in my truck."

Gwendolyn nodded and continued to the stands.

Dwayne walked back with an umbrella and a dirty work towel that was perfect to wipe the wet stands with. It had taken him longer to return, because he had, out of habit, like part of his genetic makeup, stopped and removed his hat and placed his right hand over his heart for the national anthem. Right in the middle of the field, he stood at attention and let all the emotions of the evening flow through him. He never could explain to anyone why without fail he got emotional during the anthem. It surprised him. When he was younger, he'd brace against it, but now, he allowed the wave to build up from his gut, swell in his chest. It was pride of another sort tonight. His baby girl was being brave.

He wiped his face though it didn't matter since it was wet from the rain and it wasn't until Gwendolyn looked at him with a funny face did he remember he had an umbrella and didn't use it. He handed it to her while he wiped the seat down with his hand towel.

She pointed the umbrella at him—he should use it.

"I guess all that and I'm already wet."

Gwendolyn opened it and held it over her head, but leaned so he could seek some shelter with her.

The rodeo had begun but Dwayne felt the first part of the night was particularly quiet, hushed. "Maybe the rain is muffling the speaker's ability to send sound out this far," he wondered out loud. Gwendolyn asked him what he said and he shook his head *I'm not sure,* turning to look at her, watching the tie-down-roping contestants run to the middle of the arena after a steer, rope it, jump off their still-moving horses, flip the calf on its back by the horns, and tie three of its legs. It was smooth, looked effortless like a ballet.

Dwayne knew it was grueling work. The calf had to weigh at least three hundred pounds. At least.

He couldn't help but see how much Nikki was maturing to look like her mother. He had apologized to her for the Bolton jowls, he joked, but the silhouette of her face, the way her nose rounded to a small tip, how the bottom lip hung just slightly into a forever-pout—that was all Gwendolyn.

He cheered when the crowd cheered, clapped when Gwendolyn did, and checked out on the field to make sure he didn't miss Nikki or Sonny, because he realized the more he looked at her, Gwendolyn, skin a bit dewy from the mist, the quieter it got around him. He couldn't trust his ears to listen for their names to be called.

What was this moving inside him? He knew it to be dangerous work to exist in a space of hope for something long gone. Ms. Mozell taught him that. How many times had she caught him looking out the window at the empty field across the street, and she urged him to move on.

"You can remember the good, but don't be weighed down by the sad. You have a life to live."

He had a life to live. For himself. For Nikki. He couldn't be weighed down by whatever he was feeling in this moment: cool Friday night, with what he knows might be the only woman he'd ever love, but who was also impossible to love. She had smooth, soft sides, and glass-sharp angles that she wielded like a knife when she felt cornered. He remembered why they never worked, despite being rocked into a place of remembering only the soft sides of each other, sitting in the rain together under a singular umbrella watching the only good thing they made together conquer her fears.

"Ladies and gentlemen, the rain isn't being so nice to us tonight but we want to thank you for being a cowboy-tough audience out there. We just got word that we're going to do a bit of a rodeo shuffle—no, no, not a newfangled dance—and bring out our cowgirls a little early for the breakaway. We're afraid the dirt's only gone be mud by the time they gallop out on those fast horses and would be hard to rope a calf stuck in the mud, wouldn't you say?"

Everyone cheered.

"Listen to that. Wet as a noodle but still y'all ready to rodeo! Let's show our cowgirls how much we love them!"

Dwayne snapped to his feet. As did Gwendolyn.

"Can you believe it?" she asked.

"Not at all," he said. "Not at all."

Dwayne looked in the back galley of the arena for Nikki. Wondered how she was doing. If her nerves were taking over? Did she get that from him? Debilitating performance anxiety? Or, did she always know what she wanted and he was witnessing her get after it, like her mother did, for better or worse?

He never wondered of himself, until those moments between finding Nikki in the ocean of cowgirls lined up to rope a young calf in the rain, who he might have been if horses loped beside him all those years to now. He can't say he'd be brave enough to showcase—in some ways, he could imagine the backstretch as a place perfect for an introverted horseman like himself. How the intimate relationship between man and horse translated to the stables and it was the horse that had to brave the public eye. No substitute for those who were extroverted, like he believed his grandfather to be, who wanted to showcase his talent to the world, like Nikki now, or how he might have imagined his father to weave that same hunger for recognition into owning his own racing operation.

Gwendolyn shook Dwayne back to attention.

"Oh! Nikki's next!"

"Ladies and gents, I hear we have a rookie cowgirl tonight stepping up to the plate. Let's give a warm rodeo welcome to little Miss Nikki from up the road in Fairfield County!"

The crowd screamed and cheered for the new cowgirl.

"Little Nikki, you're gonna nod to that nice cowboy by the chute when you're ready, then you're gonna let that rank calf get a head start, and you're gonna ride that cute red horse after him 'til you rope 'em, and then you're gonna stop your horse to let the calf break away. You got this, cowgirl—let's go!"

Nikki lined up in the box and Easy started prancing; shifting his weight from front two feet to back two feet with each roar from the crowd.

"What's happening? Nikki OK?" Gwendolyn asked.

"Easy's hyped up. Nikki's got her intensity up. She's ready. He's telling her he's ready."

Finally, all four feet on the ground, Nikki's exhale visible in the stands. She nodded and the chute flung open to release the calf, who blasted out into the arena.

"Alright, little Nikki, get after it! Let's show her we're rooting for her!"

Nikki pushed Easy out of the pen and kicked, increasing Easy's speed after the calf.

"Give him his face! Let him open up!" Dwayne said. He saw Sonny come into his view from the galley. He was up soon for bulldogging but made his way to cheer his girl on.

"Swing the rope! Attagirl!"

Nikki lifted her arm and swung the rope into a loop, pushed the left hand holding the reins further up Easy's neck to give him room to stretch out into the gallop behind the calf.

Nikki swung one more time and released the loop. Dwayne held his breath the millisecond the rope was in the air.

"Sit back! Stop!" he yelled. No way she could hear him above everyone else, but that wasn't going to stop him from trying.

Easy's butt dropped towards the earth and they both slid a few feet before stopping completely.

"What a stop, cowgirl! What a catch! Didn't look like a rookie run to us out here! Way to stop the clock at 8.6 seconds—we still got a lineup of other cowgirls gunning for the bucket, but you're a winner to us! Keep going, kid!"

The crowd chanted her name until Nikki strutted off the field.

Chapter 14

Nikki's first rodeo was like a fever dream. She had never felt a rush like that before, and all she wanted to do was chase that high.

Nothing else mattered. Nikki found herself hungry for the wins of the arena. A small salve against the ways she had felt torn down by school—every day, little chisels picking away at her. Every day, reminders of the peace she found in the company of horses and what it had meant to her to find her herd.

She'd daydream while the hours passed until the school bell rang. And then she'd run to Sonny's place, to Easy, her safe space, partner. She was his herd member. They were emerging on the rodeo scene as a team to watch. Regardless of whether they won, she noticed while walking the grounds after a run, folks would look and point and smile.

But then, all that stopped when the incident happened—after she was escorted off her high school campus by the cops.

Dwayne had been called to come to Nikki's school in the middle of the day on account of an officer had, and he quoted, "removed the threat"—Nikki—from her classroom, and she had resisted, and so the officer had "yoked her up" (another student witness said) while she was still seated. Nikki had grabbed the top of her desk so the cop had lifted both her and the desk into the air, and when Nikki still wouldn't let go, that same student said it was like watching WWE wrestling: the officer swooped her and the desk, and then slammed them both to the floor.

When Dwayne went to ask Nikki about what happened, she still wasn't speaking. She had just looked up and to the left and her lip started to quiver, and it made Dwayne stop all of his inquiries. It didn't matter what happened. It didn't matter to Dwayne what anyone said happened before the officer entered the scene or whatever anyone says the inciting incident was or if Nikki was at fault or not. What mattered was that someone had put their hands on his baby girl, and no one stepped in to stop it. Even thinking about that fact made his blood boil. When the superintendent told Dwayne he was going to send Nikki home for some time, he used lines like "should have known better," and "respect the badge," and tried to use their military service as a point of understanding. "I mean, when Sarge says move, we moved, ain't it?" and tried to chalk it up to *kids these days.*

But Dwayne's refrain: *He put his grown hands on my baby.*

That's all he said to the news anchor who stormed him that afternoon outside of the school, on the day it all went down. The day he became a parent of a police brutality case. And when they asked, he told them firmly that no, they could not interview Nikki. That's the least he could do to protect her; shield her from the intrusive lens of a camera, and from a journalist who was surely going to ask what his child had done or not done or how she had gotten in that predicament. It was very clear that everyone—even the Black superintendent—expected him to discipline Nikki for causing a scene, for getting suspended, for "making" that officer do what he had done.

After that, walking around Fairfield County, rather than greeting Nikki with a smile, like folks did after her rodeo début, they pointed and shook their heads. So, Nikki retreated to the solace of Sonny's barn and let a few rodeos pass her by.

After a couple of months of keeping a low profile, Sonny finally convinced her to sign up for a small local rodeo over in Blackstock, South Carolina. It would be a little space from the big, bright lights. Some same players, sure, but an audience who might not know any of the drama floating above her like a rain cloud. Nikki agreed. No one imagined the same news anchors would cover that rodeo. But of course, they would: it was the Midlands of South Carolina.

"We know you've been having some trouble at school, but you seem to excel in the rodeo arena. Did you always ride horses, or come from a family of horsemen?"

The woman holding the microphone shoved it into Nikki's face. Nikki smiled, thinking it reminded her of an ice cream cone, and that was how she focused during the interview, imagining one thing for another. She looked up and to the left, her nervous tic, one she used in place of blurting out the first thought that came to mind. When she was put in counseling after the incident, the woman in the big chair across the room suggested she take a deep breath, think of an appropriate answer, then respond. So much of Nikki's having been misunderstood stemmed from how quickly her thoughts came to her and then how quickly the words passed to her lips. She had thought them before they were spoken out loud, but she hadn't considered who would be the recipient of those thoughts, and the woman she was mandated to sit opposite from, weekly, had told her to consider who she would be in conversation with. When she and Sonny were preparing for this news interview, scheduled to happen just after her first rodeo event of the day, Nikki told herself to consider her answer before she just blurted out any old thing.

"I don't know, really," Nikki started, feeling her heart pump in her ear, chest tighten. It was funny, she had more adrenaline thinking about what she was going to say on live television than when she was in the arena in the box, waiting for the steer to rocket out of the chute and for her and Easy to track and rope it in record time with Sonny. She cleared her throat, realizing then that she hadn't answered either question. Dwayne was right at the edge of her vision; she could see him clearly without it looking like she was looking away from the news anchor. He had made a circle motion with his finger, *keep going.*

"I mean, I didn't grow up with horses, but my dad's best friend, I call him Uncle Sonny, he had some horses and one day, I came over and he just let me ride them. Said I was a natural. So, I kept riding, and working with him and his horses, and then I did some rodeos last fall, and here I am again," Nikki said.

She adjusted her hat on her head, which was more of a secondary nervous tic, rather than that her hat needed any straightening. Something she got from Sonny. He'd say his few short words in greeting or goodbye, then reach up with his free hand—whichever wasn't holding a rope or reins—and grab the crown of his hat and lift it off his head and set it back down.

At first, Nikki wondered why he ain't just wave? It was near the same gesture: bent elbow raised away from the torso. Nikki had asked him why he was always reaching for his hat and he shrugged. Said it was a habit he got from his daddy who got it from his daddy and so on *until the beginning of time.* He explained when it got to him, probably the context changed over the generations—like maybe, back when his grandaddy did it when the whites was being territorial and such, he had taken the hat all the way off, how you do at prayer or the Pledge at the rodeos. They removed any shadows from the face so folks could see their eyes, know their intentions.

Sonny had told Nikki that afternoon in further explanation about the hat gesture, that one day when his daddy was about her age, a woman said a Black man with beady eyes had looked her up and down like he was undressing her. A woman everyone called Miss Mary was passing by when it was all going down, and she had lifted her hand to the crown of her own head and reached up, as if she was wearing a ten-gallon hat herself. It was only then that this boy everyone called Bubba got the memo and quickly moved his hat so the shadow cleared his brow. But by then, the white woman was already hollering, and no one saw Bubba after that. His horse, his saddle, and his palm hat was gone the next morning. No one blamed him when he disappeared under the cloak of night, leaving no note no trace no nothing. Everyone knew what woulda happened if he had stayed. So Sonny say that's why he lifts, not tips, his hat—out of habit and maybe fear, his nervous tic too. And so when the local news anchor started asking all them questions, Nikki looked up and to the left and then she moved to lift her hat, but stopped and just pushed it further over her eyes instead while she thought the best way to respond.

Dwayne tried his best to smile through the questions and Nikki's answers. When she had first answered "I don't know," Sonny had turned to him with his look like, *You see what you doing to her?* Dwayne just shook his head: *Not now, not now.* After Nikki's record run back in Newberry, when the interviewers asked permission to showcase Nikki ("We just don't see Black cowgirls!"), the news anchor also asked Dwayne if he had wanted to be interviewed. He thought back to how different that energy had been from the encounter he had with the journalist outside of Nikki's school. After the officer had put his hands on Dwayne's baby girl.

How different it had been from the first rodeo, cheering Nikki on, with Gwendolyn, in the pouring rain. How no dream of theirs could have brought them to that moment, and yet there they all were. So when the news spread like wildflowers across the stations that a Black girl was suspended because of failure to comply with the SRO's demands, it was a surprise to everyone—especially Dwayne and Nikki—that instead of checking in, Gwendolyn began to grow more distant.

The thread was already loosening since her and Dwayne's official separation and Nikki expressing her desire to live the majority of her time with her father in Fairfield County, and not in Columbia, where Gwendolyn had moved. It was supposed to be a weekdays/weekend setup, but between the demands of the rodeos, practicing for the rodeos, and general disinterest in the arrangement, Nikki adopted an irregular schedule.

When they had finally decided enough was enough, and the separation this time would be final, they had promised they would try everything they could to not let it impact Nikki's life, even though of course it had. She had two houses. Had to be taken between one house and the other every other weekend. The house Gwendolyn had left but that Nikki grew up in, with its proximity to Sonny's place, was, of course, her preferred place to be. There was land, the outside. Horses down the road. Gwendolyn had moved to the outskirts of Columbia into an apartment complex that had popped up in the last few years; comfortable for her, and she had made sure to get two bedrooms so Nikki would have her own space when she came, but that was about it. There was a pool, but it had shut down after the young boy drowned that first summer they got there and no one had it in them to push the property owner to reopen it. So Gwendolyn was hyperaware that there wasn't much for Nikki to do at her place, and that she had more independence with Dwayne, so she had tried to find things for them to do together outside of her apartment.

Every time Gwendolyn would bring Nikki back, though, it seemed as though they both were relieved to be free of each other. It was hard to tell if it was the breakup or the tension of this growing mother-daughter warfare as a girl starts turning towards womanhood, but Dwayne was thankful that he had a buffer in Sonny when Nikki was with him. But the incident at school pushed Gwendolyn over an edge no one knew existed; how could she not see that there was a system designed for Nikki to get caught up in—no matter what she did? She was a broken record: *I didn't raise a child to be like that.* Everyone tried to show her that she hadn't, that Nikki *wasn't* like whatever version she was seeing against whatever version of a perfect child Gwendolyn had built up in her head.

The biggest blow, though, was when Nikki announced that she did not want to go back to school—that school, or any school—because everyone knew her as the girl who got slammed to the floor by a school cop. Gwendolyn all but threw up her hands and walked away from it all.

Sympathetic to Nikki's desire to be shielded from an environment that did not let her thrive, Dwayne was the one who ultimately honored Nikki's ask. How could he not, given all that she'd gone through? When he was deployed, some of his brothers were married with school-aged children, and when they were in the thick of

Operation Desert Storm and no one knew when they would return home, many of the wives said it was that uncertainty that pushed them to homeschooling—one less variable to manage as a mother, alone. All those years listening to other men serving with him recount the journeys of their wives and how they felt like they were single parents and how they navigated it all, and who knew Dwayne would draw upon their stories later?

And then, Gwendolyn did walk away, for the most part. There was no way for Dwayne to anticipate how personal Gwendolyn would take it all—the incident itself, the fallout, Nikki advocating for her own future—or that she really would one day drop Nikki off at Dwayne's house on a weekend that was not his weekend, and start going about living her life—with only so much left of her daughter in it. Only now popping in to see her here and there. But isn't that what they say? You live your life so much in search of your original wound, you end up feeling like you married it?

Since he was pretty singular in the big decisions concerning his daughter's welfare, he would let Nikki choose what would be next for her life—'cause she was the one living it.

||||||||||||||||||

The deal was that Nikki would have to find something to give herself over to, a trade, if she was opting out of school. In a perfect world, Nikki would have chosen a more objective trade like he had: small-engine repair. When he had chosen the path for his life at a not dissimilar juncture, after his grandfather died and he had watched Ms. Mozell count out how many spoons of beans there were, and then herself not eat, Dwayne had to consider what his vocation would be that was not horses. Horses were too hard for him to consider after all his losses. He remembered the rainy afternoons with his grandfather tinkering with all the farm machinery—the tractor, the mower, the chainsaw, and whatnot.

"To be a farmer, you can't choose the one thing," Moses would say every so often, so much it became a comfort and Dwayne stopped finishing the statement but let him tell it whole: "You have to master the heavens, the earth, the rocks and the metals, the deaths and the births."

For Dwayne, tinkering was metal mastering and seemed the most controlled of all of the elements that come with farming. Your talent—and as such, your ability to name your price—was indisputable. Either you could resurrect a long-dead tractor, or you couldn't. Everything else was subjective and conditional: Folks had to find value in how you trained horses by their ability to ride them. And so on. So, to be a horseman for others, you had to translate what you might want in a fully trained horse, knowing all that you know, into a horse that anyone could ride, not at all knowing who will eventually ride them or what that rider might know. So, whoever ends up on the other end of a horse having been trained by you and what they think of your skill depends on the buyer and not you. Crop farmers got the weather and seasons and whether or not you can amend your earth. Livestock folks got weather and seasons; price of grain, disease, predators, breeding moons, all. Metal masters got their tools and all that knowledge in the brain. After all he wanted, that's what Dwayne chose to bet his fortune on. And so even when they went over to Sonny's, he'd tinker with some metal, hoping Nikki would be attracted to it, maybe by osmosis kind of how he was. Instead, she could not resist the earthen wheat-grain smell of horse dander, pulling her towards them like gravity.

Dwayne wasn't surprised when she asked if she could see if

Uncle Sonny would show her how to do horses better . . . which was different from her sneaking and running after school for the thrill of a pony ride or to hear the nicker of Easy across the pasture as she waved a carrot or a core-soft apple. No. She wanted intention. And study. And depth. *To know* as well as *to do.* And Sonny, more ingrained in that space, had connections and did not come with an ocean of hurt so big as to live a life as though it never happened.

Nikki was asking more than to have the bus drop her off at Sonny's after school, because she was asking for no more school. It took two weeks for Mrs. Esther to understand that she no longer needed to stop at the end of their drive in the morning for pickup, but she slowed down and honked the bus every morning until summer break. Nikki actually woke up earlier now, because Dwayne had passed the morning chores on to her, before she headed out to Sonny's: Feed Butter, their outside orange tabby mouser who always made his way to the back steps just in time for her to drop a sausage link and refresh his water. She knew he also drank from the creek and just about anywhere he found it fresh, but Nikki also wanted to make sure he had it at the house. After Butter was the chicken coop, and King, the guardian dog. She had to drop the scratch, and then scooped out some fresh ground pork to top King's kibble—a full belly keeps him on vigil of flock protection and not licking his lips at the juicy egg-layers. She stuffed whatever she could find in the fridge or pantry into her mouth and then she could set out for Sonny's.

The first day of her new arrangement, Nikki idled around the pasture, twirling her fingers in Easy's hair. He had met her at the fence like always, but both of them cocked their head at an angle. What to do with a whole day, not just the sliver of daylight at the end of one? When it was only waning-light hours of the day, Nikki got to enjoy the spoils of an already-fed horse. Sonny put out their oats and corn at seven A.M. and three P.M. He said he liked to give horses time to digest their food before nightfall because that's when horses don't want to move as much and as the temperatures drop, that's how you get a colic on your hands.

Nikki looked around for signs of Sonny milling about on the farm, and didn't see any. She walked over to the shed where the feed and tack was, figuring he'd be there. When she got closer, she heard rustling in the back and called out to Sonny so as not to startle him.

"Yeh. I'm back here. Might as well stay where you at," Sonny answered her call. "I'm coming 'round with something big and scary."

Nikki stepped back. Asked what it was. Sonny emerged from the brush that backed up to the shed carrying a metal rake with a big snake dangling between the tines.

Sonny jabbed the rake and caught the snake quickly in Nikki's direction and chuckled, attempting to elicit a fright. Nikki double-checked its markings then reached out to unwrap and let the snake creep up her arm like a tree branch, probably no different from the branch it fell out of.

Sonny smirked. "I shoulda known a girl who runs around a farm barefoot, who used to catch caterpillars and fishing worms, wouldn't be 'fraid of no rat snake."

Nikki held the three-foot length of the snake between both hands. She knew, if frightened, it would start to coil, and even if nonvenomous, still had teeth that could bite. She jabbed it near Sonny, chuckling, and he took a step back.

"Watch it now, youngin," Sonny said, shaking his finger at her and also the snake. "Put that thing far out in the field behind the barn if you want him to live." He pointed just over Nikki's left shoulder. She nodded her head in agreement and turned in the direction of the cornstalks that were only to her knees—slow growth for these late June days.

"And then what, Uncle Sonny? I come to start working with you with the horses, not snake trappin'," Nikki called back on her way to set her new friend free.

When she returned, Sonny was standing next to two large metal cans and at his feet were ten feed buckets. Nikki knew he had more horses than Easy and Patriot, but honestly only had eyes for Easy since the day he let her climb atop his back when she hopped out the school bus, so the sight of the ten buckets seemed a surprise. She raised her eyebrows. Sonny handed her a scoop what looked like a mix between a metal spade and an empty beer can.

"Everybody gets a scoop of oats from here," he said, tapping the metal can closest to him. "Easy, Patriot, Remi, and What's-His-Name get one scoop of corn." He looked up to the rafters of the shed for a moment. Nikki knew not to interrupt so she just started to unstack the feed buckets and then waited. "Ace. That's it. I wanted to say Spade—I knew it had something to do with cards. Anyway, Ace is here for training, so he's in work. So is Remi. You'd run the oats off Easy, so I upped his ration, and Patriot needs extra for all the hours he's carrying me or dragging them growing colts off in pasture trying to teach them some manners." Nikki hummed, signaling she was listening while working. She glanced up to meet Sonny's eyes for good measure.

He walked to the other side of the shed, about seven steps, or the size of a two-car garage. Nikki watched him run his hand over the bales of hay stacked in the corner. He picked up a straw with a little flower and leaf on the end and stuck it in the corner of his mouth. It dangled like a cigarette while he talked, explaining that his pastures were big, and sprigged with Bahia and Bermuda grasses and that summertime that was enough forage for horses, but again for the ones in work, and for the horses in winter when the grass is dormant and gray, he fed fescue—the piece dangling from the right corner of his mouth.

"But do not under any circumstances take this to the field with the colts and broodmares. That's how you cause abortions. With fescue. My man Russell brings me round bales of Bermuda for the winter, so you only got to know our horses and the ones in work get this."

Nikki stood up straight. "Our horses?" She smirked at the clarifying question. Sonny sucked his teeth.

"You know good and well the fit you'd throw if anyone besides you rode Easy, like you haven't claimed him. Hell, somedays I feel like *I* gotta ask your permission to ride 'im."

"You can ride him!"

"See, that's exactly what I'm talking 'bout! I won't asking and here you go, lording over me with my own horse I raised from the day he dropped onto this here green earth."

Nikki started to gather the buckets and called out, "I think I hear Easy asking for his breakfast, which I better do if we gone work him today."

"We using him and Patriot to check fences. It'll be too hot to do much else by the time we get to saddling. Mr. Buck wanted me, I mean us, to come help cut out some cattle to take to weigh and inspect and then load up to take to the sale up in Laurens, but since we got a late start today"—Sonny looked at the buckets in her hand. He twirled the straw of fescue in his mouth—"told him we'd be there first thing in the morning if he'd let us practice some roping before we cut, sorted, and shipped them out. You up for that? Gotta be here before the sun's up, then we feed, catch our mounts, saddle here, then trailer over to his place before the sun gets too far over the pines. I promised Mr. Buck we wouldn't sweat his steers out too much—you know, keeping they water is money—but I also know you and Easy need time on some cows before the next fall rodeo if you want to get in the buckle territory."

Nikki repeated the term "buckle territory" and lilted her voice up, a question.

"Winning circle," Sonny answered.

Chapter 15

"My hands are really starting to callus up like yours and Uncle Sonny's," Nikki said, twisting each hand left and right at the wrist like a spatula flipping burgers on a grill. "Mama would die if she saw 'em. She already say I wanna be a boy so this would really send her. Maybe I'll get my fingernails painted pink, then."

Nikki laughed and held her hand across the dinner table and wiggled her fingers towards Dwayne as if already lacquered.

They had both finished their dinner of steak tips and potatoes. Nikki had added a salad, hearing her mother's voice in her ear droning on and on about a balanced plate. Protein the size of a fist, a starch, a veggie. It had frustrated Nikki to no end to always think of her food as a slate of—how did the pamphlet say it?—checks and balances; good energy and bad energy. It had started a while back when she was still in school. One day she had been sitting at home after class in between sports seasons, and the next she was accompanying her mother to a "nutrition meeting," which was in a small shopping center next to the Bi-Lo not far from where she knew her cousin Mika lived in Columbia.

They checked in to a front room with a scale by the folding table. In her little pocketbook that she used mostly for these trips of "going into town" with her mother, Nikki kept the folded cardstock with weekly sections: a place for a date, a place for the receptionist to write the number that appeared on the scale when she stepped on it, and then a place for a plus or minus sign. For the most part, Nikki was thankful that the receptionist—also herself a member—didn't call the number out, but Nikki knew when folks had a good week. The receptionist would smile or say she had to know their secret. But if it was the end of a bad week she would say something in a small voice, like a mouse, and slowly hand their pamphlet back, offering only: "See you in the meeting."

Nikki hadn't asked to participate in this program, but it was one of the things she and her mother would do during their weekends together in Columbia. Fancy things like mani-pedis. Thrifting. Shopping at Village at Sandhill's. Grabbing a coffee at Books-A-Million and flipping through the rows of magazines in the back, after having browsed her favorite book sections to see if anything new was put out since the last visit.

They'd have lunch at Andy's Deli, and even though she wanted to have the roast beef sandwich with the special creamy sauce, her mother would say, without looking up from the menu, "Maybe we should get a salad, huh?" and Nikki would flat-lip smile in resignation and order the Big Greek when the waitress returned with their two waters with lemon. Nikki was conflicted most often because it was over meals that they caught up with what was happening in each other's worlds, but with the addition of the weekly meetings the meals became hyper-focused on food, whether she should have asked for salad dressing on the side or not. Thankfully her mother never asked to see her weigh-in card, but she would ask if Nikki had a plus or minus week. Nikki convinced herself that sitting through the hour meeting was a minor inconvenience compared to the rest of the activities they would find to do on a Saturday in Columbia.

When those days ended, though, after the incident and everything about their relationship had changed, it was the small things that still lingered: adding a salad to her father's cooked meals; trying to find ways to remind herself that she was once a girl who liked "girlie things" like nail polish and lip gloss. Things she actually did have in common with her mother, despite their differences.

That was then. Another life, almost. These days, working at Uncle Sonny's, whatever problem her mother saw fit to address with those meetings literally had melted away, even if the small residue of diet culture reared its head from time to time. For the most part her mother's efforts were irrelevant because she now shuffled sixty-pound hay bales across the acreage, picked pastures and stalls daily, and trucked full wheelbarrows of manure across the farm to the big pile cooking between the pokeweeds, tall as pines. The last time she saw her mother, Gwendolyn looked her up and down before embracing her and asked, "What's your secret?," not unlike the receptionist at the nutrition meetings. Nikki rolled her eyes.

"Oh, just living outside, doing farm stuff," Nikki answered, then slimmed her sides. A knee-jerk reaction to the years of thinking of her physical appearance, how she tried to make herself small, or even invisible in the days after the incident. How those were the kinds of things that drove a wedge between her and her mother.

In her therapy sessions, the woman across the room once asked Nikki to think about any other times Gwendolyn might have shown a distancing to her or her father.

There was a time they tried to work it out, for her, and they all lived under one roof. But when she thought in the small silence between question and her answer, Nikki saw her mother leave the house for hours at a time, and no one knew where she went. But everyone could guess: into town. Gwendolyn had made her current disdain for Fairfield County loud and clear as often as she could until she left it, and everyone saw it coming. She had made the move to Columbia before, when they all thought it was a phase, but when she moved out of Dwayne's place and into her own in Columbia, even with the chore of ferrying Nikki back and forth up the interstate or Highway 21, everyone knew this time was permanent. And then time had passed and the energy with which Gwendolyn gathered Nikki each weekend had dissipated little by little, and Nikki would be sitting in her room and hear her mother pull into the yard in front of the house and sit in the car. Sometimes, it would be for more than an hour.

"No one ever talked about what was really going on inside," Nikki said one day to her therapist. Though the sessions were recommended in the days immediately post-incident, when it seemed Nikki was going to try to find her way back to school, she kept going to therapy even when she decided she wasn't going to return. "So I didn't learn to talk about how I felt on the inside. I get so mad about something, then I just—"

The woman put her pen down and rested her other hand on top. "Shut down?" she asked. Nikki nodded.

"Like that morning. You were mad or upset at the lesson. Processing what the teacher was saying, so you shut down then, too?"

If you really asked her to recall what had happened before she found herself on her back, she couldn't. Eventually, Nikki and her therapist landed on it was her body's way of trying to protect itself.

According to her friends, who offered without asking, Nikki had made an audible moan of disgust when the teacher had said something snarky. The teacher turned to her and asked if she had something to contribute? She sighed again. The teacher said if she was so tired she should have stayed in bed. Nikki rolled her eyes, and of course that set off the teacher's attitude, talking about respect, how she had none, and maybe, if Nikki were to guess with the information about that day that she had been given because she truly didn't recall, she had said something snarky back to the teacher, and the class must have laughed. And then, instead of handling the issue teacher to student, the teacher must have called the resource officer, Mr. Harris, who had conveniently followed them from her elementary school to middle school to Winnsboro High School. Many parents saw the consistency as a point of comfort. Mr. Harris had even sung "Greatest Love of All" at Nikki's fifth-grade graduation, saying the children were the future, and stood behind them at class pictures. Her mother, even, remarked at the idea that sure, there had been increased incidents of resource officer violence in schools across the county, and around Columbia, but it had only happened to "bad" kids, the rough ones. Besides, Gwendolyn had tried to reason until she no longer tried to reason, she had introduced herself to Mr. Harris and made Dwayne introduce himself, too, "so he can see Nikki comes from a good family, even if a separated home," or whatever justification she had made back when Nikki was in elementary school. And wasn't it a good thing the resource officer had followed the kids those years because then they didn't have to do the introductions all over year after year?

"But you know those resource officers are either cops who need to step down after a bad situation or they are honorable discharges from the military?" Dwayne countered often, almost any time the topic of police presence in schools was brought up. He was adamant that servicemen who couldn't hang with the demands of service not seek similar state-structured jobs, but the way they had introduced resource officers over time, folks really didn't associate one with the other. Even with the billy club dangling from the waist. Even with the not-concealed weapon. He had sang Whitney Houston to the kids who had hugged him after they received their fifth-grade graduation diplomas and moved their little tassels from the left to right side of their little caps.

"You don't hear me when I tell you how hard I work to not bring the desert home," Dwayne once said, loudly, in the middle of an argument with Gwendolyn when word made its way that Mr. Harris had pushed a kid a little too hard, and he went on his tirade again about how there just shouldn't be cops in schools. That was just before Mr. Harris moved to high school kids. Gwendolyn had said something to the effect of how kids aren't made the same anymore, more mouthy, more looking for things to get into—more things *to* get into.

"And yet, here you go thinking it's the one kid—our kid—and not the system," Dwayne would continue to push, his voice and hands raising. "When a system buys into a Black kid as the threat, won't matter what they do or don't do. Breathing would be enough of an offense."

Gwendolyn shook her head. Pushed back. "The resource officer is Black, 'Wayne. He's Black."

"The officer could be purple, but all they see is the enemy and they been trained the enemy is anything but white. Don't matter who *they* are."

"How's that work, huh? Wouldn't they attack themselves?"

Dwayne said something under his breath. Then cleared his

throat, "Don't you see the news stories about the Black undercovers getting assaulted or more? How he deals with himself when he looks in the mirror after he does what he does is surely a mystery to me."

"I just—" Gwendolyn started and looked at Nikki. "I just can't imagine a child who was raised right to find themselves in the crossfires. They would have to have *done something.*"

Nikki told her therapist that *this* was the biggest fissure that drove them apart—her mother's belief that kids who find themselves in the locked jaws of the police must have brought it on themselves. At first she thought it was because she was spending more time at Sonny's. That horses were taking over all of her free time. That may have been what started the crack, sure, but it was this belief her mother held that widened the chasm between them.

"I didn't do nothing" was all Nikki said to anyone who asked.

"And no one ever asked what had been done to you," the therapist responded. Nikki nodded.

"Daddy was the only one who believed me. The only one."

PART III

2014

Chapter 16

Nikki squinted her eyes as she tilted her head to the sky. She filled her stomach with each breath through her nose and released through her pursed lips like she was cooling her breakfast grits. Her "reaction breathing exercise." That was how this method of controlled breathing found its way to her, but she discovered even in moments like today, when she didn't think she was particularly anxious, she could unconsciously pull the air from around her into her center, hold it, then release.

It was a robin's-egg-blue-sky day with puffs of clouds occasionally moseying in front of the sun. Thankfully, this time of year, it wasn't a punishing sun. That's why she smiled—she didn't mind being out at the cemetery placing flags on graves with her father.

Nikki turned to him after her third deep breath: "Seems like the sun always shines on days some folks might feel as though it's raining inside them. Like today." She held a handful of miniature American flags fashioned on small skewer-like pieces of wood and pierced the ground next to the tombstone of SP4 Wilson Davis,

Vietnam War. Her father stood up at her observation, having been kneeling for so much time she saw that he was now walking with a limp.

"That's God's way of clearing the way for us to celebrate our patriotic angels, and do this honor with love, not resentment, like maybe we would feel the weight of it all if we were out here and it was raining," Dwayne said.

He was right. They had done this every Memorial Day for as long as she could remember. And every time they set out to place flags, it would be bright and shiny, no matter what the weather station predicted. Even if they were caught in a monsoon later. Always, for this ritual, the sun was out.

Dwayne had said "this honor" was like a penance served before the grills were pulled from underneath their tarp covers, or sometimes, before trekking down to Lake Wateree. Dwayne had looked up one day and proclaimed to almost anyone who would listen how it was such a shame that there were generations of folks growing up these days who say that the last Monday in May was the "unofficial start of summer," and not what he believed in his heart his ancestors set out for it to be: a day to honor those who had perished—during service to country.

So, he dragged Nikki to their local cemetery in Fairfield County, and once the National Cemetery at Fort Jackson opened to burials, they folded drives down to Columbia into rotation some years.

"What's worse is it seems like folk moved the date to late May because the first day, May 1, 1865, started getting wrapped up in maypoles and cakewalk dances."

Nikki smiled, because May Fest had been one of her favorite moments in school. Her mother would bake her famous German chocolate cake for the cakewalk, and when she walked down the halls the whole week before the big day all the teachers—even the ones she never had in classes—would stop and ask if her mother was baking *her* cake? She was an important somebody. As a result, Nikki got a whole sleeve of tickets for free to use at the school fair. One time she played the cakewalk and Ms. Littman pulled her aside and smiled. "Wouldn't it be more fair to let everyone else play? You can get your mama's cake at home," and so Nikki used her tickets on face paint, cotton candy, and some ride that was hollowed-out rain barrels with wheels attached and linked together and pulled by a tractor 'round the bus pickup lane.

Her father was right. If you just looked at how her school had celebrated May Fest, there was no indication for why this day existed at all. The town square would erect a pole higher than a light pole and attach from the top of it large pieces of ribbons to dance the maypole at will. Word was her Aunt Weesie won Miss May Fest back in the day, wearing this bright chick-yellow dress that sloped off her shoulders. It was corset-tight at the waist and had waterfalls of frills that spilled out from the bow in the back of the whole dress. (No, she was not really Nikki's aunt, but that was what she was told to call Weesie because "cousin" didn't feel reverential enough.)

Anyway, in the photo Nikki saw once—because it was black-and-white she couldn't capture the way the family talked about how the seamstress had used thread that had a line of gold through it—it was like Aunt Weesie shined that day. The glare from the sun drowned out whatever recognition the sash might have conferred, and there was a winner's bouquet of yellow roses. Thinking about that photo, Nikki laughed. Won't no indication at all that this holiday, capped off with a beauty pageant and a game to win cakes, started out as a way to honor and mourn the soldiers lost to the battlefield. No. It was a picture of Aunt Weesie at fourteen and she was there because her mama had dragged her to Fairfield County's May Fest activities because it was 1951 and there won't no way Weesie wasn't beautiful enough to win, but Columbia's May Fest was still for whites only. So for cultural events like this the family gathered up the road.

Nikki continued to place her flags at the graves, and had placed four more flags next to tombstones, walking each row methodically, looking for mentions of military service. Her father was two rows north of her and about six plots down, so she had to raise her voice above a library whisper, which, for whatever reason, was always the level she adopted near the dead—inside or out.

"Did that May Fest get it right?" she hollered.

A family pulled up in a white Pontiac. Five penny-brown faces peeled out of the doors; two girls small enough to consider any open field—even pocked with granite headstones—a playfield, two adults, and what must have been the matriarch of them all. Dwayne nodded in their direction, lifted the brim of his Operation Desert Storm cap just ever so slightly off his head in greeting, then fitted it back down. The gentleman, probably around his age or younger, brought his straightened hand to his forehead in salute. His sharp, crisp elbow pierced the sky.

The elderly woman reached her right hand over her heart and bent her head at the neck. She had reminded him of Ms. Mozell. How proud she was of his service, his survival. The few years she lived after his return from Kuwait, Mozell paraded him around town: *My soldier is back whole, y'all.*

He didn't want to think about who she might have been if, having claimed him as her own blood-born son, she had to bury him. So, he was glad in some small way to show his gratitude to her for keeping him all these years as her family by surviving. Coming home. As whole as he could, considering. That's how he had come to think of it. He showed his thanks by being alive. Being her son. And that's how he had come to think of it even more now, having survived her. She never had to bury anyone else she had loved. But he was losing something like a parent, again.

Those last moments with her: she had tried to lift her right arm to her heart, but only made it to her stomach, and said, *Thank you.* What was she thanking Dwayne for? Being a boy she rescued from the flames? A frog in his throat, he shook his head. No, *thank you.* And in that instant, though he never had the occasion to say it, he had thought to say: *Thank you, Mom.* She smiled anyway—the corner of her mouth curled up as best she could. All those years when he had come back, she had been asking and asking when he was going to give her grandbabies, and he kept asking what her rush was?

How could he have known she'd never live to see his girl? But somehow, Ms. Mozell seemed to be in the mix there—as if Nikki had descended from Mozell's line and had caught Mozell's determined and independent spirit on the way into this world.

The woman at the cemetery said out loud in Dwayne's direction, "Thank you for your service, sir," and Dwayne held up a flag in his hand for a moment, brought it down, then turned back to Nikki.

"Even then. Those early May Fests, there won't no real honoring of the ones who served and died. Especially no honoring the Black ones. And we was the ones who started it all. Grandaddy used to say that at least someone would say a prayer at the opening events and mention 'the real reason' for this day, but that happened so lightning-quick. I kinda expect that from the Columbia May Fests, but here," Dwayne pointed to the dirt. "Here, when we know so many of us fought in every single battle and lost so many of our lives for . . . for an idea that didn't even include us, it just feels strange to cut it out."

He brushed some dirt off the headstone that was nearest to his hand while he was talking. The sun was back out from behind the cotton-candy clouds, and lower, right into Nikki's eyes. She had moved closer now.

Later, back at the Spot, Dwayne was unimpressed with the whole setup that Nikki had thrown together hastily for the brothers—a splattering of flags left over from this morning's venture placed in red Solo cups here and there. Someone had pulled out the flag-decorated tablecloth that someone's wife sent with them last Fourth, and another someone placed atop it a bucket with a few longnecks peeking out, and besides that, some bottles of store-brand soda for the folks who were straight-backed on the wagon. There were a few canisters of roasted peanuts left over from a past Saturday gathering, and two bags of chips crumpled like old receipts. It would be a miracle if whole chips remained, Dwayne thought, surveying what had been presented as a cookout. He was glad he had dropped Nikki and gone to the store.

Sure, they had talked it over, the idea of having a cookout, while playing cards Saturday past as a thing to do on Monday, together. They would be together, remembering their gone—both the known gone, the ones on the battlefields with them, and the unknown gone—those who fought in the fields as their forefathers.

This particular holiday ticked away at his heart more than almost any other holiday tasked with highlighting those who fight for country. Veterans Day of course was a county-wide celebration, especially now that they brought it to Fairfield County. The Fourth, with its big fanfare and "Freedom is not free" slogans strewn across town. Before that, Flag Day snuck by practically unnoticed except in the eyes of other veterans and servicemen out and about their days with their caps proclaiming it was this land they defended with their lives, and were blessed enough to come home to.

Dwayne was blessed enough to come home. He tells Nikki that whenever they set out this time of year for their own maundy Monday.

Today, Nikki was more talkative than before, and honestly Dwayne had grown used to not having to fill the day with words or stories, only had the physicality of the rhythm of bending to the earth to set the flag, standing straight to walk to the next grave, and do it again and again—how he followed his grandfather Moses through the corn and soy fields.

He was thankful her talk most often went in a single direction, even though many days he had wished she had learned the art of conversation: pitching ideas and stories and questions across time with another person like a game of badminton. But she was a teenager, and her words and thoughts and stories—almost never any questions—were a stampede on a one-way street that dead-ended with him. He had to gather inertia, and the words and stories, to start the passes back across the net.

Lassoing teen energy was supposed to have been Gwendolyn's job. They had planned it: He'd get the fun years when it was still cool to be a daddy's girl, before hormones would take over. Gwendolyn would swoop in and handle it from there. But now, they were rarely in each other's orbit at all.

And so, Dwayne was left to navigate Nikki's moods that came with those adolescent years. That's how she was outside the Spot, offering Patriot some water because the sun slipped through the pines and the horse was no longer in the shaded place where Sonny had tied him up. Dwayne had only shrugged and said, "Teenagers" when the guys looked at him like *why is she here?* and then pointed outside to Nikki when they peeled in, one by one.

She was with him for the whole day, except when he sent her inside to "spruce the place up" while he ventured out for some vittles before the stores closed early to observe the holiday. Now, looking around at his daughter's attempt at making the Spot "festive," Dwayne was thankful that he had grabbed some seeded watermelons from the guy with the truck just down Highway 21 and halved them—at least their bright red flesh speckled with black would offer additional color to their "collective man cave"—what Nikki called it.

The boys of the Spot had settled into their usual corners of the place: four around a card table, a couple on the couch, a gang of them floating near the refreshments. When the door opened and Nikki floated back in to ask across the way if she could ride Patriot to the barn and pony Easy back, then maybe take Easy out for a trail ride? Both Dwayne and Sonny were at the card table, but it was Dwayne who stirred first. Meaning to look busy or otherwise occupied, and even though no one had called out what would be the game of the evening, Dwayne picked up the stack of cards and cut the deck open and started to shuffle.

"I mean, I think you gotta ask Sonny 'bout all that running around you mean to do with his horse," Dwayne said, turning to Sonny and winking. That girl had been running around with Sonny's horse since the day she first laid eyes on it.

Sonny put his first finger and thumb together and rubbed back and forth near the corner of his mouth. He wasn't a smoker but he was known to walk around with a busy-fidget like a smoker: a piece of hay or straw hung out of his mouth almost to the same effect, and so everyone knew that gesture just then to be him spinning his imaginary straw between his lips before he called out towards Nikki.

"I reckon, yeh. You can gone do that." He winked back at Dwayne, acting like he was even considering saying no, given she never asked in all those hours in all those days since she started being an apprentice of Sonny's, but knew Nikki caught the wink.

Nikki chuckled and asked if they were hillbillies now, out at Green Acres?

Someone from the couch asked her what she knew about that? Nikki said 'cause her daddy old as dirt, before she squealed almost like a wallowing pig and ran off about her business.

Someone huffed, "Teenagers is right," but Dwayne never caught who.

"You *was* raised by someone old as dirt, tho," Sonny offered to Dwayne. Dwayne turned back to the table. He knew immediately what with the timing of Nikki asking about horses and Sonny's reference to his grandfather exactly where Sonny was looking to take the brief pause in the room after Nikki's interruption. Dwayne hedged it by turning attention back to the day. He pointed behind him.

"We got up before the sun and went out to the cemetery to raise some flags for our brothers," he said. Brian Newport, his and Sonny's comrade killed in combat, was the reason Dwayne came back from Iraq and started decorating graves. Even though everyone in the room knew someone lost in battle, Brian was shared among two of them. He looked at Sonny.

"I cleared the weeds off Brian's footstone. Looks like it's been a while since the grass been cut, or else the landscaper ain't keeping up with the May sprout surge," Dwayne said. Sonny looked down at his hands, started to pick his cuticles—another busy-fidget—and hummed in acknowledgment. All those years, and Sonny never went with him, but Dwayne still provided updates. It had been Dwayne that instructed the recovery crew where he saw Brian last. It was Sonny who went back out into the desert on horseback, leading the way. It was Sonny who trekked on with his mount, even after the bigger machines with their armored sides and bullet-proof windows peeled off due to heavy gunfire, having calculated the casualty costs of this single recovery from what was otherwise a successful extraction of a high-value Iraqi target. But Sonny had trekked on—because when they had dropped them into the middle of the desert only fifty-five hours earlier, and given their assignment to go out on horseback in the cover of night, only two of the six of them had ever been on horses. Before they left, it had been Brian who stepped out of the line and proclaimed, "This we'll defend," and pointed to the flag hung up in their barracks and then pointed to the men gathered in the room over the maps, over the bridle leathers, over the artillery. He looked each man in the eyes, and repeated, "This we'll defend." Sonny was the first to nod and offer, "No matter what. Leave no man behind. No matter what."

At the table, Kenny asked who Brian was right at the moment the Spot fell to silence except for the rattle of the window air-conditioning unit coming back on. Dwayne snapped out of the desert, snapped himself off horseback, and centered his body back into Memorial Monday in Fairfield County.

"He went to battle with us," Dwayne said. "We lost him, but Sonny went to go looking for him. Only came back with his body."

Kenny always came to conversations with a bit of levity that everyone said was his defense mechanism for his own war wounds. Every so often he took a misstep. For the most part, it went unchecked. He chuckled, "Yo, you pulled 'em out of the sand and carried 'em out like Forrest Gump?"

Dwayne cut his eyes in Kenny's direction. Sonny still didn't look up from his cuticles. As uncomfortable as it was to talk about Brian, rest his soul, Dwayne was glad that the attention stayed on the aftermath of the event and not the tactics. How they rode horses across the desert dunes into battle. To not defend Sonny left a lot of room for conversation about who exactly knew how to ride horses. Command had made an educated guess: three Black boys from the country in South Carolina born in the 1960s—truly a big chance at throwing a rock and hitting horsemen. At least one. At least one would know the head from the ass, and which way to set it all to ride out. They had struck two among the crew. At the time, it had been years since Dwayne sat on the back of a horse. What was it? More than a decade since his grandfather Moses had perished in the fire? But he was the oldest of his crew, and even Sonny looked up to him, especially when it became known they both had roots in Fairfield County. And of course, Sonny knew horses at the time, too, the way one knows things natural but has a hard time explaining. He had hopped on the back of enough horses and stayed on. He could show. He could help the four other men get atop those wire-thin desert mounts and place their feet exactly where he knew they needed to be.

"If you feel like you're falling," he'd said, tapping the leg of a mounted soldier. "Use your feet. Catch yourself."

Confused, the soldiers, Brian especially, had looked to Dwayne to explain what Sonny meant in plain English. Dwayne had to dig deep to recall the words of his grandfather, but they came back, smooth as a lullaby. He didn't have time to sit in his emerging sorrow with all that was at stake before the men. He didn't have time to ruminate on all he lost that day in the fire. All he walked away from: Horses. A life of horses. He didn't have time to contemplate how he'd have to reach deep to both access the parts of himself whose embers had cooled and died down over the years and to acknowledge the deep grief of it all, resurfacing. This felt different than when he imagined a new life with horses in it with Gwendolyn. "This we'll defend," he said to himself, faced with the task at hand: Get himself and five soldiers onto horseback with their weaponry and tack. Get the asset. Return home. Alive and accounted for. He can put it all back in the root cellar of his forever-longing when the mission was completed. And when he saw Sonny weeping, holding on to Brian's body draped over the horse's withers and saddle as if a ten-point buck, and when he saw the horse even, stranger to them but trusted enough to walk through fire and battle and unknown sands, drag its feet in a line, perhaps also mourning, he knew this part of him would need a fallout shelter within a fallout shelter to keep it contained, and himself protected as he waited out grief's half-lives.

After a few moments of playing with his own cuticles, Dwayne sucked in a full belly of air, tapped the table with the deck of cards and declared, "Well, isn't this the saddest cookout on this side of the Mississippi? Been here all this time and I have yet to feel the crunch of a burned hot dog with a thread of mustard. Let's go fire up the grill and get some fresh air."

Chapter 17

Nikki smelled something burning while she was out riding a new trail that she and Sonny cut only a few weeks ago. There was a thin sliver of a path with a blanket of trees on the left (if you were riding out), and on the right a twenty-foot sheer drop to a small ravine. Certainly different from her usual haunts, this part of the trail tested her mettle and her ability to ride with confidence, and showed the importance of it. Nikki knew that sensing the rider's fear, horses could become unpredictable and dangerous. But growing as a horsewoman meant accepting new challenges. First it was the rodeo scene and competing. Now it was riding out further from Sonny's place alone. Trying new trails.

As she stepped into the ravine pass, smoke entered her nostrils and her heart skipped a beat. Easy lifted his head just then, and she breathed into her belly, rubbed his neck, and gently tapped him along. His slow-moving feet matched the tempo of her rising worry: it had been a dry spring, shaping up to be a drier summer—the pasture crunched under her boots these days whenever she walked across it. Anywhere she went about town it was always something about the weather: How many days it had been since a substantial drenching rain. How much rain was needed to keep up with the planted crops. Estimates on losses. And so on. There was a statewide burn ban; forest fires popping off everywhere. Still, folks burned their trash rather than pay a dump fee, and lit their evening bonfires for the hell of it—don't they know we're all just sitting in the middle of one big kindling bundle here in Fairfield County? All this pine. All this underbrush waiting to catch alight.

Nikki hadn't heard the whistle, crack, or boom of fireworks, so it wasn't fireworks, though too far away from the day to be lingering Memorial Day celebrations. The Towne Center had posted warnings and advisories all over the week before: potential for woods fires from fireworks, bonfires, *and trash burning*—danger. She wasn't too far from the Spot to where she left her father and Uncle Sonny and the rest of their crew, but she'd have to get to the other side of this tight pass then turn around and would have to do it with utmost confidence. She was breathing with her shoulders and with each tight breath, Easy tightened.

Sing a song, Uncle Sonny would say, after telling her to correct her breaths. *You can't worry and sing, so just sing a song.* All that occupied her brain just then was if she was going to be caught out on the trails trapped by a brush fire. What song accompanies that? She picked a nursery rhyme to hum—even solo in the woods she felt too silly to make such a noise, but the humming still had a similar effect. Easy lowered his head. So she relaxed her own shoulders and kept walking back to the Spot, but it was also the direction of the smoke smell.

Nikki asked Easy for a stop. She had thought she heard the

sound of more footfalls above the crunch of the fallen leaves and pine needles under Easy's feet. It wasn't fall, but the woods thirsted so that the trees dropped leaves and nettles to save themselves. Though he had stopped walking, the crunch sound kept on—like an echo. *What now?* Nikki had crossed these trails morning and dusk, sure, with Uncle Sonny, but no one had ever found their way back here. She guessed it could have been a deer—all of the animals acting like it was Freaky Friday every day of this early long drought with high temperatures close to a heat wave. Dwayne saw the chickens had stopped laying eggs a few days ago and Uncle Sonny remarked Patriot—ever the horsey gentleman—at first tried to run away rather than be caught, and once haltered, nibbled on Sonny's belt loops and T-shirt while Sonny bent over tending to his monthly hoof care. He was ornery and bad-tempered. It was the heat. Everyone blamed the heat that made animals do things out of the ordinary, so it would be of the times for a deer to come marching out into the open at three P.M. though they were a strict dawn–dusk crew—leaping from the weeping love grass when Nikki was out for chores.

Squinting her eyes to try to discern, Nikki started humming *merrily merrily merrily* when Easy started his narrow prancing—standing still in the middle of the trail, an indication something should be watched for. Ears pricked forward, he snorted, looked around, trying to locate his rider's search to know where to place his increasing worry. She ticked him forward, remembering her reason for turning around, and then caught movement out the corner of her eye: an amber animal body began emerging from what looked like a new path that opened onto this one, and then finally she saw it clearer—a horse. A rider. Someone she recognized—it was Chris, a boy from school, in her last history class. She had seen him hanging on the edge of the arena at every rodeo. When he had fully emerged from the woods, he nodded in greeting. Lifted his hat and wiped his brow with a bandanna then stuffed it back in his back pocket.

"You ride?" Nikki asked. It was all she could think to ask, still waiting for her heart rate to simmer down so she could process someone being out in her woods, much less someone she knew, and also on horseback.

"Yes ma'am. I guess it seems so."

"What's with the 'ma'am' talk?" Nikki scoffed.

Chris lifted a hand, half-shrug. "Country-boy habit, I guess. You a lady, you get 'ma'am.' How it's been taught to me." He ticked his horse fully onto the established trail. Nikki and Easy backed up a couple steps.

"I'm trying to—" Nikki started.

"—I'm sorry, you know," Chris interrupted whatever Nikki was trying to say. They both stopped, waiting for the other to start back.

"Sorry about what?"

"What happened to you at school," Chris said. That was nowhere she was expecting his "sorry" to go. Apologize for making her skin jump off her bones in the middle of the woods, sure.

"What do you have to be sorry about?" It was a knee-jerk response. She looked in the direction of the smoke . . . further down the trail. "You weren't even there."

Chris nodded. Grabbed his bandanna again. Nikki was a broken record. "What do you have to be sorry about?" The change in her voice brought Easy's head back up. His ears pricked towards Chris and his horse now.

No one had apologized to her, now that she thought about it.

The school, after weeks of retribution and investigating, found a trail of incidents in Officer Harris's employment history, and out of the blue called Nikki up to offer her a seat back with her class in the fall. In therapy, Nikki considered she could see it like an apology? Still, no one had ever said the words. Not like this. She wiggled in the unease of hearing "I'm sorry," and Easy took it as a sign to move forward. She corrected his feet, and pulled him back into the place she had asked him to halt.

"You heard about them stories coming out of the correction facility in Columbia? The one where the man turned up dead in his cell? The officers tried to clean it up, but the body tell the story what happens to it, every time. Don't even got to study science to know that. Just watch a half episode of *Law & Order.*"

Nikki chuckled at what Chris had said, then quickly fixed her face.

"It's OK. Anyway. That man in there that was killed was my uncle. They rounded him up on some nonviolent charge and we had tried to scrape up some pennies to get him out, but he had to wait for his trial. They kept pushing the date, pushing the date."

Nikki interrupted him this time. "I'm sorry." Made a loud sniffing sound. After some silence, she started again with a new subject. "I'm trying to see where the smoke is coming from."

Chris took his hat off. Wiped his brow again.

"Maybe you wouldn't be so hot with that long-sleeve shirt on," Nikki pointed. He lifted the corner of his mouth. Then breathed deep.

"Red oak burning. We're in pine woods. Any oak in here not big and dried enough for that. That smoke is cured oak wood. That's cooking fire. Somebody 'bout to eat good."

Nikki's shoulders relaxed. She loosened her rein grip. Of course. Memorial Day was a good day for a cookout. For some, the start of the cookout season. Burn notice be damned.

"They're all the same," Nikki said. Chris squinted, calculating where she had jumped into the convo.

"Cops," Nikki clarified. "They don't care about us." She had finally said it out loud.

"Sure don't. Sure don't. The official story, the one they telling the public, is that he died by self-inflicted wounds, but the thing is, the thing they don't account for when they round us up like cattle is more often than not we end up knowing several folks in with us at once."

Cousin Junior. Cousin Mike. Terry. Peter. Chris was right.

"So my uncle's friend finds a way to get word to us that his boy was in the cell across the way pretending to be asleep so he could live another day. But. He saw it. Officer knee to the middle of the back after he was commanded to lay on the ground. Ten minutes. DJ says my uncle flopped around under him like a fish until he didn't. Then the officer put him in the bed and tucked him in like a baby."

"They all the same."

What else was there to say?

"Yeh, so I knew you didn't have to do nothing to get Officer Harris's crazy. We don't hardly ever be doing nothing."

Chris and his horse walked closer to Nikki.

"Wait. You live over here? I thought this my Uncle Sonny's land."

Chris shook his head, smiled. "Probably is. I'm just passing through. I'm about an hour away on horseback, longer when I don't catch this trail. Jet and I meander here and there. He's an old guy who won't quit, so I tack him up and let him walk all over the county."

"Say, why don't you ride in the rodeo?" Nikki asked, remembering how Chris cheered for her after she caught that steer for Uncle Sonny. The crowd was already going wild, but Chris, hanging over the corral panels, screamed, "Go Nikki!," and hearing her name, she turned and saw his clapping and pumping his fist in the air. Before she left, she hadn't considered talking much to him at school. But now she wondered why not? Chris took a deep breath and scratched his horse's wither.

"Oh, this boy is an old retired racehorse. Grandpa says he inherited it from a friend. We 'bout ready to get out of horses altogether what with the cost of everything going up up up."

Nikki nodded. Then she searched through the trees for the sun's position. About ninety minutes left of daylight. Calling off her internal alarm to make her way out of the woods for fear of a brush fire, she allowed herself space to linger, since it seemed Chris was, too, or else he'd have been on his way, having found the path he was looking to connect to. Her lips were dry. She hadn't thought to pack water. But she didn't want to leave now.

Chris hopped off his horse and wrapped some leather around the horse's hooves to keep him close.

"Are you coming back to school?" he asked. Still mounted, Nikki looked down on him as he asked the question.

He reached up his hand in a very gentlemanly way, not that she needed help dismounting, of course, he had to know that. She rode out alone. But his gesture was really an invitation to join him for a pause. Nikki considered.

"Easy is so tall. If I get down, I probably won't be able to get back up."

Chris tilted his head. "How'd you get up there in the first place? Won't born there!"

Nikki chuckled. He sounded a lot older than he was.

"Uncle—well, he's not my uncle, but my daddy's friend—Uncle Sonny has enough stumps and logs and things 'round the barn that are the perfect height." Chris looked around the small clearing in the woods. The heat had cooled enough to allow the cicadas' songs to fill the air. He pointed to a fallen pine just on the edge.

"That looks made just for ya. If not, happy to give you a leg up too," Chris locked his hands together at the knuckles and pretended to lift.

This was the most they had ever spoken, even though, in Nikki's before-times, they had several classes together. Mrs. Esther had picked him up on the bus before her and he always sat near the front and maybe, maybe once he had nodded as she boarded or departed, but she couldn't remember. She smiled to herself as she tried to think what he felt like to her then, in school. Like the Feed & Seed store's fake flowers hanging year-round, maybe: noticeable, but barely. Chris was quiet; unassuming in announcing his presence. Yet here he was, with loads to say. She hadn't answered his initial question or invitation.

Whatever. Nikki swung her leg over to dismount, stumbled a little at the landing, and Chris grabbed her elbow.

"I told my dad that I don't think I could walk into that hellhole again, and he agreed. We are trying some homeschooling modules or something the district sent when he explained, and when the superintendent agreed, it would be best for all parties. I look at it every once in a while, just in case," Nikki said.

Chris had grabbed a bottle of water from his saddlebag. Offered Nikki. She accepted, took a swig and passed it back. Chris asked *in case what?*

"I decide I still want to do the school thing. But this," she lifted the reins, scratched Easy's neck, and he let out a sigh. "This is my school for now."

Chris made a toast motion with the bottle of water. "Amen."

They chatted during the last slivers of light and let the horses graze on what green things they could find. Having quenched their thirst, they offered the horses a palm of water from the bottle. The chuck-will's-widows had started their evening calls through the trees, and a cowbell sounded.

"You hungry? I'm sure there's plenty on the grill if my dad has anything to do with it. You know Sonny? This his horse."

"My people do," Chris said. "I might have met him a few times when he came to do some day work, but I would be out waiting for the bus. We don't do any organized rides or anything. This my pop's horse. He said at his age, and with this old racehorse we have, won't no use in trying to make another horse like him, so he's all we got. Horse-wise. When he goes—" Chris turned, and the horse was giraffe-necked munching the oak leaves off a young sapling. "When he goes, I guess we'll be out of horses."

Nikki, only having just got in with horses, and got in so deeply and assuredly, couldn't imagine a life without them, not now. Not ever.

"I never want to be out of horses," she said aloud. Then looked around at the darkening sky. And after a beat, "I should get back. You're welcome to come."

Chris laced his fingers near her left boot, and she stepped in, and he launched her over Easy's back, just like that, just like Uncle Sonny used to grab her from the bus stop and scoop her into the sky so she knew what flying must have felt like, or the closest on earth she would get to it.

"Maybe next time. I need to get back, give my boy his oats. He's very regimented as to when he expects to eat. I try to ride out every weekend, Sundays 'bout this time, unless it's a holiday. We could meet next week?"

"Same bat time. Same bat channel," Nikki said, tipping her hat then immediately regretting it. There it was, her Daddy's dorkiness seeping out of her. Chris grinned.

"Yep."

He mounted his steed and went on in the opposite direction.

Chapter 18

Like a new ritual, Nikki rode out almost daily into the dense woods—as summer approached, prickly vines covered the ground, reaching to their next tree-limb rung to climb, snagging her jeans with their prickly tines. Even the young pines under the white and maple and water oaks' broad leaves struggled to locate the sun. Uncle Sonny explained that the hardwood canopy was choking out the mature pines, and stopping the new ones from coming in. Nature's changing of the forest bed linens—he had counted it like generations.

When he came back from the war, he was able to buy an old family parcel—a thing Sonny didn't think he wanted, but that seemed to be waiting just for him. Mr. Bruce, the man who sold it to him, said that when his great-great-grandfather came out this way as an independent sharecropper, the land was mostly cotton and soy as far as the eye could see. Some Bermuda grass fields—to stock up to feed the livestock when the grass gets bare.

Mr. Bruce told him the woods then were like it had been when his people were enslaved. "Only difference was, they became like small business owners. They got paid a wage for what they had to do for free just a few years before."

It stayed fields and fields until the land could no longer bear it, and that forced his father to look for work and so took to the railroad and that was when nature began its work in the absence of man. Pines grow fastest, and seeing the writing on the wall, someone must have planted a field of pines. Word was then the land was rented, and whoever had it only got to harvest once before the land changed hands again, but then finally, the last owner before Sonny logged every five or ten years depending on his own financial need and how much he had to supplement the small salary and tips as a porter running the Copper Cloud rail line from Columbia to Philadelphia. When he died, and the land lay dormant, the earth took it all the way over until Sonny and Dwayne carved a horse farm out of the wooded parcel.

The big fallacy about timber farms, though, was that folks assumed you could sit back and watch your money grow. Trees get pests and blights—like the great chestnut blight that knocked out whole orchards across the United States. Every few years the tree out front, blocking the living room window, after being chopped down to its stump (too dangerous to leave a standing dead tree so close) would reseed itself and folks would think they'd have the big tree back only to chop it down again.

Anyways, whenever Sonny was asked where he was from, it was hard to say Fairfield County, because he left so young and with so few blood remaining. His family land withered away to heirs and property taxes. He could never come home again. So he went out into the world in search of himself. He thought he'd find it in the army. He did a tour here, a tour there, then Operation Desert Storm and that wild horse operation. That event changed his life completely. Doctors said it was "probably exhaustion and adrenaline" that allowed him to go back to find Brian after he was shot in the shoulder; prevented him from fully registering his injury. That, and his determination. But when it came to be, it was his left shoulder, and now he was at least happy at that, because he wanted to continue to learn horses and know them—be in a herd with them, even—and he needed the full range of motion of his right shoulder for roping steers and so on.

So, horses had become his thing. And he bought the land and dreamed up this life. A new one for him, but somewhat familiar. Sonny decided to wait the time it needed for the woods to turn to hardwoods—it would be a greater reward when the time came to reap, if he could wait. In the meantime, Sonny went through each fall to thin his woods out: cut the standing dead pines, mulch the underbrush, clear new trails and paths. In midsummer he believed it must have felt not unlike the jungle he heard about that swallowed whole battalions of men in Vietnam. A whole other atmosphere from around the barn, a great reprieve when the temperatures made the air like a thick curtain. Sonny started clearing paths to let the air in, to make the trails a cooler place to be.

Like Chris, Nikki started riding those trails with a cloth to wipe her face—she had asked Dwayne for an old T-shirt, and had chosen an army-green one, to cut into hand cloths that dried faster than terry cloth and didn't bulk in her back pocket. As the days got warmer and the deerflies crept out to join them on the trail, she also understood why Chris wore sleeves in the heat—suffer one thing to avoid suffering another.

She had texted Chris while she was grooming Easy, preparing to ride out. She was running a little late so hoped Chris wasn't already in the no-contact zone of the woods. Now that they were meeting up on the regular, she had a reason to ride out, a destination, a purpose. Every day this summer if the weather allowed—and, for better or worse, they were still in the throes of a mild drought, so while the farmers who grew things in the soil did their rain dances—Nikki and Sonny and Chris enjoyed the spoils of clear skies.

"About to ride out. You in?" Nikki texted Chris, then lifted the saddle onto Easy's back. She remembered how at the beginning of all this, she had to ask Sonny for help—the weight of the saddle and the height of the task felt an impossibility. Her phone buzzed.

"Was waiting on you. Same spot. See you soon."

Now Nikki thinks to bring water that she stuffed into a makeshift saddle sack from an old tote bag and slung around the horn of her saddle. Beef jerky. Enough to share if Chris asked. A few weeks ago, Chris had come with his father's machete attached behind the back of his saddle, and rode the whole way with one hand to allow him to carry bush clippers. They had decided the spot where they first met each other—as horsefolk—would be their spot, and so set about intentionally clearing the space. There was the log that became a bench. Two trees mature enough to hold full-sized horses became hitching posts, and Chris hacked notches at the horses' ear level to allow the lead ropes, when tied, a place to nestle so that they wouldn't fall and they'd have a horse loose in what the two were calling the Hundred Acre Woods, a nod to their favorite childhood book, having found out they had that in common, too. That day, Chris showed Nikki some of the trails (he used air quotes) he rode, and back there had even more drop-offs like the one pass Uncle Sonny cut, and even more jagged.

"The wonderful thing about Tiggers—" Nikki sang, belly-breathing. She was getting tight, anxious.

"Is Tiggers are wonderful things," Chris turned his head to answer.

They laughed and continued singing the silly song until they reached another clearing where Chris's path crossed Sonny's. At their clearing, both dismounted and hitched their horses to their designated spots.

As the weeks progressed, they agreed to meet more often, when Chris wasn't at his summer job, cutting lawns and various landscaping gigs with his dad's friend who needed a young boy's energy and strength the deeper they got into summer. The months went by in this way—Nikki and Chris meeting week after week at their designated spot in the woods, until one day Nikki could smell it, and feel it, too: the slight tinge of cool in the humid undercurrent in the mornings. Soon, since they could see the hem of summer's end, and with it, things were bound to change.

"What are you gonna do when it's time to go back?" Chris asked, this time using his sleeve to wipe his mouth after taking a gulp of water. Nikki had pulled the pieces of beef jerky from the saddle sack and handed him one. She answered, mid-bite.

"I told you I ain't got no reason to go back to that place. I feel like you're the only one checking for me there, and I see you all the time now."

At first, Nikki recognized that her going out to ride—especially on Easy and not a training horse—was not in any way part of the deal she had made with her father or with Sonny. But Sonny pushed her out into the woods.

"You got to be as brave as you want the horses to be," Sonny said. "It'll be good practice before I put you on the young ones who go around looking for a reason to be scared, to bolt and run away."

So she braved it alone, and enjoyed stretching her limits. But then, she'd had her appointments with Chris. Something else to look forward to, to fill her days. They'd often sit in silence and let the sounds of the Hundred Acre Woods wash over them. She didn't know how to tell Sonny or her father that there was a boy at the end of that ride, because automatically they would think the worst or make a bigger deal than just someone her age who liked what she liked: horses. She returned the question to Chris.

"What about you? What you doing when it's time to go back?" She really wanted to know the answer. Isn't it funny? She was just filling her days before, and now couldn't imagine stealing hours, daydreaming. Of course his answer was going to be that he's going back. From what she had gathered, Chris was a rule follower. Regimented in the familiar rigidness of her father and his friends. A same-meal-at-same-meal-o'clock—with no deviations—kind of guy. It wouldn't surprise her if he came one day and said he was joining the military.

"I mean, I know you're going back," Nikki said. "Anyways. I realized, all this time we never talked about who or what you want to be when you grow up."

Chris tore through the last piece of jerky he asked for.

"I dunno. I kinda am waiting on the wind to blow me in the right direction. Some days I consider staying here and seeing what I can do about my folks' parcel—I think I could find my place, if we keep it. Other days, I want to see the world. I hear there's a world outside of Fairfield County that's not Columbia."

They both chuckled. Nikki sat in the echo of his possible leaving, even though that would be years from now. At least two. If things had gone different, she had dreamed of going to the University of North Carolina. They won basketball national championships, and her father wore so much of their apparel. Who doesn't dream of a school who calls its color Carolina blue, and it is as blue as the sky in Fairfield County?

Outside of her teachers, when she had them, she didn't know anyone who went to college or desired to go. Her father learned what he had to learn to keep the farm machines going, and he said his specialization in the army was about what he heard college was like. But he chose home, or as close as he could get to it, and the land, and—he had chosen Sonny, too, in a way. A lineman before shrapnel tore through his left shoulder, Sonny could build any structure you dreamed of, from the ground up, inside and outside, and with the way Columbia was extending its arms out in all cardinal directions every time some farm or large parcel was sold, he did not hurt for general contract work . . . even though Nikki knew his heart won't in it like they say your work should be your passion. There were still enough livestock operations that needed a good hand, and he was one.

What did her guidance counselor Mrs. Boyd say folks like her—before—should be on the lookout for? A possibility model. When Nikki dreamed of college life and what it might be like, she'd go online and see kids reading books in the grass. A bell tower just like the clock in Ridgeway. Mrs. Boyd had affirmed her choice because UNC did have a good journalism program, and journalism was what Nikki was interested in back then, but warned they liked to see higher test scores, though often would make an exception for a compelling story, so she'd have to think of one to gain a competitive edge. She superimposed herself onto the pictures pasted next to the options on the online course catalog: Mass Communications 101, Newspaper Writing in a New Age, Diversity in Journalism—in the photos, students sat in lecture halls the size of concert venues, her staff position would be op-ed for *The Daily Tar Heel,* and so on.

The wind, as Chris described it, blew her in another direction, though.

Chapter 19

Nikki tried to fill the silences on the ride down 321 from Mr. Jim's place. They had caught a loose cow and returned it to the pasture and mended the fence. Then, on horseback, Nikki helped deliver books and small items from Dollar General up the dirt road just behind Mr. Jim's place—the summer rains had washed it out, and since it was a dirt road, it was the responsibility of the owners and they were sick and shut-in, and so the answer was to help deliver things they needed on horseback.

We take care of we, Nikki thought as she took a swig of water.

Sonny started up some conversation about horse shop, who had emerged as his favorite quarter horse line to work with and train (beyond his own string, of course). What she was learning about the qualities of horseflesh she liked ("A thinking horse. Loyal. Strong bone. Looking for a partner not a master"), mimicking some of the terms she heard Sonny or a client use here and there. How they talked around her as if she had nothing to contribute, and maybe in the early days that was true, but now Nikki had language and feel. She could walk out to the pasture and—it sounds silly when she really thinks about it—hear Easy greet her. Can tell when he wants to work and when he wants to play: a bath, long grooming, hand grazing. One day, holding the end of the lead line while he munched on the weeds grown almost to her knees in the middle of what she called Sonny's lawn, Sonny walked up and declared, "You sure know how to spoil a horse, ain't it?" and moved his chewing straw from one corner of his mouth to the other.

Usually on those drives further out into the country and back, she and Sonny had long exchanges because his old boxy Ford could pull anything you hitched it to, but didn't have a radio to speak of.

Sonny chewed his straw slow like a cow chewing cud—lower jaw going left-right, while he kept his eyes on the road. He never felt the need to fill the silences, but appreciated the conversations mostly.

"I've been thinking about how I don't think I'm ever going back to school, but also thinking about all I'm taking in. Don't they say there's different types of learning? Folks who need to hear, folks who need to *do*? I guess I get to *do* horses with you."

Sonny hummed.

"So many more people do horses than I think! Like you can go about town and folks don't know you scratched a horse muzzle just a minute ago, or you show up clean to wherever you going, and no one knows you were fixing a broken fence in your pajamas; mud all on your hands. You know my friend Chris? I know him from school and then ran into him on the trails. I wouldn't know he rode horses. Like at all. That's not the vibe he gives at school."

"I seen him at the rodeos all the time. Some guys say his daddy was into bush racing."

Nikki nodded.

"Yeh, the horse he rides out on is an old winner, he says. He saying his folks want to get out of horses. Can you imagine that?" Nikki turned to Sonny and widened her eyes in disbelief.

Sonny kept his eyes on the road. "I can't."

"But also, like, riding out into the country with you like this, meeting these folks—I'd have no idea there were so many Black folks who owned horses. Who ride."

"Who? You mean cowboys," Sonny said.

"That's what you call yourself? I mean, I know that's what they call me at the rodeo, but that's just a term they use when competing, right?"

"What else is there?"

"Chris says *horseman.* I guess I'm a horseman. Woman. I dunno. Ain't cowboys only out West in the past like those black-and-white movies? Ain't they all white?"

"Maybe you do need to go back to school then, how you talking out the side of your mouth!" Sonny pushed her shoulder, playful like a brother. But a bit exasperated, repeating into the cab of the truck, *"Ain't cowboys white."*

"Lil lady, you do got some learning to do," Sonny said.

"That's my whole point. But it's not in school. You know, I think about how it all happened that got me here. How folks would say something about fate or destiny or whatever. When would I have ever had the chance to do horses like this? Like more than just playing with you. You make it work, like this is your job. Your life. Did you always want to be . . . a cowboy?"

The question rose at the end like the end-of-summer heat sneaking over the air-conditioning, working hard, but barely. Sonny did two thinking chews on his straw.

"I didn't really pay horses no mind, you know. Sure, they was always around me growing up here and whatnot, but they just existed in my life as a chore. Another thing I was looking to get away from when I could. I didn't even really want to ride. I didn't get it then. What my daddy called the *magic of being in partnership.* I thought it was all fake. Hokeypokey. Daddy would say shit like he could understand and hear the horses talking to him, and he would have full-blown conversations and arguments with the herds, or whisper into his main horse's ear—he called him Cricket—he'd whisper to Cricket and Cricket would nod just like he spoke English, too. He'd tell me: good horses speak English, and I'd roll my eyes, and count my days until I could get out of the country. I figured, it was all the quietness out here that must have done it: make a man believe he could talk to horses, that horses could hear and understand and even speak back to you, was just too much for me to comprehend. So I left as early as I could."

Nikki listened, and wondered at first if Sonny believed now that horses might understand English. Certainly, there were times she'd said something under her breath—a command, a direction—and the horses would do the thing. He had never really said *use your words* in their training together, it was mostly about feel. "You got to get a *feel* for what you want then use your body and energy to get a response from the horse." Really, more than the question of if horses could speak or understand English, Nikki wanted to know if they could read minds.

One day, while she was grooming Easy, he had started to jig his feet around, real nervous energy. The kind that happens when they feel something because their riders do. She was just brushing his body, braiding his hair, but her mind had wandered away from him, from the task, and he stomped once. Then turned to her. Nikki had focused back on Easy. Then, in a hypnotic lull of the rhythmic brushing, she thought about something—can't even really recall it now—and as soon as the not-thinking-about-Easy thought came up, he stomped again, with a huff, and a nudge with his muzzle. She tickled his muzzle and he wiggled his lips and breathed deeply. Finally, to confirm her suspicions on her unscientific experiment, she intentionally turned her attention away while still engaging with Easy physically, and he used his teeth to softly nip her fingers to redirect her focus. So, she determined, it was true.

Sonny kept on, like the road unwinding before them. "I mean, I guess I didn't get it until I had to. When my life depended on it. In the desert, in the army, I had to ride a horse I didn't even know. And yeh, sure, I had horses in my backyard and whatnot, but I really didn't bother with them like that. I knew how to ride 'cause my daddy and granpops said I couldn't live there and not ride, but it won't until I was in the desert and literally my life and the life of my brothers depended on that knowledge did I just have to reach deep, pray some of it stuck by what do they call it?—osmosis—and faith. I tell your daddy 'bout every other week: I found God and horses on those desert dunes. God and horses."

Nikki sat with the revelation, pondering where to enter: Horses? God? Her father's place in the story? Every time Desert Storm was mentioned in her presence it felt like a secret. *A soldier never speaks of the realities of war* and whatnot. Or that seemed the code under which her father and Uncle Sonny operated. She looked out the pickup window and saw the Blackstock Fish Camp and knew they were getting closer to the barn and for some reason Nikki started realizing the conversations Sonny had on the road were drastically different from the conversations Sonny had at the farm. At the farm, there was nothing but distractions: the animals and their needs. On the road, the winding pines like a lullaby, Sonny often seemed transfixed by the quiet and so filled it with stories Nikki could get nowhere else. She learned to not interfere with the telling, just let the stories spill. But the mention of her father raised her antennae. She'd better tread lightly at the opened door.

"How did the desert change your mind on horses?"

Sonny talked in generalities about the details of the operation but landed mostly on how he had to really learn—with no time really—to trust, to give himself over to the horse. He had to be raw so the horse could see he was for real. Any pretense and it was over. So he had to walk through the ordeal like an exposed fuse. That's how horses feel vulnerability. You have to show it. Sonny said he told the horse before they went out that he hadn't intended to die on that operation, which meant the horse couldn't possibly die on that operation, or else they'd both be in trouble.

"'We gotta work together,' I said out loud, and wouldn't you know that horse grunted in agreement. They gave them to us in such a hurry we had no information, only: four legs, kinda broke. A horse. So I named him Grasshopper. My daddy would have laughed at that, but I imagined he was a brother to Cricket, and you know I told Grasshopper about Cricket, hearing my daddy in my head saying *just talk to him, son, just talk.* And when I finally got on his back, it felt like we had known each other the bulk of my life, and I knew we were soldiers, in it together."

"What did Grasshopper look like?" Nikki asked. They were not far from the farm now, so transitioned to maybe pieces of the convo Sonny might not mind continuing while they finished out the day's work.

"'Bout the size of a colt, really," Sonny said. "Too small to back. Too small for what we was about to ask him. You know white folks gone be white folks no matter the context—like here we were, in the middle of the desert in the middle of a war given this wild-ass assignment to go out into jet-black night without the cover of tanks or trucks. No. They weren't looking out for us—we had to be our own cover. We're trying to figure out who should ride what and figure out the herd that was dropped in our laps and the good ole troops was calling out what horse belonged to them. So, no one picked my Grasshopper. He was the smallest, probably youngest. Still had the wild look of living off his mother's milk in his eye. If he had more hind development, would probably be a cow horse. Petite head, just like that. Liver-blood chestnut color—so dark you'd think he was bay—with a big stripe blaze from his ears to his lips. I didn't fight it because you need a horse not soured in experience to do what we was going to ask them to do—they needed to be brave because they didn't know any better. That's what I had with Grasshopper. Wild, blind bravery. We put the bigger guys who could barely keep their balance in combat boots on the big horses and packed those horses down with what all we needed to carry out the mission: rations, ammo, sleep packs, first aid kits, and whatnot. Grasshopper was small, sure, but he had feet as big as dinner plates which meant he was gone be good across the dunes, probably float across them—and he did! Them other ones—big as they were—had petite feet, so dainty. Looked to be glued together with their horseshoes. Like Thoroughbreds or Arabian horses—all engine, no brakes or brain, definitely. Grasshopper had the best brain."

Nikki heard all what Sonny was saying, and even understood the distinctions—why they were invested now in riding horses bred explicitly to do cow work, how important the small stature was for quick-footed stops, turns, change of direction. She had watched the Kentucky Derby on television and marveled at the long strides of the young but big colts, barely fitting on a screen. The long necks. Long faces. Long legs. How, standing near their grooms, the horses towered over them like skyscrapers. One that was designed for use, the other for . . . spectacle? Taking her own size out of account, a size-to-work ratio also seemed apparent in the rider's ability or inability to mount the horse independently from the ground, and she could imagine Uncle Sonny, like Chris, giving those men legs up onto their mounts with strict instructions not to get off until the plan was to be off horse for some time. Which had to mean their butts *had* to feel as though they were ready to abandon the mission. Nikki chuckled at that thought, remembering each ride in the beginning and the ache that went on for days.

But she also couldn't help but pause again on one thing Sonny kept repeating. Nikki heard there were six men out there with them, and it had seemed as though most of them did not know horses, but he had worked with someone to assess the herd when it got to the point of figuring out their assignment. "*We* had to . . . ?" Nikki repeated out loud, just as she and Sonny were turning off the main highway, minutes from the farm.

Sonny chewed long. Longer. He turned in to the driveway and crept over the gravel so that it sounded like the growl of a wounded animal. He had slowed down so much he barely had to use the brakes to stop the rig. For Nikki, there was still the chores of unloading horses, untacking, cold hose, and turnout before they considered the trip done. That's what Sonny taught her: from load out to load in, the trip begins and ends with horses in pasture and everything back in its place before moving on to the next task of the day. Usually, they do this piece together because often they are both settling in horses after a job, but this time there was only Patriot to unload. Like clockwork the two went to the trailer. Sonny opened the door and Nikki stepped up to bring Patriot out. This was their dance. Usually, some banter would float between them, but Nikki was still waiting for Sonny to respond to her question, which she felt she was coming to know based off her own understanding of Sonny's relationship to her father. But she needed validation. Who was *we*? She took a different approach.

"This year, for Memorial Day, Daddy took me to the cemetery and we placed flags. I remember Daddy telling you he placed the flag and cleared Brian's footstone. Did y'all do this horse operation together?"

"Renegade," Sonny said, almost a whisper. He tapped the trailer because Nikki was inside with Patriot, interrogating, and he was ready now for this trip to be over so he could mentally and emotionally switch gears. Nikki had started moving but got distracted by Sonny's response.

"Renegade?"

"Brian's horse. That's what he wanted to name his horse," Sonny said. "No, he didn't know how to ride before we started, that's how . . ." Sonny trailed off and turned away.

Nikki led Patriot off the trailer. Sonny's gaze was still elsewhere, as if looking for something or someone to emerge from the woods. He didn't turn back, even when Nikki made motion to hand Patriot over. Failed in her attempt, she let it go.

"I'll untack Patriot and put him out with fresh hay," Nikki said.

Sonny turned, but still didn't seem to be looking at Nikki before he just barely let "thanks" slip from his lips. He closed the trailer and called back that he was going to walk the hayfields and he probably wouldn't be back before Dwayne came to pick her up for the day.

He said he'd see her in the morning, bright and early.

Chapter 20

And just like that, the county had come and staked four notice signs on the frontage line of the Bolton property without Dwayne having seen it happen. Not unlike how he looked up and it was late summer already. Usually, he'd have the occasion of Nikki's return to school to mark the countdown to his crazy time: farmers kept their machinery as close to their chests as possible during planting season and then rush and dump all their problems in Dwayne's lap and expect all expediency, and the timing is usually always perfect because Nikki would catch the bus to school, then the bus to Sonny's (or catch Sonny on the bus route), and then, when he was ready to end his day, he'd drive over and sit a spell, gather his daughter, and head home.

But now, of course, things have changed. It made sense it was time for his life to change. Nikki had changed in just a little over a summer. He knew why. Her desire for discipline and consistency was in partnership with her desire to be a good steward and partner of Sonny's herd. He used to have to peel Nikki out of bed for school. Remind her every few minutes in the morning how she needed to get a move on to the end of the drive because Mrs. Esther maintained an army-tight ship. "And she *will* leave you. And no, I won't sign you in late." Threats. He had had to use veiled threats or bribes for their farm chores, their household cleaning, and so on. He wasn't ready to explore a driving learner's permit with her, not yet. That would be a whole new can of worms in an already changed landscape. So, Dwayne was locked into driving Miss Nikki to and fro, which meant his own schedule had shifted earlier than he would have liked to accommodate and on days like today, when he sets aside time for town and city errands, he'd grab breakfast—steak and red-eye gravy over grits and over-medium eggs—at Waffle House until the Feed & Seed store opened.

Between Waffle House and the Feed & Seed store on Tuesdays, Dwayne used the lullaby of syrupy summer days to catch up on county gossip. Mostly by way of eavesdropping. Other times, folk would drag him right on into whatever news was swirling about town. That Tuesday, he recounted what he heard to Sonny when he made it to gather Nikki later that day. They paused for two longnecks because Dwayne had approached with the *I need a drink* exasperated look and Sonny didn't ask, just went to the fridge in his carport and emerged popping the caps off and handed one over. The bottles clinked and Nikki peeked over Easy's back in the barn, where she was braiding his mane. That her father had settled into one of the camping chairs around the firepit signaled that she had more time, maybe even enough to braid Patriot's mane, to her Uncle Sonny's dismay.

"I'm not a horse-crazy teenybopper," he'd said the first time Nikki asked if he wanted her to do Patriot's mane. "What cowboy horse you see with braids?"

"Mine."

"Touché. I see you done learned something!" Sonny chuckled. "Wait, no. I still stand by my statement. You're a cow*girl.* I rest my case."

Nikki shook her head and let it go but it was always hard to resist raking her fingers through Patriot's thick mane. One time, she did sneak in some braids on him on a day they weren't expected to ride out or be at a job, and when Nikki had taken the braids down, she caught Sonny fluffing the horse's waves, trying to preserve the look. He hated the braids but loved the after . . . so with the way her father and Sonny were settling in and she heard fire logs fall onto each other and the *snch-snch-snch* of the fire starter, she'd probably have to find something else to do after finishing with Patriot, too. The spoils of not having a school night anymore, even though she actually woke up earlier these days.

"So I walk into Waffle House after I drop Nikki, right," Dwayne says. He lowered his voice and looked over his shoulder for evidence she might be actively listening. "And you know Marcus there like he always is, running his mouth to anyone with ears. Waitresses. Cooks. Folks who just want to eat their steak an' eggs like me. You know how in the movies, folks open doors to a joint and the record scratches and music stops playing? And there's an ominous feel about the space? That's what it felt like as soon as that door creaked open. I mean, even Marcus stopped and turned to look at me. I almost wanted to check that wasn't something wrong with my face."

He pointed to his forehead. "Ain't nothing there, right?"

Sonny shook his head while taking a new sip.

"Thought not. Anyways. I'm sitting there, ordering my usual, and Marcus come over and ask me if I'm going to try and buy the land. That's all he say. And I say, what land? And he has this puzzled look and goes, 'Ain't the Bolton Plantation land your land?' and I say technically, why, what's up? And he says there's announcements in the paper about a tax sale and whoever got their eyes on the acreage already trying to change the zoning from agricultural to residential. 'Don't you live right across the way? You ain't seen it? I saw the notice in the paper, just the address, and I thought it was what it was, and I drive that way just about every day and I drove by on my way here, and sure enough four signs announcing their intentions to rezone it, so hopeful owners jumping 'bout ten guns.' "

Marcus wasn't quiet while he was saying all this—he had the sizzle of the griddle to contend with, the metal scrape of the spatula flipping breakfast meats, the call of orders to the cook in the open kitchen. But that was also how Marcus operated, about six decibels above normal.

"They say a new housing development, what they always up to," that was Harvey, jumping into the conversation.

"Of course I live across the street. Y'all all know that. So, I was there this morning, and won't no signs out there," Dwayne announced to the whole of the restaurant.

"County work quick-fast when they want to," that was Paula, behind the register. She wiped her brow with the back of her hand, then wiped both hands with her apron before cashing a customer out.

There was a collective hum in agreement.

Sure enough, when Dwayne drove back home after he left the Waffle House, just to see, the notice signs were there. Sonny asked Dwayne what he was going to do over the crackle of the firepit. His question snapped Dwayne back to the farm, after the events that had unfolded that day. He recounted them all: since he was already set for a day of errands, he went over to the tax assessor's office with a copy of the classified announcement of the sale and inquired about it. Mrs. Harmon was in, thank God, and so he knew if he showered her with enough *yes ma'am*s and *thank you*s and syrupy-sweet talk asking about her family and so on, she would be glad to help, and be more helpful than folks working in county offices are known to be: Slow to move. Full of red tape and arbitrary rules. Hassles begetting hassles. Closed doors. It worked. She spoke quietly while she told him to take a seat in her cubicle and leaned in to announce, "Baby, this property's taxes had been paid for years like clockwork. You know when Mr. Moses and Ms. Lillie went on to be with the Lord in the fire, the property passed to your father." Mrs. Harmon looked at the computer. "Lloyd. And according to these records, the tax was paid religiously, like I said, except the last two years. We sent notices to the last known addresses, and I even tried to extend it, which is why all this is happening now, after two years and not one payment. Last few notices came back *return to sender*."

Dwayne thanked Mrs. Harmon for that background information, armed with the knowledge that the property was going up for a fraction of its worth, a fraction of all he invested in the whole of his life to keep the land as manicured as his grandfather had taught him. But even at a fraction of what he believed his birthright to be worth, it still exceeded what was possible for him to gather in time—the sale was to take place in less than ninety days. Of course, expedited. After the tax assessor's office, he went to the Department of Health to see if there had been any death certificates submitted. How could today have been the day it had become so? There was no evidence of it having turned this way. Wouldn't someone have notified him? They were veterans! Wouldn't someone show up at the door and say, "I'm sorry for your loss"? That would hinge upon if Dwayne had been listed as last known relation, and as far as his father really knew—according to what Ms. Mozell said in the early years—Dwayne was just to stay there until he had come of age and joined up. So as soon as he turned eighteen, what little money his father did send along with what little greeting or half-tidings stopped, and that was exactly when Dwayne joined up so as not to be a burden any longer to Ms. Mozell. It had been how long? Thirty-three years. Jesus's years worth of silence. Longer if you count before his grandfather died, when Lloyd disappeared almost altogether except for his occasional handwritten missives. The Department of Health lady said there would only be something if his death was registered in South Carolina. There was no record.

Then, Dwayne had also found his way to the county library, and asked the nice young librarian if she could help him look up on the computer the names of property owners for the last two addresses that Mrs. Harmon had written on a scrap of paper. The first address listed Lloyd Bolton as owner and included a phone number. The next address was listed as Sandhills Properties LLC, posted to an Angela Fisher, owner, and there was also a phone number. So had he moved, sold that residence to live elsewhere, with a woman? Or was he renting? Why did he sell? Both owners had addresses in Jacksonville, Florida. The nice librarian showed him how to use a mapping website in order to calculate the fact that those two properties were within ten minutes of each other. Armed with more information and more questions, Dwayne sat in his truck wondering if he was going to try to salvage his day during his busy work season or follow the trail of clues about a man—his father—who may or may not be dead.

He sat in the truck and flipped open his phone. As he held his finger over the first digit, a man walked his son into the library. The son practically floated down the sidewalk—how Nikki rushed the doors of the library of her elementary school; how he walked as a young boy hand in hand with Moses to the barn each morning for chores. Dwayne dialed the first number, the one listed next to Lloyd's name. He breathed deeply, then held his breath. When the computerized voice announced the number was out of service, Dwayne jerked the phone up and contemplated throwing it, and at just that moment a young girl bounded out of the library holding a stuffed plaything in one arm, and cradled three books in the other arm. He thought about what his grief had denied him all these years. What his father had taken away, caught in the rapids of his own grief. Whenever he would ask, Moses only offered that Lloyd had to take care of himself for a little while. No matter the time that had passed, that was always the answer. All those years, too, Dwayne had justified his own distancing from the life he had inherited, from the life coursing through his bones, through Nikki's. He had built a protective barrier, like the Lake Murray Dam erected to keep a reservoir of water as a source of recreation and energy. But if you think hard and deeply enough, whole towns, mostly Black, were drowned for that reservoir to exist. And no one speaks of it anymore, just keep on living. Whole lives lost in the damming up of his river of grief. He dialed the second number, belonging to a Ms. Angie Fisher. And she answered.

"And Sonny, this woman was saying how—I'm quoting her here—'All Lloyd ever talked about was trying to figure out how to make it right with his son before he goes.' You believe that?" Dwayne said.

He snapped back to earth. He needed centering. He recounted to himself: Sonny's place. Picking up Nikki. Tuesday night. The fire had almost died down. Nikki had found the barn light and another horse to groom. Sonny came back to the firepit with an armful of logs, shaking his head.

"Man, you want me to put some chops on the grill? I can see if I have some corn, too."

Dwayne looked at the darkening sky. There was still so much more he had to say. How much had Nikki heard?

"Sure. Yeh, man. Thanks. That'll be nice to have one less thing to think about today."

Sonny went to gather dinner, and Dwayne watched the embers turn to flames around the new logs . . . turning Angie's conversation in his head, thinking about how amber-orange the sky was this morning in the early hours, as the sun was rising on an otherwise normal day, how there was no indication of what he would learn: that his father had died over a year ago, apparently full of regret and remorse, but with a guilt that paralyzed him from absolving himself of any of it.

Lloyd had made Angie promise not to get involved. She had asked him to settle the rift for years, she said. She was the first person he called when Dwayne's mother died, the day he was born. They had all been friends in school. "That's how long I been loving your father. But he chose Delores, and I loved them both. So much. We didn't get together immediately after, but he had come by for a spell to get his head right here and there before he drifted off to wherever next. Then, what was it, about fifteen years ago, he moved here. Bought a house. Asked me to marry him. I told him won't no use marrying now, but that we could love each other for whatever lives we got left. I told him, though, that I wanted him to make it right with you. I'd watch him gather pen and paper and then toss it in the fire. 'Bout seven times over our time together. Each time, I swear it looked like his body was weighed heavier with grief. One morning, I had decided to sleep in a little later because my arthritis acts up during storm season—air pressure and all that. My room was cold, and I guess I thought he had gone out and hadn't started a fire, but he had. The dining room was warm in the way a room holds warmth when all that's left is embers and ash. He had his head on his arm, pen in hand. I just thought he had gotten tired writing because it was still so early, even though I'd slept in. And you know the fire had been going enough to die down so he had to have been up for some time, so I thought maybe he had just fallen asleep. So I called out to him to come back to bed. I called out to *come back to bed, honey,* but he didn't move. Dwayne, he was gone. Gone trying to write you a letter."

Sonny had returned, dragging the small gas grill nearer to where they were sitting, and lit it up. He put the ears of corn in a buttered foil packet on the grill and seared the sides of the chops before closing the top to let them cook. He had also somehow managed to gather more beers and tossed one to Dwayne, along with the opener. Where had he left the story with Sonny?

"So yeh, man. Come to find out, the bastard's dead," Dwayne said. He had a dry laugh and drowned it out with a swig of beer.

"The bastard is dead."

Chapter 21

It was all anyone could talk about at first: Sonny coming into town—"off the mountaintop"—to the Waffle House and didn't order any food, just asked out loud if anyone got one of them county land notices, too? He had just gotten his. They had come in waves, so at first Sonny thought it was only Dwayne's problem, but it turned out to be a county problem that had prompted Dwayne into action over something years old. For Sonny, this was news. Big news. From the looks of it, it was news for others, too. A few hat brims nodded in the affirmative, and the cook—wearing a paper hat without a brim—sucked her teeth. That was the intent anyway. She had lost her front teeth years ago, and anytime anyone asked *did she miss them?* she said she eats everything she wants just fine, and her man still say he loves her and comes home every night so what use she got for vanity? She got a man and kids to feed. A whole county, too, if you think about it. Sonny looked around at half the counter nodding and then shaking their heads. Not a *no, they didn't receive the notice,* but a *can't believe,* an *always something,* a *sick of this shit* head shake over their smothered hash browns and hard-fried eggs. He ordered a to-go tea and asked Ms. LaTarsha to throw two lemons in there, left a five-dollar bill on the counter, winked, and said: "Meeting at the Spot Saturday, y'all welcome to come."

At the Feed & Seed store, two elders smoked a cigarette with James at the counter. Sonny could tell by the tenor of the conversation that they were discussing late-summer fishing techniques—what's biting now, how sometimes it's easier and cheaper to string up a few kernels of corn instead of worms: won't make no difference. Sonny considered the proposal, listening in at the tail end, and thought maybe he should try it. He lifted his hat.

"Mornin', y'all. Excuse the interruption," he said. The men turned in unison as if for the first time acknowledging his presence. They exchanged gruff pleasantries in the ways of old Southern men suddenly trying to find something else to do.

"Alright, James, I'll be seeing ya," one said, tapping his hands twice on the counter then lifting into a wave.

"Let me let y'all go now," another said.

Sonny sped quicker to his point: "I was wondering if y'all own your parcels, and if so, did you get the county notice like the rest of us?"

One gentleman had cowboy boots, a red-and-white patterned button-down shirt tucked into his slim jeans, and a handkerchief in his front pocket. He looked as if he was a mean steer wrestler back in his day, could probably still hook one. Sonny could feel the pride oozing out of the starched-pressed lines straight down the front of his legs, but his globe-round knuckles and missing pinkie finger told a story of his probable team-roping retirement. He spoke first, after shaking his head in disgust.

"I'm actually over in Blythewood, but on the Richland County side. Every few years they try to test the waters, see who's ready to give up the ghost of rural life while the city pressing you at the seams—pockets of houses popping up where folks threw in the towel—usually, you know the next generation kids don't want nothing to do with the family business 'cept to sell off to the highest bidder and you know them developers give good checks. I seen 'em. Some would make you think yeh, maybe this is my retirement or something, you know, pay off some debts. Then no sooner than that balance from that check clear your account because you settled some of your scores, one house on one-fourth of one of them acres is worth least two times more than that check you thought was written in gold."

He slid his hands into his pockets. James sucked his teeth.

"Yeh, I heard Blythewood on Richland County side started annexing as much property as possible, promising to 'preserve our county ways of living,' " he lifted his hands in air quotes. "Prolly just packaging all the parcels of the owners who believed that crock of shit into one nice city package while taxing extra, waiting for the big fish. These housing developers, they little fish, you know. I'm watching. Blythewood tried to cross over into Fairfield County with that annexing business—that's how I know they slip was showing."

Sonny interjected and asked Mr. Crisp-Pants his name. "I'm sorry, y'all. I'm Sonny. You are?"

"Nate. Nice to meet ya," he tipped his hat again.

"See, they running a marathon; we sprinting from tax bill to feed bill to gas bill trying to catch our breaths before we plumb out of steam," James at the counter said.

Everyone hummed at the testimony.

"Them some real true words," Sonny said. "Wonder if more folks could use them words like I do right now. I gotta be thinking long distances. Meanwhile, I'm trying to be the fastest sprinter."

"Them's two different training techniques, pedigrees, and resources needed," Nate said, lifting his hands near his face, rubbing his pointer finger and thumb together.

"Dollar bills, lots of them," Sonny agreed. "A few of us just outside Ridgeway, who got several hundred between us, all got the county notice. I just come from the Waffle House, there's folks there got it, too. Mr. Nate, we could use your knowledge of Richland County antics; seems like Fairfield County trying to be a citified county, too. I'm hoping folks would gather at the Spot me and my brothers got out at my place. Someplace private. Y'all know how white folks get nervous when a gang of us gather anywhere 'cept church on Sundays. Maybe we can put our heads together. I know if the proposed tax bill for my place is real, I don't know how I'm going to make it happen. I know a few others feeling the heat as well."

"I'll be there," James said, then looked at Nate. "It's right up 21, a bit past where we go turkey hunting." Nate nodded, but didn't confirm his attendance.

Sonny thanked the gentlemen for their time and turned to the door. "Anyone is invited Saturday. Need as much Fairfield County there as possible."

He turned back to the counter. "*Black* Fairfield County. We need to think about how to send a message."

James winked, and the men chuckled when the bell above the door rang out at his exit.

||||||||||||||||||

Sonny's last stop was the OBAMA gas station that popped up almost simultaneously with his first inauguration—when they all thought the Great Recession was over and Obama promised there would never be another one. And then, everyone everywhere was losing their houses and jobs and gasped at the price of milk and the price of bread and the diminished size of eggs, considering how much they cost. At the back of the station used to be one of the best places to get biscuits and gravy or fish and grits. You'd come in for gas and leave belly-full of buttered toast. They lost the grill in those early Obama years, and some lone volunteer scoped the back corner of it out as a campaign outpost and made their promises again to anyone stopping by that if they voted Obama back in things would be different, even though folks whispered their realities: *Won't they better before this? Won't they better?* Corn yields and oat prices were their canaries and as soon as Obama took office, it seemed like "progress" was for the city folk. They had to choose between feeding themselves or their livestock to feed themselves later. It was hard times, and lately the Obama station—erected with such hope and promise—was a memorial to times changing.

The restaurant long gone; the tables still huddled around the back of the gas station. It was a rest stop for the wayfaring, the folks just trying to get back on their feet, the ones who—if they were quiet and clean enough—could slumber overnight as long as their things were out before the early-morning crowd came for their gas or vittles on their way into town for their workday shifts.

When it came about, everyone within the county was filled with the same hope. But now, the hope that moved the owners of the old gas station to rename the place after the first Black president and the promise of prosperity is gone. Soon after his reelection a hurricane sent its wind and rain up to Fairfield County, but federal aid only went to the coast. It was so early in the season, what was the storm called? Some name started with a *C*—and so all of the late-summer crops hadn't been gathered, but were drowned by all that rain that stayed for days, never letting up enough for the hay to be cut then dried then gathered. Corn turned moldy on the stalks. Okra wept so, the pods laid down on the ground like fallen soldiers. When the dust settled and the rains stopped, the *A* at the end of the station name was found four blocks west—one of the grill-seat regulars brought it back to the gas station, handed it to the cashier then reached his hand out across the counter—expecting some sort of cash reward no doubt—but the woman shook her head: ain't no use for it, the owner's already talking about changing the name back to Texaco anyways. So the name came down but somehow folks still called it the Obama station, or jokingly, the 'Bama station depending on if they are referencing the folks who gathered there or not. *Those 'Bamas over there talking they shit again. He's one of the slowest-talkin' simplest-minded 'Bamas I done ever did see!*

On weekday mornings, the old folks used to make their rounds about town—those folks on disability or some other assistance that demands one keep on keeping on without steady work to reap the benefits of the state, what else were they to do with their wide-open days? They would gather at the tables in the back of the station late mornings sharing a newspaper—one reading aloud to the others—sharing gossip, sharing company of the dispossessed. Sonny knew some of the crew: older veterans who never made their way to the Spot despite numerous invites; those who lost part of themselves and tragically, their family, to drink or something harder. So many folks rendered them invisible. So invisible, they had access to information normal folk might not: people strolling about the county discussing very intimate or important financial affairs in front of those they deem of no consequence. Sonny whipped through the Obama station, nodding at the folks he knew and those he didn't, and made a beeline for the back table.

"My man, my man! Jack-attack!" he said, his voice booming to announce his approach so as not to be a surprise. There were two men back there this morning. One smoking a cigarette and ashing it in a well-used Styrofoam cup. That was Jack.

"Boy! Sonny Boy!" he said. The other man huffed a bit at the disruption. He was reading through yesterday's paper—the only way he could get it without paying was after the cashiers changed over the paper for the day, at four A.M. when the new issues were delivered, and he was very often there to gather a copy before the rest went into the garbage. Jack introduced his sitting partner as Earl. Sonny tipped his hat.

"What's the news, Sonny Boy? Ain't seen you 'round these parts for some time, like you shame to be associated with riffraff like me." Jack's words whistled through the gap where his two bottom teeth used to be, a war wound he called it, then if in the presence of other veterans (usually marked by their trucker hats), he'd quickly apologize and say he ain't mean to offend and go on to explain he was helping his friend Jonny trim this rank-ass horse's feet, "and you know them white boys let they horses get away with the devil and swear that fucker better trained than your'n." Tim had, in fact, said that his horse stands good for the job, and it wasn't until Jack got the hoof straight to his face did he determine that that was, in fact, a lie. He was only able to find one, but it didn't matter nohow, what the dentist said it would cost to fix it was more than he got in four monthly checks from the VA. And anyways the care he got didn't cover cosmetic dental stuffs, which is what the folks at the dentist office determined. So that was that. He'd be a fast-talking whistling Dixie.

Sonny cut to the chase and asked had they heard anything about this county assessment tax notice? Earl mentioned hearing a few folk around town complaining a few days ago. Jack said he was cutting the lawn of one of them fast-box-builds that popped up on Willis's old tract—rest in peace—and it won't no more than a soul patch of grass but them folks buying them overpriced new builds ain't themselves built for manual labor, but they'll run their mouths and said they had heard that a big manufacturer was coming to town and had started hiring their first employees, you know, the bigwigs, and Jack was cutting the grass of one of the bigwigs one day and he was packing up to leave and so had to wait for his thirty-dollar cash payment and could listen in—he won't eavesdropping, but he won't *not* trying to listen. You get it. You can tell the developers a mile away: Walking around in casual wear. Highlighter-colored shirts. Raccoon face from wearing sunglasses every day. Jack said, he had confirmed to whoever he was on the phone with that two thousand acres had been approved to be converted from rural to industrial. They were owned by the county anyways, so no fight. They was gone build a new railroad. Move a road. Build a new highway overpass. Expecting four thousand jobs, so now they gotta scope out parcels for the population boom. They buying up as much land as they could, as quickly as their investors pump monies into the banks. Then they got the county on their side transferring without the middleman, the council votes, you know the roadblocks. Looking for tax sales, you know what they did to Richland County. He said they got the blueprint, won't no need charting a new path. State gave an open permission slip to go in and do what they need.

"Same script, same cast," Earl said.

Sonny chimed in, "Just different Blacks."

They all laughed the laugh of the surrendered. The machine that was moving had made moves over years without anyone clocking it. By the time the moves were made public, Sonny began to realize, it was *fait accompli*—there was so little ground to stand on. This news changed the agenda for Saturday's meeting.

The meeting day came heavy with the promise of answers. Reserved mostly for use by former military men, the Spot opened its doors to anyone who heard by way of Sonny's messaging that there would be a safe, private place to gather and discuss just what to do about the notices, the taxes, the rising costs, the whole idea that there were forces out there trying to change the nature of things: folks seeking city life—their quarter-acre plots, or no parcels at all, car exhaust, highways and freeways, sidewalks and five o'clock traffic—could and should go to Columbia. Streetlights that ticked on for comfort. No pre-dawn deer crossings. Patches of grass cut like checkerboards. The only greenery cut like geometry in Fairfield County were row crops or pastures. City folk who weren't sent to bed by the lullaby of cicadas just cannot appreciate what it is to watch dragonflies hoverboard over horse pastures, hungry for mosquitoes. Or the melodious crunch of a horse grazing. The backaching dailiness of stacking hay bales. Even the armyworm's ravenous night crawl, decimating whole acres of hayfields by moonlight. Or the high-pitched yips of a gang of coyotes closing in on their chicken coops, their rabbit dens. The blacksnakes bringing omens and slinking away with their eggs. And the hats. The ten-gallons. The hawk feathers. The jangle of metal spurs with each footfall. The jeans dusted golden and yet creased with care. The folks congregating at the Spot on meeting day wanted to keep it all.

It wasn't until the large gathering of them, the countryfolk, the Black countryfolk, that they quite grasped what they collectively stood to lose with one sweep of legislation by folks down in their brick county houses who never in their life waded in the oxblood muck witnessing a sow push nine piglets into the world and, with their own bloody hands, coaxed the runt of the litter to latch on to a teat. Their livelihoods in the balance by folks who say things like *I don't eat chicken on the bone,* so of course they won't have ever watched with wild abandon a headless hen scurry around the yard, or with their hands plucked each single feather, boiled every carcass for broth. The folks in the brick county buildings who pull their cans of beans from their shelves and have never known the simple pleasures of fresh-churned butter spread across a loaf slice still warm from the oven. No, they wanted the whole of it gone.

And so, in the waning light of late summer, that Saturday, the Black countryfolk came together to account for what might have already been done, and what there might be left for them to do.

To no one's surprise, Mrs. Harmon was there front and center. Mr. Nate and his starched jeans beside her. Every face and more poured into the Spot. Earlier that morning, after her house chores and Sonny's chores, Nikki helped transform the Spot into lecture-style seating. It was its first public event open to absolutely anyone—though the assumption was that it was open to Black folks, and Black Fairfield County land-stewarding folk. Generally, there was a smaller smattering of chairs here and there—no fewer than two card tables with their requisite four chairs flanking each side. All four of the tables not used for refreshments were slid into a line formation like newlyweds at their wedding reception, and even though he hadn't thought who would sit at those tables Sonny felt he needed them to anchor the seriousness of the business at hand.

Dwayne filed in with the bulk of the crowd even though Sonny asked him to arrive a bit early. He was dragging that day, still coming to terms with his own situation. Last week, the mailman pulled into the yard and honked the horn. If he was just dropping the circulars, bills, flyers from random solicitors who somehow procured his address, Clyde, the mailman, would slip into his yard, then back out as quietly as he came.

Before he left for Kuwait, Ms. Mozell would find things to complain about in Dwayne's presence until he fixed them. She'd wander over to the bathroom and sigh loudly until Dwayne asked what was wrong. Then she'd sigh again and then say she wished her toilet seat was higher because her old knees just don't bend like they used to. So, he got her a seat extender. Then installed a bath bar in the tub. He built a stool and placed it near the sink. It had two legs with wheels so she didn't have to lift it to move it, but it also had two peg legs so it wouldn't roll across the slanted kitchen floor if she sat at her wood stove while cooking. The last thing he did for Ms. Mozell before shipping off to the desert was install a mailbox next to the chokecherry tree just outside the kitchen door—the real main entrance—so as to limit the chances of her falling on the crushed-gravel-and-dirt drive to the mailbox along the road. He spoke with Mr. Davis who delivered the mail at the time that he was planning to move it, and why, and Mr. Davis nodded his head—these are the things we do for our folk. *We take care of we.*

But back from the desert and all the lives and mailmen since, Dwayne never moved the mailbox back to the edge of the road—maybe one day he'd need the proximity for his own knees should they give out. So every day Clyde comes in and drops the letters. If it is a delivery that requires a signature, Clyde knows to honk. Won't no need going to the house—nine times out of ten Dwayne would slink out from his shop. Most deliveries, he expected. And so he would be waiting by the mailbox at the usual route time. Last week, he was sharpening a chain saw for Mr. Johnny and didn't hear the first honk. Or the second. Finally, Clyde came into the shed waving a large manila envelope and squiggled his hand in the air.

"Looks like you got someone sending you important mail from Flor-ee-dah," Clyde said, adding staccato to his already tinny voice. "A Miss Angela Fisher. Just need your John Hancock and I'll be out your hair."

Dwayne froze at the name, then moved forward. He scratched Clyde's stylus across his handheld apparatus and they exchanged smiles.

"You good?" Clyde didn't release the envelope until Dwayne looked him in the eye. "If you were white, I'd say you looked like the blood done drained from your whole body like a goat hanging in the meat locker."

Dwayne chuckled. Nodded. "I guess I will be. Thanks, man."

In the house, his pocketknife slid slowly behind the sealed flap as smooth as slicing through fresh tallow. He flipped the whole envelope over so that the contents would spill out like he was afraid to touch whatever might be enclosed in there. A note card and a few stacks of stapled pages slid onto the counter. Using the tip of his knife, Dwayne pushed the contents around and saw folded stationery with ink bleeds through watermarks. The pages were folded into themselves so he would have to unfold them in order to read. His chest expanded as he caught his breath once he realized what it might be. He moved to the note card first.

I finally found the strength to go through his things. It's been so hard. The Fairfield County notice was forwarded here, and I remembered Lloyd talking about his family land all those years. I looked and found these papers. I knew you should have them. He loved you how he could, Dwayne. That's what I wanted to say on the phone. I know it will never feel like he loved you enough. There's more things here, should you want. Just let me know. —Angie

Dwayne went to the white-papered packets. TRANSFER OF DEED typed in large black letters on the top. Skimming the document, he saw his grandaddy Moses's address in Fairfield County—his family land, though it never felt like it—described as "ONE HUNDRED ACRES, FEDERAL GIFT TAX PAID IN FULL, TO MY SOLE HEIR, DWAYNE BOLTON." Signed by Lloyd Bolton, witnessed by Angela Fisher and Avery Fisher. Authorized by Mary Whiteside, Esq.

When he caught his breath, Dwayne walked out onto the land where he raised Nikki and looked south across the road. He looked past the tax-sale signs. Past where the faint brick foundation of the house pocked the land. The westward sun flickered on the green leaves, and the alcove, flanked with cypress trees, was fantastically lit this time of year. What had it meant, to his people, all those generations ago, to know the land so well as to pick a final resting place that shimmered in the golden hours, no matter the season?

Chapter 22

At the meeting, the space hummed like an engine. Sonny made his way near the established front of the room and the hum quieted to a purr.

"Thank y'all for making the time to gather our energies 'round this latest news. I know it's hard for some of us to peel away from our Saturdays."

"No more important place to be, really," a voice called out from the crowd. Sonny nodded and noted the temperature rising, or else his nerves. He quickly removed his cap and wiped his head with the palm of his hand.

Ms. Clinton, who everyone knows has the best pecan trees and whose house everyone comes to every October and November with their grocery bags to gather from the ground, said from the back, "Barbara. Tell us what *they* saying *they* plan to do with our land. What's the real plan?"

Mrs. Harmon looked at Sonny. He nodded *go 'head.* A resident of Fairfield County herself, she watched her colleagues print out all of the notices and offered outright, "Might as well just hand it to me now. Ain't no use letting Mr. Clyde the mailman do your dirty work." And then sucked her teeth, right there in their faces as she read out loud "Countywide Adjustment" at the top of the notice. In the meetings after meetings she attended as scribe she marveled at how, over the course of the last decade, the faces of the folks around the deciding tables had changed. More white. There was a time when the county officials mirrored the county. Everyone knew Fairfield County was the plantation hotbed of the Midlands of South Carolina. That the descendants of those on whose backs the empires stand stayed close—even as the empires crumbled to industry on the coast and riverways and industrial plants. Mrs. Harmon cleared her throat.

"They know my people been here six generations, so they whisper 'round me most days. Talkin' 'bout ten-year economic-development plan. Land-use plan. Talking about affordable houses, higher-density living. Getting rid of single-family residences. Catchphrases like that. Councilmember Jenkins was at the weekly farmers market the day after most of the county received them letters, and trust to smile at me and reach for a hug. If I didn't know by now, I knew watching him slither 'round the way that not all skinfolks is kinfolk. When he come reaching for a hug or whatever, I step back so he can't reach me and say just as straight as I'm talking to y'all gathered here, I say, 'So you the one trying to take my farm I intend to leave to my grandbaby?' And no sooner as I say that beads of sweat gather 'round his brow like a gambling man who just lost his kingdom. He goes, 'We'll leave some green for y'all,' and cups my shoulder like I'm one of his lil bros, then floats off to the next."

Heads shake in unison.

"We voted that man in. Who's he representing?"

"His self."

"Eyes greener than the pastures he's planning to bulldoze."

"Calling it progress."

After Mrs. Harmon opened the floodgates, many others took the opportunity to gripe about their dissatisfaction with local representation. The wolf-in-sheep's-clothing campaigning led them here. *It be your own who lose sight of it. It be your own.*

After a period of unspooling, Sonny wrangled the conversation back around the common theme of: if the train has already left the station—that is, if there is no big political backtracking that can be done because the plan had been ticking off year after year for some time now—all that was left was to figure out how to emerge from this next battle with as few casualties as possible. Surprisingly, there were some in the crowd, hearing the grim outlook, who offered they had spent their fighting years to keep their land this long, but their children had fled for the cities and had no desire to keep ahold of the properties. Like a man knowing when to fold, they pushed their cards to the middle of the table and tapped out.

"Developer folks all know we got them notices, and my phone been ringing all week. Each call, the offer gets higher and higher. I know folks say they gone flip it to the next highest bidder, but these are numbers with commas I ain't never seen in my lifetime, and finally one sounded good enough to accept. What use would it all be for me to stumble around holding on to all of it when don't none of my blood kin want it?"

"Now." That was Nate. "They don't want it *now.* I'm thinking about some of my folks and neighbors in Lower Richland County, in Eastover, and over near the Congaree Swamp on the south side of Columbia—similar story. Them folks slaved in the muck and mire over indigo and rice and then stayed and stayed and sent their kids to school, who got a taste of big-city living and couldn't for the life of them understand the value of the legacy of what was held for them all this time because they were blinded by promises of corner offices, of big checks, or whatever. Sold sold sold. To any bidder. Prolly not the highest. That's how we getting all that development. Then, when they realize them offices just ain't gone love you like a dogwood blossoming in spring, or the first ripe pear in August straight from a tree, they want it back. Wish it back. Go hunting for it. Then come to find all we got left in its place is smokestacks."

Folks hummed in unison. Nate pointed to Nikki and Chris standing just behind the lined-up tables, to the right.

"I mean, I look around and I wonder where the next generation is at? Sure, them two babies is here, and that's nice to see, but they not ready to take this on. We can't pass the baton to someone ain't on the field warmed up. Where's our kids at? The next gen?"

"Printing and signing the notices and licking the stamps."

There went the amen chorus.

When she was called out like that, Nikki straightened her spine to attention. She had been listening, but also felt, just like the gentleman who had a line in his jeans said—she wasn't near ready to take this fight on. If the property across the street her father said used to belong to them hadn't had that large tax-sale sign, and if Uncle Sonny hadn't been on his mission to talk with every Black resident of Fairfield County, she might have been oblivious to the intentions of this meeting altogether.

No one left the meeting with answers, but the hours spent leaning into the evening were cathartic for all the holding-in folks had been doing—holding on to the panic, the pre-grief, the anger, the forfeitures. From the looks of it, there were folks ready to stop the yearslong grip on the idea of a family land. Either they were the last of their blood, or estranged, or, as it was for several folks: had children who hadn't felt the internal pull, about a third in attendance. The second third had ways and means to fend off this attack and hold the lines. It's hard to ignore the longitudinal game of it all: folks in those brick buildings planning generations at a time, when so many of the folks gathered at the Spot could only—if at all—see one season at a time.

And each season of that year had its own losses: every pear tree was tricked by a warm March moment to push to blossom, and the next week a hard freeze. June had come, and with it, a heat wave then drought, so no water to plump the blueberries, the blackberries. Even the birds left the bushes with their blue shriveled fruits alone. The corn dried out and browned on the stalks. Only the larger commercial operations could afford to ship in water from elsewhere and the trucks had arrived, two by two up Highway 77 like the animals seeking shelter before the great flood.

No one in Fairfield County used their well water to water their lawns, so everyone mourned while listening to the crackle and crunch under their feet. They knew what no rain at the end of summer meant to their water supply, and for the folks who had row crops and livestock, there was a tight calculation between who or what got water, how much and for how long. You never want to go to the well for water to find it dry. How to account for all the losses? First, it took too long for the night temperatures to reach sixty degrees so the hay out in the field could take off. Then the heat hotter than hell. Then the weeks-long deluge. Was it hayfields or rice paddies—bogged down by bone-dry land being demanded to take on a month's worth of water in a week.

So then there weren't enough dry days to harvest anything. The markets responded.

And now the persimmons and pecans are dropping from the trees, signaling daylight's soon departure. They all still had so many summer crops in the ground, so no monetary return, right at the time the soil should be resting before the collards and broccoli, brussels, sweet potatoes, and so on. The only thing to make it out of those seasons with any type of abundance were the peanuts. Thank God for the peanuts. Everyone knows when we start planting peanuts, sure there's relief—if brief—but almost always the peanuts come before, attempting to stave off any future suffering.

PART IV

Chapter 23

A few days later Nikki rode Easy into town to pick up a few small things from the Feed & Seed store: carabiners for hanging the hay nets in the barn, a halter chain, a grooming brush, a lead rope because the new filly that was dropped off for training in the middle of the driest season anyone had known for some time was really the owner's plea for help. Mr. Tony wouldn't have to find hay for that horse—it would be Sonny's burden. So if the filly was sent home with too many ribs showing, well, Mr. Tony could withhold his training fee or argue for a discount, or whatever, even though the filly wasn't really old enough for formal training. Sonny said as much. He walked over and she barely lifted her head tall enough to reach his waist. She had just come off the teat, so also her mama's protection and guidance and sustenance. She was unruly because no one had taught her what being in community with humans was like, so she sat back or ran through three lead-rope snaps in as many days. Nikki didn't mind the errand. She got to ride Easy through town, and it reminded her of her own early days with Uncle Sonny sweeping her off the bus after school. She also didn't mind she got to hear the town news or gossip or scuttlebutt now that folks started taking her seriously as a young woman who stood to be impacted by county decisions, instead of just a young girl who could be talked around as if invisible. Or the other Nikki, the one on the news. Folks seeing her around town with Sonny and with horses seemed to change their minds about her. At the Feed & Seed store, Mr. James was praising the peanuts when she made her way to the counter.

"This must have been the same few seasons Washington Carver went through when he looked at the peanut like the last survivor of a nuclear blowout, and thought: *What can I do with you?* Must have been days like this that gave us peanut butter."

Nikki smirked. These days she couldn't go anywhere off farm—hers or Uncle Sonny's—without getting entangled in some conversation about the weather and its adverse effects on whatever market folks was in. If it wasn't weather, it was land. Often, it was both.

"Least Carver had land to dream on season after season." That was Ms. Carla. She had come up behind Nikki with a garden soaking hose and a few packs of seeds for her winter garden. Everyone believes she might be another of the folks ready to march off their land. Her oldest daughter was a manager at Applebee's in Charleston and indicated she had no desire to come home, and her youngest ran off to New York City just as soon as she could. She had stayed within arm's reach for college, made promises to come home more often. When the home-beat got less and less frequent, Ms. Carla stopped asking. Janelle had come home after college, started working in a pizza shop. Ms. Carla had to temper her feelings about all those bales of cotton, all those soybeans, those lean winters, blistering summers, the years of borrowing against and paying back so she could lift her head and say her youngest had gone off to university with a huge smile on her face. That summer Janelle was home *was* good for her, and also, how could she say with the same amount of pride that she was working at the pizza shop? Turns out, it was a temporary matter, because the next thing Ms. Carla knew, Janelle announced she was moving to New York. They say when the tax announcements floated into her mailbox, she called both girls and both, independently, asked *Why don't you just sell it, Mama?* Offering she could stop worrying about money, and there were all of these cute townhomes popping up? Maybe those might suit her now.

"Yeh, on former farms just like this one. Sell the land to pay them back their money?"

But this eighth year without William had worn her down. It wasn't the first time someone offered a chunk of change for their parcel. William had greater fortitude; his hands had spent the most time in those fair fields turning it over and over. She even used that wonderful line William gave to the last developer come to make an offer.

"Generations of my blood done soaked this soil. Made something of it, even when we won't seen as nothing more than a piece of machinery. We built this land. It's ours as long as I have breath in me to say it."

As long as she had breath, it was her land. Lately though, she had stopped using that last line, because *breath was 'bout as hard to come by as the rain that season.* She had called out "I can't breathe" at William's funeral, and everyone thought it was the widow-grief that comes on time, right as the casket closes. But she was gasping in a way that wasn't linked with her cries. The ushers came with their covering cloths and if it weren't for Mattie who brushed over

Ms. Carla's clammy wrist and felt the heartbeat run—no, gallop—to a stop, just as her body fell limp, everyone would have missed it. Would have said the Holy Spirit came and gave her comfort. But Mattie insisted someone call an ambulance and at the hospital Ms. Carla was diagnosed with this ailment that, when you say it, sounded like you had marbles in your mouth, so no one said it, just the conditions: "bad breathing," or "hard lungs."

Everyone shook their heads when they thought about Ms. Carla, her four fireplaces and wood-burning stove and the oxygen tank almost as tall as her. When Nikki heard the squeak of wheels on the concrete floor behind her, she let Ms. Carla scoot to the counter for her purchase.

James greeted her. "You got someone to put those in the ground for you, young lady?" James called the elders young, and the young ones were called sir or ma'am.

Ms. Carla shook her head and waited for the burst of oxygen before she spoke. "Getting my hands in the soil 'bout as healing as anything else I can do right now."

Ms. Carla stayed to chat with James a bit, and scooted over for Nikki to complete her transaction. Nikki smiled at Ms. Carla, paid for her things, and left. Looking at the sky, she was going to make it back a bit later than expected—she got tied up both eavesdropping at the counter, then meandering her way through town, the woods, back roads, dirt roads. It was the time of day she would have been coming home from school, and so she was caught behind the bus. Mrs. Esther hooked her head out the window, asked how she was, how her father was. When the kids piled out of the bus two girls squealed and Easy's ears perked to attention. Nikki scratched his neck under his mane. He grunted in approval. One girl bounded off the bus then ran straight up to her and asked if she could pet the horse. Nikki nodded. The little girl's friend hung back, her initial excitement waned having faced the horse now.

"He's big!" she offered. Nikki smiled.

"A *big* puppy dog!" she called back. The girl shook her head. The first girl had moved to Easy's chest, scratching, calling out *good boy, good boy,* Easy stretched his neck out in satisfaction.

"A giraffe!" the distant girl called out. "His head's in the sky!"

The not-afraid girl turned to Nikki. "Can I ride him?"

Nikki's initial response was caution. Then she softened. If Uncle Sonny had said no that first time, where would she be?

"What about your friend? If I let you ride, who will walk her the rest of the way home?"

It had been some time since the buses dropped you in front of your house like when Nikki was younger. Traffic had begun to back up longer because there were more school-aged folks now . . . a by-product of the microdevelopments. One thing begat another, and so on.

A few years back, when they made the announcement, folks protested: sure it's fine for kids to walk a bit in the days of the year when the sun stretched out its time in the sky well past dinnertime. But the closer they crawled to the cooler months, the kids would have to walk to the bus stops in the morning and back in the afternoon in near darkness. County Council and the superintendent didn't budge. The number of car pools had increased, according to the school—they had to invest infrastructure to widen the roads for folks who refused to feed their children to the darkness and could afford to rearrange their days for drop-off and pickup. For everyone else, the parents insisted on the buddy system as best they could.

At the prospect of potentially being left behind, the frightened girl stepped closer. The brave one answered Nikki's question.

"We're just around the corner. Well, my house is. Mya's house is down the road a bit more. It's still light out."

"Danielle! Don't leave me," Mya called out.

"Stop being a scaredy-cat."

A few cars crawled by. Nikki waved at Ms. Carla. Ms. Jean. Reggie. She hopped off Easy and brought everyone a few more feet away from the road's edge. Thankfully, most Fairfield County folk knew horses still had the right of way—for now—but Sonny had warned Nikki when she had started venturing beyond the trails and into town that there were more and more folks who didn't abide by that rule, no matter how many yellow signs popped up along the roads with a horse and its rider.

"I'll let you sit, but maybe not ride today. Mya needs you," Nikki told Danielle. "Have you been on a horse before?" Danielle shook her head.

Nikki figured the girl—tall but slim—might weigh just more than a hay bale. Like a good summer bale when they're stuffed to the gills and tip near seventy pounds. When she was younger and rode with Uncle Sonny, if they took a break or made a stop somewhere, he'd offer her a leg up—grab her left ankle and instruct her to push as hard as she could off the ground and swing her right leg over the saddle. So Nikki had a script to follow. It took three valiant tries—one failure was Nikki's, the other two Danielle miscalculated how high she had to go. Mya had gotten closer now, considering. Easy was of course nonplussed. Nikki scratched his withers for being such a good boy.

"Hold here." Nikki cupped the saddle horn, noticing at this angle how much she needed to rewrap it. The last few jobs with Uncle Sonny saw her roping and dallying steers about as big as Easy, and the protective wrapping keeping a barrier between the leather and the rope was tearing.

"Look at me, Mya!" Danielle called out squealing again. "I'm on a horse!" Mya was close enough to touch Easy, but kept her hands to her sides. Nikki reached over to Mya and grabbed her hand. Eventually, Mya relented and let her hand be held by the older girl, who was also holding the gargantuan horse.

"Breathe," Nikki whispered in Mya's direction. "It's our fear that horses react to. They want to know what you're afraid of, so they start reacting, not knowing that you're afraid of them."

Nikki modeled a deep breath, exaggerating lifting her shoulders while opening her mouth wide. Mya followed suit. Nikki pointed to Danielle—"You too! Let's breathe together." Easy took a deep breath in unison. Then licked his lips.

"Your heart gallops like a horse when we're scared. Did you know they can feel your heartbeats before they can see you? When we relax, they relax, just like he's licking his lips like after a good meal. He's not thinking of anything else—not running, certainly—except being here with his friends."

Mya smiled at that. Nikki, still holding her, pulled her closer and together they rubbed Easy's shoulder.

"Deep breath," Nikki reminded. "See, he breathes when we do. A nervous horse is how we get in danger." Mya snatched her hand back and Easy's ears followed.

"He also doesn't know what quick movements mean, so we have to move with confidence and purpose. Slow."

Danielle played in Easy's mane, perfectly content to sit atop the steed, and found herself in no rush to be anywhere else. Finally, Nikki got Mya to run her fingertips along Easy's chest, neck, jowls.

She no longer needed to remind Mya to breathe; Mya was smiling now, cooing his name. Transfixed.

"Okay. I have an idea," Nikki started and broke the two girls' trance. "Mya, if you're brave enough, I'll swing you on top of Easy and I'll walk y'all both home." A glimpse of terror turned over to intrigue very quickly and Nikki knew she was now trying to calculate how two girls would ride one horse. Danielle scooted to the edge of the saddle and patted the space between her and the saddle horn. Nikki repeated the steps on how to give a leg up and Danielle leaned out of her way. Mya was lighter, so only one try got the job done. Nikki smiled when Mya smiled and patted Easy's mane.

"Okay, do y'all know the cowgirl words to get a horse moving?"

Mya, eager now, clicked her heels against Easy's shoulders and Easy lurched forward. Both girls squealed and laughed.

"Giddyup!" Mya said.

"Giddyup!" Danielle echoed.

Nikki tugged on the reins she unclipped on one side of Easy's mouth to move him forward, and clicked her tongue so he'd know it was real.

"Come on, boy, giddyup!"

The girls were chatty Cathys asking a barrage of questions that Nikki had to sift through and choose which questions and what order.

No, I haven't been riding my whole life.

No, Easy isn't my horse. My Uncle Sonny lets me take care of him like he's mine though.

I stopped going to school. I want to train horses.

Yes, I like learning! A lot. I'm learning every day on Uncle Sonny's farm how to keep, train, and raise horses.

Nikki was very glad they hadn't caught her on the news that time. Didn't know her by that one bad thing that happened to her. That, in this case at least, she wouldn't be defined by that video that traveled across Fairfield County, and wherever else it may have gone to, in what seemed like milliseconds.

Yes, I want to be a cowboy . . . girl when I grow up.

On and on like a friendly interrogation. The walk felt like it stretched on forever—the road unfurling like a red carpet. Between the questions were giggles. The girls saying Easy's name like a nursery rhyme. Looking at Easy, his ears twirling back and forth—looking at Nikki, then the girls on his back—he was so proud of himself that his lips curled up at the corners.

"I know, boy. You are taking such good care of them," Nikki said in his direction. He snorted. *Yep.*

"I can't believe how brave you are, Mya! You're riding a horse!" Nikki called back, smiling.

"Danielle, you're a natural."

Danielle sat up straighter, a true horsewoman. Proud of the compliment. Then to no one, maybe her friend, maybe Nikki, maybe herself.

"I wonder if my ancestors rode horses."

It was a phrase that didn't stop or curl up at the end in a question. It rode the wind down the side of the road with the girls. Nikki heard it and hummed. It had been her question, too. A thing like this come so naturally, as Uncle Sonny would say, surprisingly, passed down like dimples, or the color of your eyes, or like how she had her mother's short stature with her father's family's big bones.

She had never asked it out loud so that someone might have an answer, or another inquiry or a refutation. Some days her and Sonny are so busy she didn't have time to necessarily dream out loud. And when she was with Chris, she felt like she didn't have any questions that needed answering.

But now with the girls, Nikki wondered what would it have been for her to have a model at such an age? Sure, Uncle Sonny was there, and has given her all he knows, and made a way for her to figure out for herself what kind of horsewoman she wanted to be, and how, and for whom. Most days, that was more than sufficient. Most days she went home to Dwayne and recounted all of what she was up to with such pride she could not imagine anything else she might have done with a day in her life.

This morning, Pepper, a colt born just a month after the unruly filly who broke the lead rope that sent her out into town in the first place, joined up with her. She had been pushing and pushing, applying a force field of pressure to keep his feet moving around the round pen. When she stepped back, making the bubble between her and Pepper bigger, he stopped moving his feet and like she was taught, she turned her back and waited. Pepper was still in the corner of her eye. Nikki saw him look out to the pastures for his friends, then turn to her. The wait was always the worst. When Uncle Sonny taught her this technique of strengthening partnerships with horses, especially when they're young, he warned her that most of the work was waiting.

"You gotta wait for them to start thinking, and most importantly, thinking of you as someone they *want* to be with, maybe join on whatever journey you trying to take them on."

"Like a leader?"

Sonny cricked his neck, considering the question. "I mean, you *could* think of it that way. Like a leader and follower. That's a big separation though. Like—I am human. You are horse." He beat his chest and spoke short staccato words mimicking a caveman. Nikki chuckled.

"I don't think that way anymore. Like top-down. How they say it? Vertical. Like I always say, I want them to think we're in a herd together. So we're looking out for each other. That other way," Sonny pointed his thumb over his shoulder to nothing in particular. "That other way leaves you with a horse only looking out for himself when he's not with you, and waiting for you to make every single decision for him when you're together, and if you're in danger or something, I think I want a horse that asks me what are *we* going to do to get out of this mess—'cause the other way—he down the block, prolly bucked you off, maybe ran you over because panic set in his chest and he was just thinking 'bout himself. Not, like, thinking 'bout *y'all.* Together."

So that morning Pepper turned to her. Nikki waited. He crept up to her and she felt his breath on her neck. He was asking: *What are we going to do next?*

When Nikki approached the next driveway with the girls still squealing on Easy's back, a woman who was sitting on the porch popped up and walked briskly to the end of the drive.

"I saw the bus go by a while ago! Where y'all been?"

"Granma, look! I'm on a horse!" Danielle didn't answer the question.

"I see that. Clear as day, Dani. What are you doing *up there*?"

Nikki reached her hand out in introduction. "I'm Nikki Bolton, ma'am."

The woman paused. Nodded. It felt like an eternity between Nikki's reach and the woman's return.

"Dwayne's girl?" She was holding Nikki's hand like now performing an inspection. Squinted her eyes even though there wasn't sun in them. Chewed her lip like she was thinking. Nikki nodded. Wasn't sure where the next line of inquiry was going to go: the school incident, or?

She pointed to Danielle. "I'm Joyce. This my own great-granbaby Danielle you ferrying down Highway 21 on this horse."

"Easy," Nikki said. Joyce cocked her head to the side and flattened her lips. Nikki quickly understood the misunderstanding.

"We call him Easy, ma'am." She threw in the honorific to try and smooth things over. Joyce nodded and reached her hand up towards Danielle, who hopped down, then scratched Easy's shoulder in thanks.

"Your grandaddy and great-grandaddy would have a hoot to see this! You know, I grew up with your grandaddy, Lloyd, and I swear I loved me some Mr. Moses and his horses."

Whatever was said after that, Nikki didn't remember. She didn't really remember dropping Mya off, or waving goodbye to the girl and the adult that came to scoop her up. Only, the part of the day that stuck with her the most was the moment she learned there were people in her family who had horses—information that had never crossed her path before. Nikki rode Easy the rest of the way home, holding the pulsing new knowledge in her chest.

Chapter 24

It had been a few Saturdays since the meeting at the Spot where the Fairfield County Black folks compared tax notices and griped and grieved and attempted to plan. Finding ways to simultaneously come up with thousands of dollars and not sell land to settle a bill when you already live hand to mouth was not the type of quandary that could be solved in a half-day meeting, so mostly folks left with no more answers than they came with, but they did leave with a calming sense that they were not alone. That wasn't nothing. Folks left understanding whatever fight it was they were up against, it was not their singular battle. Everyone gets rained on when the sky opens up.

Because of the meeting and because of the fact that Sonny had tunnel vision for trying to solve his own quandary with his two working hands, he had taken in more horses than he knew what to do with, which was a boon for Nikki—Sonny had deputized her to be his assistant trainer. A title that came with no pay increase (she had no pay to speak of), but with much more responsibility. Weanlings, on the verge of turning a year older when January 1 hit, whose human parents thought they had the mettle to raise once they left the teat, sat months unhandled and were rank, rowdy, spunky things with no time or respect for humans save if their human approached with a bucket of grain or oats or a flake of hay.

Otherwise, they were kites: kicking and bucking every which way. In your face. Behind your back. At the vet. The farrier. Bucking because it was Tuesday and drizzling and ten degrees colder than it was yesterday.

Sure, Sonny would prefer to put his hands on the young horses before they got to this point, but before this point, they were bite-sized toothless balls of muscle and still-forming bones. Still forming their opinions of the world, too, and it's not that with the right trainer, Sonny explained to prospective clients, a horse at any age can't come around to having some sense about him, it's just that the work is easier if it happens earlier because the transactions with the horse are all deposits: put in good interactions, get good back. Now Sonny's got a barn of near-feral opinionated baby horses and all of the transactions must start with a series of corrections, which the colts read as withdrawals: *You're taking from me, so I am mad and will show you my anger.*

It takes a series of fits before he can get to deposits.

"This is where the work gets draining," Sonny said to Nikki, holding a colt at the end of a lead rope. He was leaping up into the air like a balloon because Sonny simply asked him to move out of the three-foot no-horse-allowed invisible bubble like a force field around him.

"He thinks my space is his because this space was given to him for too long by his humans. So when I say *no—*" Sonny lifted his arm and pulsed the end of the lead rope. "All he knows is I took *his* space from him. And I have to keep telling him: *No, no,* it's *my space.* It's mine."

Sonny explained to Nikki it's not unlike raising kids, he thinks. He had never raised any, but he could imagine it was the same: at one point you're feeding the child three meals a day with your spoon to his mouth, and the next you're saying *here, you do it.* And the baby might cry because you took the luxury of being spoon-fed from him, so then your work becomes getting the child to see that he is also learning to do things for himself.

"So I'm trying to get this colt to understand that if he moves from my space, I'll leave him alone. Make the right decision for yourself, little guy."

Nikki had a string of colts she had to show how to be good horsey citizens. Almost never in her life had she been given a task with such high stakes, and she took it very seriously. Secretly, though, she began to know that she could. Even if what she knew the whole of her life up to this point were a lot of silences, and around those silences—tension. She knew what it was to walk with ghosts of past lives you wished weren't a part of your story. That was how she tried to wrap her arms around understanding what her father kept from her. Her history, her roots.

The whole ride home when Dwayne picked her up, she chewed on this understanding, even with the high-pitched giggles of the girls ringing in her ears from earlier that afternoon. Because, according to people she had never met, she had come from folks who had some horses, and that meant, she hoped, whatever task Sonny was bestowing upon her now, she could do it, and with ease. Like it felt the whole of her journey had been. *Natural.*

Nikki didn't know how to bring up what she had learned. Who to bring it up to. Saying something to her father just then felt like it could be seen like a confrontation, and ever since that day in the classroom, she had avoided situations that felt like they could combust with the tiniest of sparks, and this felt like . . . the first flare of a bonfire. And she didn't think she could take it to Sonny because Sonny didn't know her father their whole lives. How would he know the depths of who she was like Ms. Joyce?

So she leaned in, dug deeper. Tried to touch the limits of her understanding, and decided to work harder. She left the house earlier, came home later. Dwayne watched the schedule change, and as nonconfrontational as he is—did she get it from him?—he didn't say anything exactly, but Nikki could see the questions on his face, wondering what the extra time really was about.

"Daddy, who these colts become is up to what kind of deposits I put in right now," she said, sounding like Sonny, stuffing a piece of dry toast in her mouth, leaving the cheese-scrambled eggs on the stove. The other day, noticing how she moved often with such haste to the farm, Dwayne had asked if she might take it a little easier, to not burn herself out. *What will you do if you get tired of this?* Today, the request: At least finish breakfast? The next thing he knew she was in the car waiting for him to taxi her over.

Finally, Dwayne insisted Nikki call her mother to set up some time together. The horses could probably also use some time off.

"Uncle Sonny says consistency is key," Nikki tried to offer as a counter to his directive. "He says if you build a sense of predictable routine, then you build trust, then you have the foundation of a good partnership."

Dwayne raised his eyebrows. "Exactly my point. Call your mother. Be predictable. Fall into a routine."

Nikki sighed. She didn't have another retort. She could have leaned on how, after the first few months of their life, having depended and looked to their mothers for just about everything, the colts have to be separated from their mothers, and vice versa. Weaned. They needed distance. The last time Nikki saw her own mother there was an ocean between them. In Gwendolyn's absence, Nikki relished not thinking about her body, its limitations. Her inadequacies. At the farm, she reveled in all it could do. For her mother, it was always something—think about what men might want in a wife. Think about all else you have to overcome being Black and woman. Be presentable, always. The incident.

"I'm only trying to help," Gwendolyn would say before any critique. Nikki would point out how it absolutely was not helping. Her days had been filled with horses who needed her help; Nikki didn't want them to think her not being there was a withdrawal. She also didn't need her father on her case, and thought if she said OK to this, she might bank a few weeks again without having to go. A trade-off.

"Daddy, you know what more work means to Uncle Sonny right now. If he loses his farm, what do *I* have? So I'm trying my level best to help him keep it and I get all this experience out of it too. At first it was a thing to do, 'cause, you know . . ." she trailed off. "Then it became a thing I liked. But now it feels like a thing I *need* to do. You know? I never got this close to this feeling before. I can't lose it. Uncle Sonny can't lose it."

Dwayne didn't respond. She did have *it*. Sonny said it, and he heard it then, but now he felt it. He knew she had it, of course, she's a Bolton, but he had wondered all these years of her life if they—horses—would come to her and sink their teeth in as they had done for generations, even if he had caused a separation. Even if the work itself seemed to skip a generation. Even if he had made a child with a woman whose eyes light up at a downtown cityscape. He had been thinking about the blood that had always run through his daughter and hadn't responded to Nikki's last comment. She filled the silence.

"Fine. Since it's so important to you, I'll call her. I guess I could get my nails done."

Dwayne snapped back and then held her hand and looked, as if inspecting. He chuckled.

"Yep. I guess you could."

||||||||||||||||||||

Over the phone Nikki didn't respond to the snark she heard in her mother's voice.

"About time," Gwendolyn said. "Was beginning to wonder if I dreamed up I had a daughter. Then I see these stretch marks across my stomach looking like a watermelon and I remember."

Nikki rolled her eyes. Breathed deep. What did her therapist say? Every word doesn't warrant a response. What did Uncle Sonny teach her? The colts want first to meet your energy until they learn it's easier to not react, but to wait. Nikki took two beats.

"Anyways, I missed you," Gwendolyn offered. Nikki smirked because it worked.

Dwayne dropped Nikki early at her grandmother's house, Gwendolyn's mother—neutral ground for the meetup. Gwendolyn had showed up a few minutes later than the agreed-upon time, and so by the time she got there, Dwayne was gone. Classic avoidance dance.

"Like the sun and moon—almost never in the same sky," Nikki's grandma said, observing Gwendolyn waltzing through the door summoning Nikki without dropping her keys or loosening her scarf. She was talking about Dwayne and her, but it could go this way, too.

On the drive south to Sandhill's, Nikki looked for random things to take her attention: The crushed armadillo on the side of the road. The stiff-bodied doe. Vultures swooping in and out the way. Herby-Curbys strewn about the ends of driveways like old receipts. The black couch put out so long ago the upholstery was disintegrating. It had been there the last few outings. Since what, the spring? Orange cones and skid steers widening roads the closer they got. A new traffic circle. A woman in short sleeves and shorts running along the few feet of sidewalk that appear and disappear almost as fast.

Gwendolyn cleared her throat. Pointed her chin in the woman's direction.

"You look like you been running miles like her. Getting slim and trim! I saw it earlier."

Here we go. It wasn't early enough for a weight-loss meeting, so Nikki thought she'd escape conversations about it. But who was she to think that? Her mom breathed it. It was in her DNA. Everywhere she turned, growing up, a reminder of how inadequate women were who carried extra weight. Gwendolyn got off the couch and went to the backyard to get Nikki's red Radio Flyer and filled it with cinder blocks—she guesstimated they each must weigh about ten pounds—until it hit forty pounds and she wheeled it in front of everyone.

"This is what I'm holding I hope to lose. The last of the stubborn baby weight."

Dwayne looked at Nikki then Gwendolyn. Smirked. Gwendolyn put her hands on her hips. "They say it can stay on for years. For some, it never goes away. I just want this much."

It went on that way for years. Counting this, weighing that. Shake this. Cut that. Nikki found herself reading labels for numbers before she could ask to have a scoop of ice cream. A handful of potato chips. If she deposited that much fat, she'd have to walk it off, or something. It had become a lifestyle. Not a great one, but the one she had when she was with her mother.

Leaving after lunch for their outing, Nikki thought she'd avoid it too. She knew her mother hated driving through the country after dark, so she'd be home without a stop for dinner. Perfectly orchestrated to avoid diet talk over food. Body talk over food. Just nails. In. Out. Done.

Nikki read the sign of the veteran sitting on the ground at the stoplight asking for any change she could spare.

Gwendolyn pinched Nikki's thigh when she didn't respond.

"Am I right? Have you been trying?"

Nikki shook her head. "Just working. Riding. Uncle Sonny's got so many horses now, barely have time to think about what I'm going to eat."

"That's good!"

Nikki knew where her mother's enthusiasm was towards and it wasn't a barn full of horses. It wasn't worth it. Let her have it.

The nail salon couldn't come soon enough. It was busy of course for a Saturday: hair and nails. Add cleaning and you have the Black woman trifecta. The Black girl's burden. Even though they were in Sandhill's mall in Columbia, considered the white part of town, all of the customers in the nail salon were Black. When they walked in, Cindy greeted them with a big smile and said their seats were ready.

Say what you want about it, Nikki thought, but she did find reason these days to appreciate a cushioned leather seat that vibrated and beat your muscles to a pulp while your feet soaked in scalding water. Tom—he in no way looked like a Tom—always set the water too hot for her feet before, but now calloused and sore from hours of farmwork, Nikki wondered if the water could go hotter. He seemed surprised when she asked.

"More hot?"

Nikki nodded. Meanwhile, Gwendolyn groaned in approval and thanked Cindy for her mimosa. The two settled into their time together.

Chapter 25

Nikki didn't know what to think. The one-two punch of it: first Danielle's grandma saying men she never met but were her blood were horsefolk like her. And then her mother in the nail salon.

How could she have guessed the day would turn out how it did? When they moved to getting their fingernails done, her mother started reaching, reaching for anything to talk about, and Nikki prayed she'd find literally anything except how her body might look that day, or her second favorite topic, how disappointed she was in her father. Eventually, after her mother landed on Favorite Topic #2, Nikki turned to her and asked, "Mama, do you have any happy memories with Daddy?"

Even the nail tech slowed down on her work. Listening. That's how you knew they were no longer zoning out whatever it was you were talking about, and instead, leaning into what they believed would be impending drama. Gwendolyn wiggled her fingers. Cindy went back to sweeping the emery board across her nail bed.

"Why do you ask that?"

Nikki rolled her eyes—her mother's first response usually defense.

"It's just that, I know y'all aren't together. I know that. I've stopped wanting that a while ago. I just guess I don't think I have any memories of us, together, happy. Really happy. So I was wondering if *you* maybe had any happy memories with Daddy? Probably before me."

Nikki looked down at her hands the whole time.

"It was so hard," Gwendolyn said. That was all she said for some time. Nikki didn't count but remembering the conversation later, the silence felt like an eternity.

"Your father and I had so many dreams together, Nikki. So many dreams. Once, we wanted to build up a farm of our own on his family land. I would garden and keep chickens, maybe some pigs. He would have the horses."

"Horses?" Nikki turned to her mother. They locked eyes, and Gwendolyn nodded, then looked at her hands.

"Yes. I wanted horses, and your father said he'd want them again, for me. For our family. On the farm. Just across from Ms. Mozell's land."

Nikki's eyes started to blur for the tears forming. Her mother was still telling about the time she had happy memories, and Nikki could only think about why she had never heard any of this before. That there had been a plan, all along, for the property across the street. That it would have been hers. That she would have had horses her whole lived life, if her parents' onetime dream had come true.

Nikki sat on what she learned from her mother at the nail salon, still not yet wanting to confront Dwayne with everything she had learned. She couldn't quite wrap her head around the fact that there was a timeline in which she could have had a partner like Easy in her backyard, or that whenever her father looked longingly across the way at where her great-grandparents had lived, he might have been conjuring—seeing?—horses in a pasture.

In the meantime, she knew she wanted to tell Chris. But how was she going to start telling it?

There was so much to catch up on since they were last together at Sonny's meeting at the Spot. Of course, she'll apologize for standing him up the last few times he texted, "Ride at dawn?" indicating his desire to trail ride with her, and they'd settled on an appropriate time to meet—not dawn at all—but she was up to her forehead in bucking colts and day work with Sonny. Two farms calved out this time of year and Sonny had always said that if it was freezing rain, you know that on one of those days when all you want to do is curl up in front of your crackling fire with a hot drink and relax under the weight of a hand-quilted blanket, *that* was when a heifer would be belly-deep in a mud pit trying to push out a calf feet first. Never fails. So as soon as several cold fronts pushed below-average temperatures and rain, Sonny's phone rang like he was Emergency Medical Services, and Nikki figured in a way he was. The vet was all the way out in Kershaw County, and emergencies never happened during normal business hours—why would they?—and so Sonny was the cheapest, most reliable, most knowledgeable call to make under the circumstances. The books were full.

The last time Nikki had even saddled Easy for a trail ride, the leaves were bright yellows and oranges. Light winds would rattle the limbs and the leaves would fall down at her feet like confetti. It was like a Hallmark movie and she was riding out of the scene into a new life. Now the limbs were bare, and it surprised her how much further into the woods Nikki could see. Already ten minutes into the ride to finally meet Chris, and she could still make out the sun's reflection off of Sonny's barn behind her. She thought she heard the crunch of leaves under hoof-fall first, but could make out a figure about a four-minute ride ahead of her. The clearing would appear firstly, so she headed that way and waited for Chris.

When the form got closer, though, she realized it wasn't Chris. Not even a man with a horse. But a white man with a gun slung over his shoulder, wearing camouflage, his face sporting black marks smeared on his cheeks and forehead. Binoculars dangled from his chest.

"Where's your orange?" he asked.

Nikki contemplated dismounting, trying to calculate if she would be safer on the horse or on the ground. She decided she would stay mounted—height advantage and all that.

"It's the middle of hunting season and you as brown as the trees," he said, adjusting his gun. "On a thing the size and color of a buck."

Nikki had never seen this man before, and she thought she knew all the white folks in town—the smattering of them, running the coffee shop, the General Store. She had never seen him at the Feed & Seed. Not at the Waffle House. Not anywhere of her usual haunts around town. She studied him to report back to Uncle Sonny and prayed that Chris would appear into the clearing soon, before she found out if this man, this nameless man, had any bad intentions.

The man stepped forward and Easy startled. She had been trying to breathe into her toes to signal ease, but she felt Easy's energy bubbling up in his back—dynamite waiting for the smallest spark. The man stepped back at the horse's startle and gripped the shotgun sling tighter. Nikki understood who held the power, and her silence would not win.

"This private property," she started, then remembered the double-barrel peering over the bearded man's shoulder. Added, "Sir."

He cleared his throat. Nikki noticed tattoos creeping down the back of his left hand. Feathers, fanned out like on the tail of a bird descending out of the sky, and talons curled, ready to grab its prey.

"I'm sure it ain't your'n," he said. "I just bought some acreage right before the season started, ain't seen no survey markers showing where mine ends, and I guess whoever's begins."

Mr. Reamer had let the tail end of his parcel bleed into Sonny's and into Chris's folks' land; they all met in a triangle—probably this clearing now she thought of it. She knew he was one of the first folks to have trouble before all this mess, and she knew that he was getting older and one of the nephews was handling affairs—trying to settle it before his death—selling off his cattle herd, his machinery, etc. The property had just been cleared to be listed. What had Mrs. Harmon said? Folks was coming to people's doors with cash to move the transaction faster. He didn't look like someone with a lot of cash, not with his tattoos, hair pulled into a ponytail at the nape of his neck under his skullcap. But here he was.

"It's my family's land," Nikki said. Breathed deep and wiggled her toes again. "Sir."

"We'll have to get the surveyor out, looks like," he said. If he had very ill intentions, Nikki supposed, it would have been made known at this point, but she knew better than to let her guard down in the middle of the woods with a man with a gun.

She had been so focused on breathing and his hands, and frankly, her own hands—no quick movements, and so on—that she hadn't heard Chris approach.

"Can I help you?" he said, pushing his horse into the clearing with purpose. He sounded out of breath.

Chris had come into the hunter's view and Nikki said, "Hi!" quickly, and with relief in her voice and in a tone that she hoped the man would understand the young Black man entering the scene was friendly, her friend, and today maybe even her savior.

The man adjusted his shotgun with both hands and stepped back so that both teenagers were in his sight lines. Easy's back tingled again, and Chris's mount moved his feet so, like how Nikki watched the ropers or barrel racers at rodeos before they entered the arena—adrenaline coursing through their veins it was impossible to stand still, at attention. Chris tried to calm the horse, while trying to remain calm himself, offering a few *whoa boys* in vain. The horse knew he had potentially walked into a danger zone—the air electric like before a storm. He was a good boy, but sensitive, Chris had always described him—the type of horse that will do whatever you ask unless and until he felt he was in danger, then the horse would try his level best to exit the source of pressure. Jet was inching to leave and Chris was demanding he stay, and watching a nervous horse gave Easy reason to start to question his own safety and still, there was a white man standing between them with a gun.

"Where's your orange?" The man asked Chris the same question he had of Nikki—all this time and no names exchanged. "Don't y'all know it's hunting season?"

"Don't you know this private property?" Chris responded. Nikki had noticed his back was timber-straight; he was puffing his chest, and she had sworn she never heard Chris's voice so low, like it had come from the soles of his feet. He sounded like a man.

"That's what this one says," he said, taking a hand off his weapon long enough to point in Nikki's direction. "I tell her, I don't see any survey markers, so how am I to know who or what is what."

Chris finally got Jet to settle long enough to dismount. He had done it in haste, throwing his right leg over, sliding down the horse's left flank. His shirt caught on the back of his saddle on the way down and Nikki saw the flash of a grip in the center of Chris's back. Suddenly she worried more for her friend than she had when he had come barreling in and she watched the man calculate drawing his weapon.

Thankfully, he did not. But had the man seen that Chris was also carrying? No time to ask why, after all of the reasons for a young Black boy to not be carrying, no matter the reason, she relaxed her grip on Easy's reins when Chris adjusted his shirt quickly to cover up.

"What I know is this spot butts up against my and my neighbor's property, and you are straddling two parcels, with a gun, mind you. I should ask you where your license is—and what you're after. Everyone knows deer ain't on the move in the middle of the day, yet here you are. I could report you for trespassing."

Chris watched the man's hands and only because Nikki knew Chris could she tell that he was so inflated like a puffer fish—all smoke, bluff—full of nervousness. Even with that understanding, no one could have been convinced at that moment the two would have made it out alive. The statistics: One Black boy was minding his business at the convenience store buying Skittles. One Black boy was playing by himself in a playground. Two Black kids trail riding in their backyards—Nikki imagined the headline: *Hunter says was ambushed on private property, shot in self-defense.* It could happen to them. In a way, it already happened to her. Her father wouldn't be able to survive the media spin, much less the actual outcome. Her mother . . .

Nikki had to think quickly. She believed from when they first met that Chris would protect her, the way he apologized for something he didn't do, apologized that no one had protected her that day. But the stakes seemed higher, and now, she believed he needed protection. She spoke to Chris.

"I think he bought Mr. Reamer's property. I remember Uncle Sonny saying when he saw the for-sale sign go up that he should probably come out and mark our lines, even though it should be on the new owner to know the limits of his land."

Nikki looked at the man. "Uncle Sonny never got around to it."

Nikki nodded to Chris. *Stand down. Don't feed this man anything else.*

Chris spoke to Nikki. "Wild how folks put the onus of our survival on us."

Nikki nodded again. Cleared her throat.

"Sir. We are just out here enjoying our day on our property. I understand you don't know where yours ends, but I assure you, it's not here."

Nikki had used her words. Like her therapist encouraged her to do the next time she felt trapped into immobility. Words can move a moment.

The man stood, contemplating whatever men going out into woods with guns might contemplate. His own shoulders dropped; his first sign of not being on the offense like when it was just Nikki and him and his weapon, or on the defense when outnumbered after Chris arrived (and with another weapon potentially in play). The lines on his forehead above his sunglasses softened. He found reason.

"Well, neighbors," he had for the first time lifted his own voice above a deepest bass. "I'll be coming 'round the way soon to get this all sorted out. I'm Matthew Jordan. The new owner on that property back thataway. I suppose I could have led with that. I was just so caught by surprise, you know, agent said neighbors keep to themselves."

How would they know? Nikki thought, knowing it had been at least as long as since she was born that Uncle Sonny bought his place directly from its current owners—it was the only way he could without any real established credit. He promised to keep it how they had intended, to the best of his ability: as natural as he found it, as the land would allow. Chris's family been on their parcels since they marched away that new year to their own emancipation. And before—what was it? three months ago?—Mr. Reamer was the sixth generation that she knew to occupy his place. How would a real estate agent know, really know, the nature of this area?

Anyway, she'll leave that figuring to the adults.

Chris stood in front of his horse, stone-faced. Even as the Matthew guy was standing down.

"You have a day," Nikki said. Incorrect and still too gracious for the moment, but she also didn't want the man to have any good in his life. She didn't know how else to ask him to be about his way so she—and definitely Chris—could breathe again. She didn't fix her words, and she didn't smile, just flattened her lips in the beginning gesture of it then clucked Easy across the clearing towards her friend. The man nodded to Chris, who just lifted his chin. He watched like a statue until the man was out of the clearing. With the branches bare, it would be some time before the man was completely out of sight, but when he was far enough, marching away from them, Chris let the curve settle into his back again. And then Nikki dismounted, finally letting Easy rest.

The air moved again around them, and Nikki plopped down on her mounting log to catch her breath. She patted the bark next to her. Chris slogged over and stood. He was panting. His shoulders heaved to the heavens, then sank below the ground if they could have. Nikki took loud, deep breaths. Caught Chris's eyes. *Breathe with me.*

He dropped his body on the log next to Nikki. They leaned into each other. They had survived.

After an uncounted amount of time, Nikki stood up. The quick movement startled the horses, who had powered down to a nap. She reached her hand to Chris. He took two beats before they locked palms and he bounded to his feet. Nikki opened her arms for an embrace. He accepted. They had never been this close before. Sure, they leaned shoulder to shoulder propping each other up at the meeting the other weekend. But mostly there was always a horse between them unless he was giving a leg up. Then they were super close but always in proximity as the situation arose. The hug after what they had endured together felt like what Nikki imagined home to feel like. Familiar. Safe. Loved in a way, but without condition. How she wished her mother's hugs felt, when they happened. Loved, with no expectations. How she wished and wished her father's felt, but she knew deep down he had his own hopes and dreams for her, even as it felt like he held her with a loose string. She didn't know, couldn't quite put her fingers on what those expectations might be these days. He had always just offered to her, *make me proud.* Nikki knew that he supported her to an extent by letting her set loose the ghost of formalized school (*no one should be in a place that causes them pain*), and ferrying her day in and out to Uncle Sonny's, sitting in the stands at the Blythewood Rodeo, so on and so on. But she had no idea she was making *him* live a life, even if on the periphery, that he had chosen to hide from her.

Chris was the first to pull out of the hug. His right hand lingering on Nikki's shoulder.

"I started seeing red," he said. "If you hadn't pulled me back to earth, I don't know what I would have done. Maybe I would have—"

"Why do you have it, Chris?" Nikki interrupted. Now that Chris had found his words and his air.

"I've always had it, Nik." He had never called her that. No one had.

Nikki frowned her face at his response, not at the shortened version of her name.

"Truth is, you should too. My pops put one in my hands years ago. Said I should never point it at anything I don't intend to shoot and kill. But I know we got coyote, stray dogs, rattlers, and now random white men roaming these woods. It's just how we ride out. I don't think about it. But today, I did. Today, I wanted it."

"I know," Nikki said. She had protected him. "I'm glad you didn't. Who knows—"

Chris nodded. "Who knows—"

Instead of riding separately back home, Chris escorted Nikki to Sonny's. When they rode past the back pastures, Sonny was just closing a gate, having turned two horses out to graze in the afternoon sun. There were sweat marks along their backs, proving an intense workout. He lifted his hand in salutation as the two approached, then started to go about his business, except Nikki had waved him down. Not close enough to cut through his clouded eardrums busted in service, so Nikki had to raise her voice almost to a scream.

"A white man! With a gun! In the woods!"

Sonny adjusted his trousers, almost reached behind him. Nikki saw the reach.

Chris stopped him and reported the man had walked back in the direction of Mr. Reamer's property, saying it was his now, and claimed he was out hunting deer.

"Y'all good?" More nods from Chris. Except Nikki had dropped Easy's reins at Sonny's feet and started walking to the front. It was all too much: what she had wanted to talk to Chris about, how the day had turned—both of them perhaps on the brink of becoming a news item, both of them standing in possibly the last moments of their lives. At the hands of a man who walks anywhere knowing the world is his, and any obstacle collateral damage.

Sonny and Chris watched Nikki walk away. Not knowing the full story, Sonny went into protection mode of the girl in his life that felt so much like a daughter these days.

He had himself been shoulder to shoulder with Dwayne all those years: Through the final break with Gwendolyn. Through trying as two men to plan girlie-enough birthday parties. Through tears. Through Nikki's horse journey, knowing what it cost his brother, watching Dwayne tiptoe around the fact that it should be him teaching Nikki—what stronger bond could be formed between father and daughter? Instead, he saw the pain. He held that for him, and held her like his own. She was his own.

"Son, I'm sure y'all been through it. I don't know the full extent of what transpired back there, but I'm inclined to offer to you to let her have some space today."

Chris looked him in the eyes. "Yes sir."

"Thank you for making sure she made it back. You good to make it yourself? I can hop on Easy and ride out with you." He patted the place a gun would be.

"I'm good. I didn't have to use mine out there, but my father insists I carry."

"You just never know," Sonny agreed. "I'm glad you're safe. Knowing Nikki, she'll be back tomorrow like none of this ever happened. The siren song of the horses and all. Check on her then, if you like."

"Yes sir. I will."

Chris mounted his horse and rode back through the woods.

Nikki hadn't said much the rest of the afternoon and she still had a few hours of the day before her father was slated to pick her up. Uncharacteristically, she didn't remove Easy's saddle, or perform her grooming before turning him out to the pasture for the night. She arranged the chairs around the unlit firepit and took a seat, staring at nothing.

Sonny moved in a silence similar to whenever Dwayne came over and sat down waiting to talk. Or sometimes, not talk. Just be. He gathered split oak logs and kindling, and lit a fire to stave off the coming chill. After the flames began to lick the sky, he went into the house and returned with two warmed mugs of cider. Sonny settled into a chair across the fire from Nikki until her father came for her.

It was unusual for Dwayne to not have to peel Nikki away from her work: a horse, mucking stalls, stuffing a net full of hay. Instead, no sooner did he pull into Sonny's place was Nikki in the passenger seat, leaning her head against her fist, propped up against the window.

Dwayne had waved at Sonny. Sonny lifted his mug. They headed home.

Nikki didn't know where to start. With what. Or at all. Sure that her father would try the tricks the therapist taught him in those days to encourage her to use her words. She knew she'd have to say something eventually. Start with the last thing first? The gun? Or the reason she was out in the woods in the first place: what her mother had told her about her father?

Dwayne hadn't started his version of therapist talk, because he too was tipping around where to begin. They both swooshed past each other like freight trains barreling in opposite directions. Today, he knew they were on a crash course leading towards a gnarly head-on collision. He knew he'd have to choose his words precisely, so he spent the better part of his afternoon practicing how he'd begin. And then, when the time came, and Nikki was sitting beside him as if waiting for those words he had stored up, they didn't come.

Earlier that day Gwendolyn had called Dwayne. He knew Nikki was with Sonny, so alarms weren't raised in an *our girl is in trouble* kind of way, but rather as a small annoyance. What now? What could she want? He answered the phone and without greeting, Gwendolyn started.

"I have to tell you something, Dew."

Chapter 26

Of course Nikki came back to Sonny's the next day. What else was she gone do? Sit at the house while her daddy tinkered around the farm avoiding talking to her all day when there was more than enough work to be done? According to Sonny, J. D. down the road had called and asked if they had time to help him ride and check fence. Someone passing through had called around town and word got back to J. D. that on the back side of his property a heifer and her calf had reached over perfectly good grass and through the barbed-wire fence to eat the highway weeds and *both* had a front leg through. Who knows how long ago the sighting was, but they're positive the fence will need mending and maybe Sonny could catch the cows?

"Yes sir. We'll be right over."

"We? That girl still ride out with you? I'm paying two day fees? And son, it's just J. D. No mister. No sir."

"No sir. I mean, no, J. D. Just mine. I work out what the girl gets paid. She's my apprentice."

J. D. thought a minute on the phone. "Like she studying this stuff? Well, I never—"

"Yes sir. She is turning into a damn good hand. Starting to figure what kind of cowboy . . . or cowgirl she wants to be. A damned good one, I know."

"Where I come from the girls make the babies and keep the kitchen."

Sonny chuckled. He could never see that for Nikki, even if she showed up that day and said she was going to go off and marry Chris.

"Ain't you from Fairfield County like she is?" Sonny asked.

"You know I ain't never lived anywhere else all my seventy years. My parents, grandparents, great, great-great. You get my drift. Every bone buried right here. And all those girls all those generations was about the business of keeping house. Who else gone do it?"

Time was ticking. There was a loose heifer and her calf, and Sonny was still at his farm. Sonny needed to get a move on or else the whole day would pass listening to J. D.'s stories on the phone, then his stories on the farm, and like yesterday, Sonny's protective shield hardened around Nikki and won't no need for her to be subjected to this talk. But he wagered if he let J. D. finish on the phone it would be out of his system before he rode over with Nikki. If it were just one cow, he'd leave her with a list of tasks at his barn and save her in that way but—and even Sonny never imagined him saying this—he needed her out in the field with him. Even today.

"Who keeps your kitchen now that Mrs. J. D. is gone? May her soul rest—"

It had come to this. J. D. chuckled and said that's why you make friends and do small jobs for all the widows in Fairfield County—he almost never had to think about an empty kitchen and what he's gone eat because it's "in their nature to want to nurture, and it's in my nature to need it."

Sonny lifted his hands in resignation. "Alright, J. D., me and Nikki will be over shortly."

The two loaded up in relative silence. Easy and Patriot were thankfully aware of the energy and didn't make a fuss of much of anything. Not when Nikki dropped her saddle at Easy's feet, causing the colt that was turned out in the round pen a few yards away to startle then kick at the air and run his anxious energy off in circles until he settled back down. Easy just waited. Touched his muzzle to her shoulder. Nikki breathed.

"I'll be present with you, buddy. Thanks for the reminder."

Overhearing, Sonny acknowledged the moment. "I'm sure thankful horses remind us there is only the present to think about. You ever think about that?" He clucked Patriot onto the trailer. Finally saddled, Easy followed his partner in crime. They both loaded themselves into the car of the truck and headed about their day.

"A worrying or anxious horse is thinking about the future," Sonny started back. "That colt watching us saw and heard your saddle hit the ground and started wondering whatever was happening was gone happen to him too."

"And Easy was just here in today, the moment of tacking up before work," Nikki said.

Sonny hummed. It wasn't a long drive to J. D.'s place, but the route took him past the front entrance of Mr. Reamer's old place.

"Sure did buy it, I guess," Sonny said. "Never thought I'd see a gate at the end of that drive, much less it be locked."

Nikki scoffed—"Meanwhile, trespassing on other people's properties."

"White folks been full of contradictions."

When they arrived, Sonny kept J. D. at arm's length from Nikki as best he could. The work took of course the bulk of the day, but it wasn't hard work: riding horses along the perimeter of the property and if there were holes, they'd take turns stepping down off their mounts if the fix seemed like a two-person job. Months of this and they did it by rote just about. The last few days also meant they did it mostly in silence except when Sonny would tell Nikki he'd take a fix, on account of his having to get off Patriot anyway if she got down 'cause he'd have to give her a leg up.

There was a cluster of Corriente steers not far from the edge of the property when they rounded about where it was thought the two had escaped. Without instruction, Nikki broke off from the fence perimeter and worked the cattle so that their cluster would grow smaller in size due to the human and horse presence perceived as a threat, but she would not apply so much pressure—approaching pressure—so as to cause them to disperse or flee, especially careful to not cause them to run towards the known breach in the fencing. So Nikki peeled off from the cluster and the gathering resumed grazing, but she had put them in the eyesight of the two escapees who had, at that moment, decided they wanted to join the herd and mewed incessantly and failed to walk back through the fence because they had grazed away from the heifer-sized gap.

The work became coaxing the two through, and then fixing the fence. Nikki dismounted and wrapped her extra leather latigos around the lower part of Easy's legs. Sonny did the same. Being the smaller, Nikki crawled through the fencing and made noises and spoke loudly to move the cattle back. It worked. They pushed through and scuttled to their cow friends and Sonny fixed the fence and whistled.

"Aren't we a well-oiled team? I can't tell you when's the last time I had a job go this smooth. J. D. questioned why I had a girl, a young one, at my side for this work and I told him that the number of horses you've had to work, the number of jobs you've faced like this in the short amount of time was probably more than some who call themselves cowboys will face in a lifetime."

Nikki wasn't going to say it, but did anyway.

"It's almost like I was made to do it. Born for it. Horses."

Sonny half-shrugged and motioned towards Easy so he could give her the leg up and said under his breath: "Almost like it."

Both were thankful they didn't have to ride very far in silence back to the barn. When they got there, Chris was scratching Jet's muzzle through the round pen panel. He was on a loose rein, grazing the oat sprouts on the edge of the enclosure.

Nikki looked at Sonny.

"I told him he could see about you, but I didn't expect it to be today."

"We still have chores and rodeo practice," Nikki said. Nikki had decided to get back into the rodeo game, all things considered. Sonny had insisted it was the best thing for her to have another goal, another focus. Someplace to put her energy and anger and excitement. *Rodeo solves so many problems when you get out in that arena,* he said before she agreed to go again. He had made other efforts to make the transition back onto the rodeo dirt easier.

"I got the chores today, no worries," Sonny said, then sucked his teeth. "Sth. You know we the best riders that rodeo got. Don't stress it. You do more work out in the fields, here at the barn, than them ten seconds of riding. It's just another day. Another field. Only difference is the audience."

"That's a big difference!" Nikki called as she walked towards Chris. He turned to her and asked what was a big difference from what?

"Riding with Sonny roping cows out in the pasture and riding with Sonny roping in a rodeo arena."

Chris smirked. "Yeh. One's guaranteed to pay out at the end. The other got bright lights and popcorn."

He was right. Nikki didn't know why she now put pressure on herself to ride in the rodeo when Sonny kept saying it's like any other ride, any other ride. When you treat it different, you ride different. The first rodeo ignorance was on her side. Then she saw how people saw her—the only Black girl, one of a few Black folk on horseback, competing. And then when NewsOne made a deal of it, Nikki had made a deal. People were watching and it was hard to determine for her if they were watching for her to fail or if they were watching in awe—either way: the pressure existed. The two stood in front of Jet, playing with his attempts to keep one or both scratching him in the itchy spots, before either one spoke.

"I'm alright," Nikki said, eyes square on the horse. Chris nodded. She contemplated telling him what they had gone out to their spot to talk about but instead recalled that she did need to practice for the rodeo, just about ten days away.

"Say, why don't you ride in the rodeo?"

Chris shrugged. "I did when I was little, when horses consumed my life."

How could they not? If you were born into it?

"My parents had me riding sheep like they were bucking broncs. Then I progressed through the kiddie rodeo scene, drinking it all in like I was going to die of thirst if I didn't ride one day of the week."

"Now that I have them, kind of, I can't imagine my life without them," Nikki said. "Without riding as much as I can."

What must that have felt like? To have at your fingertips a thing some people dream of, and for you to think or feel that it's pedestrian and usual, like wallpaper in a bathroom? Like a kitchen with cooking pots.

"I guess when you have family pushing you into something it pushes you further away, sometimes. You think it's the last thing you want to do for yourself."

That part might be true.

"Would you ride with me?" Nikki said quickly without thinking. Chris nodded his head at first, then she could see him processing the question, so she filled in the silence. What would Uncle Sonny say? "I mean, would you practice with me, and then maybe ride with me? I got good at heeling lately, you can catch the head of the steers, that's the easier part, if you just turn him for me."

Chapter 27

Time is a mother. Enough of it between a problem and the obvious resolution, and it will birth new problems. Sure, Dwayne could bury himself in the thought processes of his father and how, for over half a century, he could pretend that there wasn't a whole human walking the earth with his face, his DNA, raising a daughter—*his* granddaughter. He could fixate on how he'd run from his grief—in that way they shared similarities. He could spend energy wondering why, for years, Lloyd had kept a tether—the land taxes—to a place he turned his back on; the place that made him, and generations before him. A place that was pocked with hundreds of years of horse hooves and that he had kept—all this time, all this time—from the greedy hands of developers. How he knew it was time to say to his estranged son—did he even know Dwayne was alive?—that he was ready to pass on his inheritance.

When Sonny heard the story, that Dwayne's father had died while trying to write him a letter, Sonny immediately asked what had been in the letter, but Dwayne just shrugged.

"What is there to say? He chose himself over raising me. Every day he woke up. Think about that, Snoop. Every damn day God gave him wind in his lungs and he chose himself. Right? The one day he reaches for his son all these doggone years later. All these lifetimes later, and he *dies.* Damned if I don't actually want to know what's in that letter. Could be cursed."

And that's all he thought about it, really. It surprised him. He didn't want to know, won't no inkling, no desire. When he was younger, maybe, he might have wanted more. When the scab of his father's absence was still sitting on the surface of the left-behind wound—sure. He'd scratch at it, looking for reasons, answers, justification. But Dwayne had chosen his daughter, Nikki. To live for her. With her. Raise her. Figure out the shape of his life with Nikki in it. It was rounder around the edges. Once, he'd say it was a dagger. Now, he'd say there was just some fuzzy spots. When he sat and imagined his life as a shape, it might have been a bottle cap—serrated edges on the underbelly that can slice flesh if you grabbed it too quickly or wrong. A thing holding other things in. It made sense. His life with Nikki and Sonny. What made his family these days just made sense. But he felt that sense start to fray when he found out that his father had died two years before; if he let his mind wander down that dark path between all of what Angela said and did not say. Between what she sent and did not send: The letter. His Vietnam decorations. Old family photos he might have taken with him when he left. Did he take Grandaddy Mo's journals from his days at the racetrack? What Dwayne understood his father used as guidebooks for establishing and remixing and running his own operation? The few times he had come home from school with handmade trinkets for his father and Ms. Mozell she would ship them to his last known APO address. Did he keep any of it? Did Angela?

But Dwayne resisted being overtaken by the avalanche of questions. There was real work to do.

Armed with the manila folder from Florida, he had made an appointment with Mrs. Harmon. She tried to remind him she was just the county administrative secretary and he should talk to someone "who wears the starched and creased pants around here." But Dwayne insisted he meet with her.

"You got all the info from all the departments anyways. Don't act like you're not the glue holding this county together."

She gave him a look that showed her agreement and reached out her hand for the paperwork.

Dwayne watched as her eyes scanned page after page. When she adjusted her glasses closer to the paperwork and hummed, Dwayne leaned in closer. She pulled the papers further away and then snatched her glasses off her face and stretched her paper-holding arm straight out and then used the lenses like twin magnifying glasses.

"So what's the diagnostic, Doc?" Dwayne chuckled at his own ability to find levity, considering the circumstances.

He counted four seconds of Mrs. Harmon gathering her thoughts before she finally looked up and they locked eyes: "Son, this is a very important document. Especially now," she said. Dwayne adjusted himself in the seat like an impatient child. "You're going to say 'but,' ain't it?"

"—*And*," she said. "It needed to be filed with the county as soon as it was signed and notarized."

Dwayne hung his head.

"I know, baby. Usually, I can help move something along if it comes a little bit outside our filing window, but especially now, especially given where the county has decided it wants to go with its rural landholdings"—

Mrs. Harmon leaned in.

—"the pants-wearing county administrators are less likely to make exceptions. And even if they did, no way they'd allow two years, especially if they don't live here and we won't have no way to verify all of the signatories. Honestly, honey, all this time I thought he was dead."

"—To me he was. To the world, I guess, two years ago."

"I see."

"So this is worthless?"

"It might mean something to you, having it. But for our purposes, I'm afraid so. I'm afraid so."

Dwayne sat processing. Mrs. Harmon held the space for him. She didn't make any gestures or big movements or attempt to work through the pile of tasks gathering on her desk when folks walked by. He adjusted himself in the chair again. Said something under his breath. Mrs. Harmon said she ain't hear him.

"I just—what do I do? This would have solved it. It would have at least made up for—"

"I don't know that anything can." Dwayne knew she was right. He nodded.

He saw Mrs. Harmon's gears working as she pored through the documents again. And then she widened her eyes.

"I have it! I have it. I remember when you were just a sapling of a boy and your grandparents passed in that fire."

Dwayne frowned his face.

"It was all over the *County Chronicle.* They announced the funeral and burial plans and I had helped Ms. Mozell clean up her place in case folks come around for the setting up, and helped babysit the two boys she had in her world, and I remember the burial was on that plat. That there was a cemetery somewhere, do you remember?"

How could he not? The grief so heavy he fell to the ground and he had never said it, but he had wanted to fall into the space of the hole and be covered in the Carolina sand with his grandparents. But Ms. Mozell gathered him and told him there was still life worth living on this earth, and it was his work to wake up every day and figure out what was worth it. All these years he walked with that question in his heart and here it was again. Of course, the answer was Nikki. He nodded at Mrs. Harmon. He did remember.

"Some folks been coming in with they plat maps and getting the family land zoned as a cemetery. If they can prove one exists. It significantly lowers the bill, Dwayne." She widened her eyes—*you get my drift?* "But I don't remember hearing of any headstones or anything was placed."

"Footstones. Prolly grown over by now."

"Or taken, maybe. Remember when the quarry dug so far down they plumb ran out of granite and then they were asking for any surplus to crush? They say folks was stealing headstones and breaking them up so you couldn't see the names, then turning them in, redeeming for cash."

Dwayne was too young to remember that, but now he had reason to walk the property, maybe take Nikki. Finally talk.

"If I can prove it, what's next?"

"Come back here and let's figure it out together."

Chapter 28

The rain echoed loudly in the Fairfield County Main Branch Library. It sounded like a big percussive cacophony that rattled Nikki's chest, even as she took in deep inhales, trying to catch her breath.

"There were no signs of this type of storm when I checked the weather this morning," she whispered. When they met up to ride, Nikki thought she and Chris could warm up their ponies and see where their minds were—both human and equine—by getting off the trail for once and riding into town, maybe for some soft serve, then get back to Sonny's to practice for the rodeo. She had convinced Chris to join in. Relive his Little Britches Rodeo days. Maybe fall in love with the sport again, and she could let Sonny retire from team roping and stick to bulldogging, the sport that holds his heart.

"Grandpa says every time they clear and cut acres and acres of woods, the climate changes around us," Chris said. "I tried to say 'climate change' was something else, something bigger, like it happens all over the world and stuff. He said our climate here has changed. That's *climate change.*"

Nikki nodded, and still attempted to wipe the rain off her arms. It had been a warm enough day to venture out with short sleeves. She regretted not dressing like the season or she would have been saved from looking homeless—left victim to the elements. Drenched to the bone. They both, in unison, looked out the window to check on Jet and Easy. There wasn't a hitching post like at the Spot, but there were bike racks. They hobbled the legs so the horses wouldn't spaghetti-wrap around the metal structures undulating above for the bike loop and then attached to the ground—shaped like waves. The horses looked miserable, but not in danger.

"Thankfully there was no lightning," Nikki said. She opened the internet browser on the computer in front of her. When they ran in, having not planned to go to the library, they both trotted to the circle of computers. The librarian saw the horses outside at the same time as the gaggle of kids clumped together for the weekly Saturday Storytime. There was no way the volunteer reader was going to get through the end of *Harlem's Little Blackbird* without allowing for the squeals of "Horsey!" over and over.

Nikki and Chris giggled. Nikki checked the weather.

"I haven't been on a computer since . . ."

Then she stopped talking. Dwayne had asked her, when she left, if he should look at having Cousin Major make her a computer, and she shook her head. What for? Horses don't need computers. No room for Facebook at the farm. Nikki enjoyed being—how Uncle Sonny called it?—a Luddite, like him.

"The radar isn't even showing rain for our area," she said.

"Microclimates," the librarian said as she was passing by the computers. Chris nodded. The librarian turned back and asked if she could help them find anything? Nikki only said they were waiting for the surprise washout to pass; she'll clean up if the horses make any mess outside. The librarian shook her head.

"Don't worry about that. Used to be we had a proper place to park those type of rides outside. Now Fairfield County trying to act like that's not who we all are."

Nikki offered, "I didn't grow up around horses."

The librarian squinted. Tilted her nose down so she could look Nikki in the eyes above the top of her glasses. She started to respond.

"She's Lloyd Bolton's people," Chris said. Nikki flipped her face so quickly towards Chris a water droplet of rain flung from one of her braids to his cheek.

The librarian gave a knowing nod to Chris and as she started to walk away reminded them to let her know if she can help with anything, and he nodded again while he pulled up the internet service on his computer, then started navigating through the library's online newspaper archives.

"What did you mean?" Nikki knew by now what he meant, but she needed him to say it. So many people talking in code, moving in code. So many people, her daddy mostly, not saying anything at all. She was tired of the whole of it being conveyed to her by everyone but her father. But also, how did Chris know?

Chris kept his eyes on the screen. "That lady was about to say you were wrong. My grandpa, when he asked me who I was riding with all this time now, first he thought it was Sonny, and I say it's you, and he was like he thought that boy—he meant your dad—didn't keep the love of horses in him."

Nikki said that's what she was coming to say that day in the woods when they practically had a gun shoved in their faces. That her mom had told her so much. Maybe everything. She doesn't know, because she ain't talked to her daddy yet. Well, she didn't mention Lloyd: her grandfather. She never met him.

"How do you know about him?" She struggled to say his name. It felt disrespectful. But saying "granddad" didn't feel right. She never used that word. Only Pop Pop for her mother's father.

"Grandaddy had a string of quarter horses he raced with your—" He had started to say it. "With Mr. Lloyd. He said one day he was sitting on top of the world, winning all the big races in the Southeast Circuit that he just about founded, and the next Mr. Lloyd asked Grandaddy to take the track on. His horses—all."

Chris finally turned to her. "Jet is a horse bred from that string of Mr. Lloyd's. Grandaddy just told me."

Nikki started.

"It wasn't my story to tell you before. And I couldn't figure out when or how. And I wanted to show you this anyway. So I figured this was the day and time."

He turned his computer screen so Nikki could see it. She was still processing, listening. Everything and everyone is so connected.

"This is my grandfather, Curtis, and here's your grandfather, Mr. Lloyd," Chris said. He pointed at a black-and-white photo on the screen. Nikki saw the two men in what looked like pageboy caps, button-down shirts. One looked plaid, that was who Chris said was her grandfather. The other man in the photo had a solid button-down shirt. Both sleeves were rolled to the elbows. Both men had their arms crossed in front of their chests, and lead ropes leaking under their arms. Nikki followed the ropes one by one—a horse on either end. It's impossible to tell the coat color, she knew, but she studied them anyhow. The man who would be her grandfather held a horse that looked like Easy. Kind eyes. Back wide as a potato. Ears forward. Again, like Easy. If she imagined her grandfather the same height of her father . . . who stood eye to eye with Sonny, and this horse—she looked at the caption—Boss—stood nearly the same height to Sonny as Easy. The other horse, being held by Chris's grandfather, was darker, with no visible markings on its face. Both horses were draped with blankets to keep them warm as they cooled off. Nikki finally read the headline: "Fairfield County Quarter Downs Track and Its Negro Trainers and Horses."

Chris waited for Nikki's eyes. He looked out the window and the deluge had ended. He could tell by the way the sky lightened at that point that the storm was finishing up, but there were still raindrops beating against the library roof. When Nikki turned to him he clicked to another screen, then pointed.

A page from the Negro circular *Call & Response*. Before she fully took it in—what looked like a child posed on top of a racehorse—she barely let the question out from below a whisper, "What's this?"

Ever since Nikki asked Chris what he might do after high school and he didn't really have an answer, he had asked himself that question more in the last few months than in the majority of his life. Once, as a young boy, he said he wanted to be a cowboy in class, and the teacher, a young woman with rosy cheeks who had just finished college and always wore a shirt that had the initials TFA on it, laughed when he said it. She said cowboys were only in the movies or out West. Defeated, he muttered that his grandaddy was a cowboy, but the moment had passed, along with his dream. He told Nikki that after that moment, he stopped dreaming it.

"But you showed me what I still loved. Community. The horses. The work of it. I can't think of what else I'm made for."

Nikki turned his last statement into a question that echoed in her mind. She turned back to the photo, the child on a horse. It's wearing the number 3. There is a woman and a man. A family. Nikki silently read the caption:

Groom and exercise rider Moses Bolton, wife Lillie Bolton, and son Lloyd, after Pal O Mine's surprise win at the Carolina Jessamine Invitational.

"My grandfather," she whispered. "That's the kid on the horse. The man standing, that's my great-grandaddy."

What was there to say?

"I was trying to think about that teacher who acted like there weren't any folks who rode horses, and yet that's all I know. You know? This year in school, they got us thinking about what stories we want to tell about ourselves for the college essay. Ms. Jones said if we reference famous folks in the essay it'll help, so I asked my grandpa if he knew any famous horsemen and he said, 'Any Bolton you can throw a stick at,' and he laughed. But I thought about you, Nik. So I came to the library to look for answers in the Negro circular, where my grandaddy said was lots of famous people to write about if it's a cowboy I want to be. And he's right. See."

He pointed at the newspaper image. "This horse wasn't even supposed to race that day, so the first line of the article stated. And he won. And it was your great-grandaddy's horse."

"That's not a cowboy," Nikki said. The man, Moses, was wearing slacks that slimmed his legs. There was the pageboy cap again, except it was crumpled in his right hand, his left hand gripping the toddler on top of the horse. She was expecting a wide brim. A ten-gallon crown. A piece of fescue hay dangling from the corner of his mouth like the leathery older men she and Sonny worked for across the county.

"He's a horseman," Chris said.

||||||||||||||||||

At Sonny's place they tossed ropes around the horns of a dummy steer. Every third toss or so, Sonny would stop whatever he was up to, and add a correction, "Elbow up!" or "Tip down!" or "Bigger loop!"

Nikki was still processing all of what she'd taken in from everyone around her, while she thought about the times she found herself in: just when she learned who she was—the very things giving her breath and purpose and meaning—her world was starting to disappear. The folks who championed the stripping away of acres and acres of farmland called it "progress." The folks who could absorb the increases of taxation on their land kept their hands in their pockets. Now here she was, understanding she was now someone who had more to lose than Uncle Sonny's farm. His fight had always been her fight. But his fight, and her daddy's fight, was hers also in a new sense. Two trains running a thousand miles per hour at midnight down a predetermined track with no station stops in sight. Sonny had said it—that's how they win. They create so many battles that we have to choose one, and even in choosing one battle, there was still the pure onslaught of county council meetings, special-called meetings, hearings for every parcel made available what seemed like every day, and add to that the normal struggles of waking up Black in Fairfield County, South Carolina. None of this was designed to be a conquerable war. That was becoming clear as the fact that not only did Nikki want to be a horsewoman like her ancestors, she was *supposed* to be a horsewoman like her ancestors.

"Nice!" Sonny shouted, and Chris echoed, noting Nikki's catch. Chris's rope had tipped the dummy's plastic horns and snaked across the yard.

"What are you thinking?" Chris asked, pulling a new loop to try again.

"Y'all need to hang ten straight legal catches before you can move on," Sonny coached from a distance.

Nikki threw again. Caught. Six.

"It's like the world doesn't want us to be here," Nikki started, pulling a new loop. She spoke low in a whisper to Chris, keeping her story from reaching Sonny's ears.

"I'm thinking about how easy it was for Daddy to pretend this wasn't my legacy all this time. The world created space for that. It was in the fabric of the county now. Those articles—they were marking time: This Black horseman here. That Black horseman there."

"Even as it changed and we left the racing stables, you're right. Grandaddy always talked about how Fairfield County was farms and farmland as far as the eye could see. If it wasn't fields of soy or some such, it was fields of cattle, fields of horses."

"How the librarian said the bicycle parking was hitching posts. How Uncle Sonny taught me about how mail and books were delivered on horseback."

"A gaggle of us gathering weekly for trail rides and fellowship with arena showcases—our own rodeos." Sonny picked up a rope, moved in closer, and worked into their practice rounds.

Nikki turned to Sonny. "I know about Daddy and horses," she said. Eight.

Sonny just swung his loop at his side, no longer intending to do it, but it was clear to everyone he needed something to do with his hands. He nodded.

"I'm waiting on him to tell me though. But I know. I know I'm supposed to be doing exactly this."

Chris and Sonny nodded.

Ten.

They all dropped their ropes when Nikki made it to ten catches. Nikki and Chris hopped on their respective horses and Sonny cranked the four-wheeler to drag the roping sled across the arena.

Loping circles, Chris called out.

"Why this rodeo and not y'all own?"

Three lope strides before Sonny turned and called out above the motor: "We been talkin' about and asking the same thing, son. The same thing."

"Y'all could keep more of the money. All of it if you make it a showcase. Like a festival."

Sonny stopped driving. Nikki and Chris stopped riding. Easy and Jet's nostrils flared from the lope circles and the sudden stop. Trying to catch their breaths.

It would be harder to run a sanctioned rodeo, hence the holdup to having their own rodeo in Fairfield County in the first place. For the few Black cowboys that made their way to the Blythewood Rodeo, they always stayed after in the slack—the after-hours riding after the official show—and ran the barrels, ran the steers, jumped from their horses' saddles to grab the bull by its horns and flip onto its back. Bronc'ed the broncs bareback—no rigging, just fistfuls of hair and vise-grip thighs. Howls into the late night.

But it wasn't theirs. Why not?

Sonny told them about the good old days and started to drive off. Nikki was up next to rope and kicked Easy back into a lope. Started her swing.

Two. She had to get to ten again.

"Y'all got me thinking, though. Really thinking."

Sonny figured if he hosted, what would he call it? Something that anyone with a horse might join in on? He could charge a gate fee, then could scrounge up a few boys to build and man some quick-built cinder-block grills for concession. Could make a weekend out of it: Trail ride Friday night. Trail ride Saturday morning. Arena showcase into the evening—any and all disciplines—bonfire gathering later that night, fellowship and breakfast Sunday morning. It could be a thing. The Festival of Black Horsemen.

"We can help!" Nikki said. "But won't make any sense paying to show and spending all our prep time for this coming rodeo."

"We could use the momentum of this rodeo though. Could recruit there, too," Chris offered. He had a spark Nikki hadn't seen before. "Maybe make some flyers and pass them around. Mr. Sonny, you might need to compete."

Sonny cocked his head. Nikki kept going with her idea.

"Hear me out. You win in bulldoggin' like you always do, and maybe the news will cover your win and then you can use your interview time to tell folks about the Black Horsemen Festival."

"That sounds so official, you saying it like that!" Sonny laughed. He pointed at Nikki. "But I'm a has-been. Nikki is the new thing folks looking for. When I called to register, they asked if I was bringing Nikki. Named her and all. She's the celeb! She's who the cameras will rush towards. They want to cover the Black girl team roper competing in a pro-level rodeo."

Dwayne had spent the day going through the box of things tucked into the back of the closet, almost the same place he had put them all those years ago when Ms. Mozell figured he was old enough to have them. He pulled back his clothes like a curtain and excavated the original box with all of its original contents, having miraculously survived the fire, and all of those years in between: newspaper articles of Moses and Pal O Mine, Dwayne's first-year baby book that Lillie started to fill out since there was no one else to do it, Moses and Lillie's last will and testaments, race recaps on the bush track, a few water-marked and flame-licked pages from what must have been Moses's journals, including genealogy of a few horses, a newspaper article about the fire and the double obituary—Ms. Mozell had added to the Bolton box—and finally, what Dwayne had come to the time capsule to unearth: the map of Bolton Plantation, hand-drawn by Moses, to include instructions on their burial.

He tried really hard not to get caught up in the whole of the box's contents, because he knew he was on a mission, but he could not resist stopping to look at the photo of his father as a young boy atop Pal O Mine—it was his own face he saw. If his grandparents had owned such a horse, and had gray and white hair in the photo, it very well could have been him. He sat with the photo for a while and tried to imagine what was coursing through that young child's body to percolate into a man who could find it in himself to walk away from a life he was building and never look back? He sat waiting for the words to come, an explanation. Instead, a tear. But he couldn't be caught up, not today. He lifted up the pile of things and stuffed the photo into the middle so as not to be faced with it whenever he'd come back to this box, if he ever did.

The map, had all of the structures of the farm remained, was very clear. He remembered everyone saying the same thing in those days just after the fire, gathered at Ms. Mozell's dining table trying to figure out what to do next. "This makes perfect sense," someone had said. And because just a few days prior each marker that was painstakingly outlined on Moses's hand-drawn gridded page had just been there, or there were still echoes of each structure marked by ashes, they found their way to the plot for the burial easily. But nearly four decades later, Dwayne would have to think of other identifying markers.

The cypress trees. How his ancestors marked it. The periwinkle. He'd just have to walk across the street, walk in the northwest vicinity, and look for two twin cypress trees, and a faint dusting of periwinkle.

But he made it there. And when he did, he took a deep breath. The kind of breath he takes whenever he prepares to step into the cemetery on Memorial Day. The kind of breath that the dead insist you take to remind you that you're living. That you're still earthside. When he exhaled, he said, "Thank you." And even when the words escaped, he had thought why had he said them? Who was he thanking? For what? Who knew?

The ancestors know. Those words came back to him. Another deep breath.

Dwayne surveyed the site, then turned around to see the whole of the property he had just crossed. He had tried to see the paddocks again. Tried to see where O'boy would have been munching on grass with the others. The clothesline just to the left of the barn that was just to the left of the house. Smoke rising from one of the three chimneys. His swing on the oak. The squirrels shimmying around the trees above him now gave him some comfort.

Turning back to the cemetery, he looked for any markings. It had been so long, so much overgrowth, even with the cuttings. So many years of rain, of the earth breathing and breathing, and swallowing. The only marker he had was the brick in his chest having approached this space—how it had started as a small pebble when he stepped across the street, and grew and grew with each step. Pulling him closer and weighing him down. He felt like he was walking out into the ocean, the water getting higher and higher with each footfall. He needed something. He walked through the passageway set by the cypress, and fixed his eyes on the ground.

A stone smooth like river rock, about the size of his palm, was on the ground in front of him. It wouldn't have gotten there naturally; there was no water source nearby to make this kind of rock. On the right side of it, a few flecks of something white. Paint? He bent at the knees to see closer. It was paint. He walked a few steps to the left of that rock and saw another. All together he counted fifteen smoothed-over rocks spaced evenly, and finally, in one spot there were two rocks.

"Hi, Grandaddy and Grandma," he said, cooing like a young boy again. The water reached his nose. He fell to his knees, sobbing.

Dwayne made his way to Sonny's to pick up Nikki and he prayed the right words would find their way to his lips. When he first recognized they should talk, Dwayne couldn't envision what words, what story would justify the generational silences between them. He pulled in and didn't get out. Nikki was ready. He saw Chris making his way home, and Sonny waved everyone on.

When she plopped in the seat with intent to speak first, Dwayne interrupted.

"I found out recently my father died. In Florida. Well, he didn't die recently. It was two years ago," Dwayne said. He was thankful to have the occasion of driving to have a place to focus his eye and not have to look direct at Nikki. On his periphery, he could see her turn to him.

"I'm not sad. At least I don't think I'm sad. If I squint I can remember his face from one of the quick visits he made when I was a little boy. If I squint. I think sometimes, I'm mad for his having left me, left the family, for not coming back when my grandparents died. When I found out he died, I realized that I'll never know the answer to the why I've been carrying my whole life. Maybe that's where the sadness lives: I had been waiting for the answer to the why. I didn't realize it, but I guess I was waiting for him to show up one day and say, 'This is why,' and I never thought what I would do if that day were ever to present itself. I hadn't thought that far. If I got the thing that was buried so deep in my heart all this time. Why he chose himself instead of me."

A few ticks of the road went by and they rode in silence. Dwayne inhaled, started again.

"I can imagine you are carrying a lot of whys right now, too. Like me. I chose myself when my grandparents died and all of the farm animals with them in a fire. I couldn't choose a life rooted in grief. I guess . . . now I think about it," Dwayne bit his lip, "I guess it was a similar juncture as my father. Grief, you know, and what to do with it."

"Daddy—" Nikki whispered. She didn't want it like this, she didn't think. Not knowing how it would go or really, what would be the path forward after, either, Nikki held space for her father. She had never seen him like this before.

"You know about Brian. Service made me unbury my grief then. For country, I did it. For my brothers, I did it. I got on a horse again. I wanted to live, so I did it. I wanted to get back home to Gwendolyn. I wanted to—" He turned to Nikki. "I wanted you."

He flicked his thumb under his eye to divert a tear down his face.

"I couldn't have it all. I didn't think about what my grief might keep from you until the jolt of knowing my father had died, on top of the possibility of losing of our land. I swear I didn't know it then, or the whole of this time, until I understood we could lose it. That I wanted the land *for you.* And I understood that I could lose my chance to give it to you."

Nikki turned her head.

"If you want it. If I can make it work."

They pulled into the Bolton plantation. Nikki got out of the car having barely said two words since leaving Sonny's. She'll later tell Chris she didn't know how, but after fifteen years of looking across the street, when her feet touched the ground that day the sky looked different. A wind blew across her face. She breathed it in, felt a tingling from her toes to her fingertips.

Dwayne rummaged in the back seat of the truck cab and found a flag—like the ones they place on Memorial Day. He stuck it in his back pocket. He started walking west, towards the cypress trees.

"I have something to show you," Dwayne said.

Chapter 29

Sonny agreed Nikki should be the star of the night if there was going to be one, but he still pretended like he was going to compete so he could get behind the scenes and talk to the guys handling the cattle. He walked over and made small talk. Acknowledged their contribution to the whole event—no cattle, no rodeo—and how thankless it must be and he knows it, so he came to say thank ya. Sonny was also scoping the cattle out. Looking for wild eyes. One that would run and give Nikki a good show, but not blow the whole thing up by being too sour. Sure it was a timed event, but Sonny believed the run should look as good as it was fast. He asked the cattleman about the steers. Some Angus. Some Corriente. Some mixed a little more with longhorn and that's how you have the straight horns like an airplane wingspan. The pure Corriente that Sonny saw was smaller, mostly black with brown accents. He watched, one eye always following. Sonny watched his ears—quiet. Broke to the chute and probably been roped a few times, but still respects a horse. The kind of cattle you want to draw. He made a few quick moves so to startle the herd and watched the little guy run around. The cattleman walked over with his paddle to help. He watched Sonny watching the black steer and confirmed: it's a good one. They made the herd disperse quicker—Sonny wanted to see the back feet hop into the air in unison. An easy heel catch when they do.

"My girl is going to head for her friend for the first time tonight. Just doing my pre-work," Sonny said.

"No problem, man, I'll make sure they get a good one so y'all can have a good night."

The cattleman tipped his hat. Sonny returned the gesture.

The crowd was loud, but there was no denying many folks got louder when Nikki and Chris lined their horses up in the box. The announcer said something like "Blythewood's Sweethearts on a date in the roping pen" and everyone laughed.

From the stands Dwayne yelled, "Fairfield County!"

They *were* the youngest. And with Sonny out of the competition, the only Black cowboys competing. Everyone settled into a hush when the horses backed up into their boxes.

Nikki heard her heartbeat thump in her ears. Everything stopped and waited on her signal for *go*. She nodded.

The chute sprang open. The black steer spilled out into the arena and Easy launched Nikki after it. She spun the rope and loop three times before she threw it. Half-head. She only caught one horn, but the rope looped around the steer's chin. It was legal. She dallied the rope around the horn of her saddle to tighten the rope between her hand and the steer's horns. Nikki turned left, made the steer turn left. Sonny called out to Chris, "Kick him up! Kick him up! Get into position! Place!" Chris urged Jet to get closer to the steer's double-barrel kicks in the air. Chris swung four times, tossed the rope.

"Turn!" That was for Nikki. The crowd rose to their feet. Hand clasps and feet stomping, rumbling the stands. Chris tossed the loop towards the ground and caught both feet after Nikki turned left. Clean.

"Great run by the Blythewood lovebirds! I'll have to check the time, but unofficially that may be an arena record!"

Sonny jumped up and down at the back and shook the hand of the cattleman who made it happen. He made his way to the front just as the news anchor was shoving the microphone into Nikki's face. Dwayne nodded as he approached.

"I'm so excited for this win and to represent the Black horsemen of Fairfield County," Nikki said. It was clear the anchor was not expecting Nikki to move the interview in that direction. You could see her visibly recalibrating how to volley the questions back to Nikki and the night, and she just landed on "tell me more."

And Nikki rattled off what they were practicing: Date. Time. Place. "Donations for the Black horsemen in Fairfield County facing displacement from the county-wide land-use upzoning." She looked into the sky, pulling the language down. Sonny gave her the thumbs-up. She had nailed it.

IIIIIIIIIIIIIIIII

The whole week after the Blythewood Rodeo, Nikki couldn't go anywhere in town or otherwise—even out with her mother in Columbia—without someone coming up to congratulate her. They had seen her on the news, on social media. Some folks remarked how nice it was for her to have a new story to tell—"You get to write your own story now," Mrs. Harmon had said. She was at the Feed & Seed store looking for last-minute bait to go fishing with Weesie and Betty at Lake Wateree.

"Our whole lives, we can be defined by the stories folk tell about us. Or," Mrs. Harmon said, sliding crinkled dollar bills across the countertop to James. "Or we can grab the pen ourself. I'm proud of you, young lady. Fairfield County must be, too."

James nodded and held up an invisible camera and made clicking noises angling it side to side—"I got to get all the angles of our rodeo queen," he proclaimed. Nikki paid for her bag of horse treats and thanked them.

The weekend between the rodeo and the showcase, Nikki took off from the farm to spend with her mother. They skipped the nail salon and the meeting, and went for brunch and the bookstore. A great change of pace. At the restaurant, Gwendolyn ordered pecan pancakes with regular syrup and agreed to the whipped cream. Nikki raised her eyebrows. Gwendolyn lifted her hands in resignation and smiled.

"It's a celebration! My baby girl is a rodeo queen!" she said loud enough for the other patrons to hear. The server smiled bigly.

"I'll have what she's having!" Nikki said. It wasn't worth correcting them. It wasn't worth it. She savored every moment. When the lattes came, they toasted.

"You've hosted people at your place before, Uncle Sonny! Stop stressing," Nikki said. Sonny was pacing the barn with a broom in his hand, not sweeping. They had a call for some daywork across the county and only because it was an emergency had they considered it at such a time: a new calf and mother in a mud pit in a briar patch in the woods where Mr. Jim's tractor couldn't reach and the temperature was set to drop that night. Sonny can't say no to a baby calf—he likes to drape the thing over Patriot's wither and waltz back to the owner like the cowboy-savior he is. But when the sun had risen above the trees so clearly as to cast light into the barn aisle, and they weren't loaded up and on the road yet, Nikki came to check and there Sonny was: pacing like a nervous wreck.

"We gotta make good on the festival, Nikki," Sonny said. Stopping only to lift his hat and scratch his scalp. She remembered when he had tried to cornrow his hair and smiled. The girl braiding it said there won't really enough all the way through—she couldn't say *balding*—for the braids to set right. She offered to clip him short and even. "Like a Caesar" and Sonny agreed only to get out of the chair, and then got home and shaved it bald. Nikki remembers that day each time she sees the shine on his scalp. And it was extra shiny because of his pacing and nervous perspiration.

"Everyone's talking about the Black rodeo coming to Fairfield County, Uncle Sonny. I know you want to have more than the normal rodeo events so I don't have the heart to tell them it's a festival or showcase and not a rodeo, but in town everyone telling me they can't wait to see me—and I'm talking about folks who made it a point to let me know they don't go to 'the other rodeo'—that's how they said it."

Sonny smiled, then terror flashed across his face. "So they'll be expecting it to be better, then. Just great." He had channeled the frantic energy to the broom and moved errant dirt and shavings out of the way. Then Nikki grabbed the broom.

"It will be better. We're riding!" she said, and leaned the broom against the wall next to the other barn-cleaning supplies. "Now. We got a freezing calf we gotta pull out the muck. Then you can worry all you need as we finish setting up."

||||||||||||||||||

When the day finally came, the energy on Sonny's farm was electric, like the first time Fairfield County gathered for its own Veterans Day parade. Many of the same players: The classic and vintage cars shined and lined up at the front of Sonny's place like a welcoming committee. Each owner posted nearby with a camp chair and beverage. A few tabletop grills for their own tailgate situation. The ice cream parlor set up next to the frozen lemonade stand manned by Mya and Danielle. Mrs. Harmon had a popcorn stand with various toppings: cinnamon sugar, ranch, Frank's hot sauce, seasoned and Cajun salt. The horseshoe-shaped section featured grills lit by firewood. A whole hog. Chicken legs and thighs. Burgers and franks. Derrick set up some Adirondack chairs and a firepit for folks who wanted to chill with a beverage and cigars. It was mostly the fellows who would crowd the Spot on the regular. Chris and Nikki dragged out some old stall mats and lined them up. "Bowling?" Sonny asked when he saw the two lines of rubber running parallel on the ground. "Looks like bowling lanes."

"Horseshoes!" they called back in unison. Chris had brought his older brother's cornhole setup as well. "Something for the kids."

Sonny chuckled and promised the adults would be lining up too.

Mr. Eliot, who runs all of the rec centers in Richland County, and so has access to a plethora of speakers, came with Major to rig a sound system that was loud enough so anywhere you were on Sonny's place you could hear the announcements.

"Alright y'all, thank you for coming to the first inaugural Black Horsemen Festival!" Nikki couldn't place whose voice it was, but everyone from the Spot said they would chip in running the event. So it must have been Kenan—she hadn't seen him yet. Chris whispered, "Isn't 'inaugural' first? Y'all doing this again?" She put a finger to her pursed lips. They were grooming their horses in the barn ahead of the grand entry and show. They were to bring in the flags.

Near the arena, folks were warming up for their respective events. The walking horses marching their high knees. The barrel racers loping slow, calculated circles. The ropers pulling loops, looping and throwing to catch imaginary steers. Folks galloping to a twenty-foot stop.

When Sonny put the call out, like the meeting, like the parade, like . . . he was met with a resounding yes. *We take care of we.* Dwayne told him it would be so, and when he arrived, he cuffed Sonny's shoulder and said it to him straight.

"We take care of we, man," he said, looking Sonny in the eyes. "You're my brother. You know that."

Sonny nodded. "Of course. What you need?" was Sonny's initial response. Dwayne smiled.

"That's exactly it. Thinking about others when you should be thinking about yourself."

"I ain't nobody," Sonny blew his statement off and looked at the growing gathering of Fairfield County residents at his place. "But it's a shame. I wanted this for so long. Exactly this. This whole time, man. A place for us to gather. I thought it was the Spot. But it was this. A place to be. To showcase who we are. For us. I wanted this, and it's at the end of my story here."

Dwayne shook his head. "Everyone got buckets or cups for donations. For you, Snoop. We want to give it to you," he said.

"It won't be enough. You saw the bill. What the county wants. It gets. Hook or crook. And if we get this year, what about next? Ain't no way to live—holding your breath from tax bill to tax bill. Ain't no way to live, man."

Dwayne took a deep breath. "I been thinking about exactly that. How you're living." Sonny cocked his head. "All the way over here. I'm not ready to give our girl a car yet, and boy am I tired of driving her here. What if . . . what if you were just—closer?"

"I barely got enough money—" Dwayne stopped him.

"Hear me out. You know that property across the street was family land. I been ripping and running these past few weeks trying to figure out how to keep it out of the tax sale. When I learned my father died, a whole portal opened up that made a way for me to get it, finally."

"How?"

"It's not the full hundred acres. I had to sell some off to settle a portion of the bill. But Mrs. Harmon reminded me my blood, Nikki's blood, is buried there. A cemetery. Anyways, a few twists and turns and I put forty-eight acres in Nikki's name. You think that's enough?"

Sonny asked *enough for what?* with his face. Then the words followed. "Enough for Nikki to—?"

"Live out her cowgirl dreams with you over there? Before you say something, I talked to her. You're family, man. We agreed. Come home."

"Home?" Sonny asked.

"Bolton Family Acres. Nikki named it. Since it's hers. Will be hers when she's old enough. I'll watch y'all galloping the acres from my porch across the street."

Sonny was silent. The weight of Dwayne's words pressed on his chest. Then the tears came.

"I know today is about you and this place. And you're right. County got its grip. We can pour money into it to try, and fail. Or, we can build on our family land." Dwayne nodded. "Our." He patted Sonny's arm like a coach prepping his athlete for a big game. "Alright, Snoop. Think about it. Come home. Now, let's get this show started."

Dwayne waltzed away as smoothly as he approached. Sauntered, really, towards Nikki and Chris. The announcer's stand crackled over the multiple speakers set up around the place, signaling that it was almost time.

"Get ready, y'all, for the showcase. As with all our gatherings, we'll open the night with a prayer for safe cowboys—er, horsefolk, I've been told to say—riding this evening, and then we'll rise for the national anthem. How's that sound?"

The gathered crowd, growing with late stragglers, cheered their agreement.

"Alrighty then! The masses have spoke. Mrs. Harmon, take us away."

Chris whispered to Nikki. "That lady everywhere, ain't it?" And they muffled their giggles.

Everyone was lined up in order for the grand entry—exhibitors, turn-backs, mounted patrol officers, Chris holding the state flag, and it was decided Fairfield County's newest darling would bring up the rear with Old Glory.

From the corner of her eye, her father approached. Chris acknowledged him first.

"Great day for a rodeo isn't it, Mr. Bolton?"

"A Black rodeo at that!"

Chris tipped his hat. "Yes sir."

Dwayne tapped Nikki's leg and asked her to listen up. She heard what he had to say, and pulled back. Her face showing shock, confusion. Then, a smile.

Mrs. Harmon had only begun to get her stride on the prayer, they wagered they had a few more minutes before Nikki and the flag were due.

"I'll be right back," she said to Chris.

The announcer named every rider and horse as they entered. Where in Fairfield County they lived. There were a few folks joining from Eastover, Blythewood, Columbia, Hopkins, and they were welcomed, too. "Anyway, we love you," the announcer joked about their not having been Fairfield Country horsemen. As they entered, each stopped their horse to take it in. It was their night. Their moment. They waved to the crowd, then loped left around the arena. Finally, it was Chris's turn. He crept. Stalling, looking for Nikki. He still needed to enter solo on his horse with the blue palmetto flag waving in the air. Except, his instructions were to lope twice, then proceed to the middle of the arena standing at attention and wait for the American flag to enter.

"Ladies and gentlefolk. Please remove your hats, and stand for the national anthem," the announcer stopped. "Looks like . . ." you could hear him try to ask off mic, "looks like Miss Nikki Bolton has passed the flag to her father. Dwayne Bolton. Veteran of Operation Desert Storm. Of Ridgeway, right here in Fairfield County."

From the sidelines, Nikki swore she was the loudest cheering, but recounting the event later, Sonny would contend that the loudest voice was his.

Dwayne entered and, holding the flag in his right hand, presented the colors. A young ROTC student began.

O say can you see . . .

Dwayne kicked Easy into a lope around the arena, circling for the full duration of the anthem. Neither skipping a beat. Like there was no wide expanse of time since the last time he let a horse go so fast that its wind would wave a flag. Sonny made his way to Nikki's side.

And the rocket's red glare

"My goodness, you did it," Sonny said. "You got him to come back to us." He hugged Nikki's side, using the butt of his right palm to wipe his face.

"And you?" Nikki asked. They both watched as Dwayne kicked Easy into an effortless gallop. The speed filled their lungs with air. The crowd, cheering.

"Yeh," he sighed. "Yeh. I'm coming. Someone's gotta keep teaching you to cowboy, ain't it?"

"Cow*girl*," Nikki said. They hugged again.

And the home of the brave.

No one planned it, but the energy was explosive, and anyone who was close felt like they were going to combust. It wasn't protocol. The festival hadn't even really started, but it just felt like what needed to happen at that moment. Everyone rushed the arena: cheering, screaming, saluting—

Rodeoing into the night.

Author's Note

After my father died in 2018, I made quick plans to return home to South Carolina—to my sick mother's side—and packed up my Brooklyn life and my husband, Curtis, and arrived in Columbia on Christmas Day 2019. You all know the timeline: we had approximately three months before the world shut down in March 2020. My home state, ever behind the curve in most things, declared COVID over later that year. Curtis and I were skeptical. We had friends and family in New York City. I still could not visit my mother in her full-time care facility. We stayed inside, mostly, one more year.

Like a lot of us who survived that time mostly unscathed, I got restless. We took a vacation to my father's hometown of Charleston, South Carolina, and on a whim I signed us up for a horseback trail ride that took us along the beach. It was magical. I had never been near or touched a horse. The one I had was a brown-gray color, the largest, and she was a perfect first-time horse for me. Scared though I was, something about the journey made me sit up straight in my back. A confidence I hadn't felt about myself before—that I could do things I had never done before, as an adult—rose up. I wanted more. It was clear I was being taken for a ride—not "riding"—and I hungered for this new adventure. I told Curtis I wanted to take riding lessons, but it felt important that I learned from a Black instructor. I'd wait until those conditions were met.

In May 2021, after a series of starts and stops, I met a Black riding instructor named Lafonta Harriet (called Tay) who was eager to take me on. We both drove an hour from Columbia to a farm where he taught and selfishly, even after only the first lesson, I wanted a closer location for us to meet. He was nearing the end of his contract at the farm; I had found him just in time. Where will you teach next? I asked him. He had no firm plans. But one started forming for me.

"What if I found a farm? Would you come teach me there? Maybe open it up to others?"

Not knowing me well at all, other than that I was a thirty-something Black woman in her first formal horseback riding lessons, Tay said sure.

A month after that question, we met at a property that had just arrived on the market, fifteen minutes from where I lived and had grown up. I already had a name for it: Saloma Acres.

"Can we make this work?"

Tay said absolutely. I purchased the land, and that fall we put the first gate up on Saloma Acres. Shortly after, we brought the first Saloma Horse, Shadrack, home.

The space was mine, but I wanted to share it. While transforming the raw land into a place that could house equines, we also showed films for the community, and I continued to develop my own horsemanship, land stewardship, large animal husbandry, et cetera. I called Saloma my living PhD program. Tay taught a handful of lessons there as well. One summer, after two sisters finished their first lesson, I remarked how impressed we were with how easily they took to the task of learning to ride. The younger sister, a middle schooler, asked out loud, "I wonder if my ancestors rode horses?"

The question is one I have pondered as well. One I may never know. It is the question Nikki feels bubbling up inside of her. I give thanks to that young girl often for voicing the eternal yearning I feel every day I walk out to my farm and have the privilege of swinging a leg over one of my horses. That question drives the heart of *Fairfield County:* is it nature or nurture that makes up who we are? Perhaps it is a sweet mixture of both.

Acknowledgments

I'd like to thank, as always, my agent, Victoria Sanders; Bernadette Baker-Baughman; Maya Millett, my editor and partner through this journey again; and the team at Dial Press and Random House for carrying these stories of ordinary Black South Carolinians to the public with such care and attention.

My equestrian friends and teachers who have embraced this utter newcomer into the fold, especially Abriana Johnson, Jasmine Lomas, Elizabeth Clavette, Tay Harriet, Kelsey Willis, Eddie Braxton & Laura Cannon Regan, and the folks I ride with in mounted shooting and cow horse disciplines. Thank y'all.

Of course, none of this would be possible without the wildly unconditional support of my New York born and raised husband who one day woke up on twenty-two acres filled with ten horses, two donkeys, two pigs, two cats, and a pup. I am thankful love knows no bounds when you are partnered with someone who gives you the room to explore a complete metamorphosis so close to midlife.

ABOUT THE AUTHOR

DéLana R. A. Dameron is the author of *Fairfield County* and *Redwood Court,* a Reese's Book Club pick and a *New York Times Book Review* Editors' Choice. She is also the author of two poetry books, *How God Ends Us,* selected by Elizabeth Alexander for the South Carolina Poetry Book Prize, and *Weary Kingdom,* chosen by Nikky Finney for the Palmetto Poetry Prize. Dameron's work has appeared in *Kweli Journal, Los Angeles Review of Books, The Rumpus,* and elsewhere. Dameron is also the founder of Saloma Acres, an equestrian and cultural space in her home state of South Carolina. She passed away in 2025.

delanaradameron.com/
Instagram: @delana.r.a.dameron